"Weber creates a fascinating future with a captivating gaming aspect, complicated political and personal relationships, and a constant watchful alien presence. Suspenseful and romantic, this intense story should intrigue teen and adult fans of Caragh O'Brien's Vault of Dreamers series."

−*RT Book Reviews*, 4½ stars, TOP PICK! for *The Evaporation of Sofi Snow*

"[*The Evaporation of Sofi Snow*] offers the best of both science fiction and romance."

−*Booklist*

"An action-packed kick in the pulse. Mary Weber kills it with this conclusion to Sofi Snow's story. You will hit a point where you just. Can't. Stop. Reading. And when you finally turn that last page, you'll be ready to jump into round two."

−Nadine Brandes, award-winning author of *Fawkes*, for *Reclaiming Shilo Snow*

"In this sequel to *The Evaporation of Sofi Snow*, Weber takes a darker tone, delving into alien abduction, experimentation on children, the machinations of power-hungry politicians, and black-market corruption . . . This is a well-paced page-turner."

−*Kirkus* for *Reclaiming Shilo Snow*

"This spellbinding conclusion to Sofi's story has all the intensity of James Dashner's *The Maze Runner*, the horror of Rick Yancey's *The 5th Wave*, and an enduring hope that will leave readers inspired to look outside of themselves to see how they can help those in need."

−*RT Book Reviews*, 4½ stars, TOP PICK! for *Reclaiming Shilo Snow*

"Told in multiple perspectives, [*Reclaiming Shilo Snow*] is a twisting, electrifying read. Weber delves into human trafficking and deals with anxiety in ways many readers haven't seen before. This thrilling sequel is unlike anything else."

−*Booklist*

"[*Reclaiming Shilo Snow* is a] heartbreaking sequel of love and triumph. Weber's sequel offers timely explorations of themes of family, compassion, genetic engineering, and human trafficking. Highly recommended for sci-fi fans."

—School Library Journal

Praise for the Storm Siren Trilogy

"*Storm Siren* is a riveting tale from start to finish. Between the simmering romance, the rich and inventive fantasy world, and one seriously jaw-dropping finale, readers will clamor for the next book—and I'll be at the front of the line!"

—Marissa Meyer, *New York Times* bestselling author of the Lunar Chronicles

"Intense and intriguing. Fans of high stakes fantasy won't be able to put it down."

—C. J. Redwine, author of *The Shadow Queen*, for *Storm Siren*

"A riveting read! Mary Weber's rich world and heartbreaking heroine had me from page one. You're going to fall in love with this love story."

—Josephine Angelini, internationally bestselling author of the Starcrossed trilogy, for *Storm Siren*

"Elegant prose and intricate world-building twist into a breathless cyclone of a story that will constantly keep you guessing. More, please!"

—Shannon Messenger, author of the Sky Fall series, for *Storm Siren*

"Mary Weber has created a fascinating, twisted world. *Storm Siren* sucked me in from page one—I couldn't stop reading! This is a definite must-read, the kind of book that kept me up late into the night turning the pages!"

—Lindsay Cummings, *New York Times* bestselling author of *Zenith*

"Don't miss this one!"

"Readers who enjoyed Marissa Meyer's Cinder series will enjoy this fast-paced fantasy, which combines an intriguing storyline with as many twists and turns as a chapter of *Game of Thrones*!"

"Weber builds a fascinating and believable fantasy world."

"A touching and empowering testament to the power of true love and of knowing who you are, *Siren's Fury* is a solid, slightly steampunky follow-up to the fantasy-driven first book that will leave you with a sigh—and a craving for the next volume in the series."

"A perfect conclusion to this delightfully brave trilogy, *Siren's Song* will leave you eager to read whatever falls from the pen of talented author Mary Weber next."

To
Best
The
Boys

Other Books by Mary Weber

THE SOFI SNOW NOVELS
The Evaporation of Sofi Snow
Reclaiming Shilo Snow

THE STORM SIREN TRILOGY
Storm Siren
Siren's Fury
Siren's Song

To
Best
The
Boys

MARY WEBER

THOMAS NELSON
Since 1798

To Best the Boys

© 2019 by Mary Christine Weber

Published in Nashville, Tennessee, by Thomas Nelson. Thomas Nelson is a
registered trademark of HarperCollins Christian Publishing, Inc.

Thomas Nelson titles may be purchased in bulk for educational, business,
fund-raising, or sales promotional use. For information, please e-mail
SpecialMarkets@ThomasNelson.com.

Publisher's Note: This novel is a work of fiction. Names, characters, places,
and incidents are either products of the author's imagination or used
fictitiously. All characters are fictional, and any similarity to people living
or dead is purely coincidental.

Library of Congress Cataloging-in-Publication Data

Names: Weber, Mary (Mary Christine), author.
Title: To best the boys / Mary Weber.
Description: Nashville, Tennessee : Thomas Nelson, 2019.
Identifiers: LCCN 2018040689 | ISBN 9780718080969 (hardback)
Subjects: | GSAFD: Fantasy fiction.
Classification: LCC PS3623.E3946 T6 2019 | DDC 813/.6--dc23 LC record
available at https://lccn.loc.gov/2018040689

Printed in the United States of America

19 20 21 22 23 LSC 5 4 3 2 1

For the girl who's been told to quiet down,
calm down, sit down, or just leave
it to the men—this is for you.
And to those who told you such things?
Watch. Us. Rise.

Also, for Judah-bear Meade & Jonathan Ulibarri.

To
Best
The
Boys

THE INVITATION

No one needed to bother opening the letter to know what it said.

All gentlepersons of university age (respectively seventeen to nineteen) are cordially invited to test for the esteemed annual scholarship given by Mr. Holm toward one full-ride fellowship at Stemwick Men's University. Aptitude contenders will appear at nine o'clock in front of Holm Castle's entrance above the seaside town of Pinsbury Port on the evening of 22 September, during the Festival of the Autumnal Equinox.

For Observers: Party refreshments will be provided at intermittent times. Watering facilities available at all times. Gratitude and genial amusement are expected. (Those who fail to comply will be tossed out at *our* amusement.)

For Contestants: Those who never risk are doomed never to risk. And those who've risked previously will be ousted should they try again.

For All: Mr. Holm and Holm Manor bear no responsibility, liability, or legal obligation for any harm, death, or partial decapitation that may result from entering the examination Labyrinth.

Sincerely,

Holm

Each family had received the scripted invitation every year for the past fifty-four years of good King Francis's reign, exactly one week before the autumnal equinox. And every year with its annual arrival, each family breathed a sigh of relief, signaling that whether they had a male youth of university age or not, their status as members of the strange little community had been remembered and, more importantly, recognized. The chance for a scholarship to the top secondary school of Stemwick University in the Empyrical kingdom of Caldon was the highlight of most men's lives (aside from the annual Cheese Faire, obviously) since it was the one time of year such things as mental and physical prowess trumped the favors of wealth and political leverage.

To the odd, underprivileged people of Pinsbury Port, the contest was seen as a step up in equality. To the wealthy, it was a good-natured rivalry among themselves. And neither cared how any of the other provinces of Caldon saw it, so long as they played hard and fair, and cleaned up their mess before returning home.

Still, despite knowing the letter's contents, each recipient opened it anyway. The wealthy wives to check the parchment type—to promptly order it for their own fashionable invites to winter solstice bazaars and their husbands' hunting parties. The poor to check and double-check the wording—to ensure nothing had changed.

Rhen Tellur opened it simply to see if she could scrape off the ink and derive which substances it'd been created from, using her father's strangely fashioned microscope. Which is how she discovered that this time the lettering was created from two types of resin, a binding paste, gold flecks, and a drop of something that smelled quite remarkably like magic.

The problem with siphoning blood from a bloated cadaver is that sometimes its belly makes an involuntary twitch just as you're leaning over the discolored skin.

The problem with being the girl currently stealing the sticky blood is that while logic says there's an explanation for such phenomena, the rest of me says it must be one of two things.

Either the good king's clerics are out somewhere trying to raise the dead again . . .

Or I've just discovered the town's first certifiable vampyre right here in the cloying cellar of the local undertaker's.

Either way, it hardly matters because—while a bloodsucker would be an interesting twist on my day—the *cadaver just moved*, and the fact that I'm not keeling over from heart failure right now is rather magnanimous of me. Instead, I stay alive and spring backward. *"Of all the—"* Only to ram into another cadaver-laden table behind me. The table creaks loudly inside the tiny room of our even tinier seaside town that sits on the border of a tiny green kingdom that believes itself the center of the Empyral world.

I freeze. *Drat.* I've bumped the table so hard the thing's starting to tilt away from my hindside (which the cadaver's face is now ungraciously pressed up against), and when I flip around, the whole thing's suddenly tipping, and the dead lady laid out on top is tipping with it.

I reach out to grab the slab. But deadweight and wood are heavier than you'd think, and the next second the table upends between my fingers and—*No, no, no, no!*—unceremoniously dumps the old gal's stiff body onto the sloped floor. Like a white oak dropping a tree branch in summer.

I stall and wait for the sound to fade. Except—

Oh you've got to be jesting.

The dead lady starts to roll.

With a lunge, I shove a hand out to grab the edge of the table she's headed for, but my blood-slicked gloves graze the wood just as the lady's body clips the base and promptly sends *it* rocking.

That table pitches and slams into the next.

And that one into the next.

And so on and so on, until five of the eight dead people in here have suddenly taken the phrase "from dust to dust" literally as they join the old gal on the ground in what looks like a dramatic retelling of *The King's Fair Predator*.

This, of course, is when Beryll starts to scream.

Not just scream, but the kind of bloodcurdling wail that's used by pregnant mountain basilisks just before they give birth, or by the sea sirens out hunting sailors. Both of which our town is famous for, because apparently being famous for things that can kill you is better than no fame at all. In fact, Mum says it's like our own version of township pride. What doesn't kill you makes you compelling.

Except for Beryll, who I doubt has ever been compelling in his life.

I swerve toward his yelping face to find it turning the color of heifer's milk beneath his high-cut bangs and lengthy nose.

Oh for the love of—"Beryll, be quiet!"

His gaze veers to mine with an expression promising I'm definitely going to the underworld and he's got a mind to help send me there. That, or he's about to lift his impeccably pressed knickers and scurry for the back door, outside of which my cousin, Seleni, is keeping watch in the village alley.

Unfortunately, he neither attacks *or* scurries.

He just keeps screaming.

With a groan, I grip my glass vial and scramble toward him beneath the low, curved ceiling that's already got the wretched air locked in too tight, and thrust my other hand over his mouth. "Beryll, shut *up*! You're gonna get us caught!"

He pulls away to shove his dainty handkerchief back over his lips, while his screeching stumbles into a strangled falsetto.

He locks his brown eyes on mine in the stuffy space that's lit like a halo by the two oil lanterns hanging from the rafters. "Miss Tellur. That thing's belly just moved. I think expressing nerves at such a time is completely acceptable, considering it's still . . ." He tightens his fingers on the linen covering half his face. *"Alive!"*

"It's not alive," I hiss, my mind finally wrenching into gear. "The body's just bloated. The belly was reacting to my abdominal incision. But if you keep up your whining, we'll likely join him on these slabs!" I point the glass vial I'm still holding toward the narrow, oil-stained door in front of us, where the sexton's quarters lie beyond and a shiny copper bell hangs above, and hold my breath. That bell's made to ring if anyone enters or exits—mainly in case the dead in fact ever do rise. Whether it's the religious rapture or an outbreak of undead, the good folk of Pinsbury Port believe it'd be equally important to know which they're specifically missing out on.

Beryll's voice sharpens to a whistle. *"What do you mean reacting? Dead things don't react!"*

I shake my head, recalling Da's mention of such things. "Sometimes they move. It's the nerves or gastrointestinal system. Now for goodness' sake, Beryll—you wanted to come." I put a finger to my mouth. "So shush!"

He shushes, although I'm guessing it's only because he just got a good inhale of the extra-thick decomposition fumes.

I flick my gaze back to the sexton's door and count six

heartbeats as I watch and wait. The spiritual man has yet to catch me. Still, he's heard my disturbances often enough to believe the room's haunted. Thinks it's our dead armies—the ones that still rise on the moor at night because some fool forgot to tell them the war ended two hundred years ago.

I wait a moment longer. *No movement of the handle or metal bell.* Then release my breath, ease my shoulders, and turn to Beryll, muttering, "Are you *trying* to get Seleni and me sent to the workhouse?"

"Of course not." He edges toward the rear door on which Seleni's now tapping sharply from the outside. The sounds of horse and carriage clipping by emerge, then fade. "And they wouldn't send you there anyway. Your cousin's father would bail her out and just convince the constable you're off your head. Best case, they'd post a sign on your parents' house to warn folks—and really, I'm not sure I'd blame them, Miss Tellur." He tugs at his shirt cuffs and waistcoat, then swallows as he turns an unusual shade of green.

I purse my lips. I start to tell him to pull himself together, but I abruptly end up bent over.

The atmosphere's just hit my stomach too.

I scramble my glove across my knitted scarf and yank it up over my nose to plug my nostrils tight and slow the rolling in my gut. The baking afternoon sun has heated this room to a steamy level—like the graveyard and underground catacombs last year when the storms flooded the marsh. The rank miasma nearly suffocated half the town and drew the sirens in with the smell of rotting flesh.

"Besides," Beryll says, still inching for the door. "The constables are about to have better things to worry about than people stealing organs and blood from the dead."

I glance up. "What's that supposed to mean?"

"Nothing. Can we just leave?"

I assess him with a frown. I assume he's referring to the competition tomorrow at Holm Castle—the one Beryll's participating in and that I've wanted to for as long as I can remember. But the fact that Mum and I can cut up a corpse or do an equation better than half the blokes my age means nothing when it comes to Caldon's long-standing tradition of gender roles.

I bite my tongue. Force my comments down. "Fine. Help me get these corpses back up, and then we'll go."

I hurry back to the toppled tables and bodies as Beryll peers at the dead man still on the upright slab behind me—the one who started this whole thing with his twitching stomach.

"Beryll!" I whisper. *"Let's go."*

He takes cautious steps in my direction. "In my defense, Miss Tellur, I'm unaccustomed to dead bodies, let alone ones that *move*. And I can only imagine how Seleni—Miss *Lake*—would react. I expect she'd be absolutely appalled."

I snort and stop at the first slab. In spite of Seleni's high civic standing, she joins me in this endeavor near monthly—and while she may be many things, appalled is rarely one of them. Mainly because Beryll is usually appalled enough for both of them. It's like the one emotion he allowed himself at birth upon discovering he'd had to travel through his mum's delivery canal. I highly doubt he's ever forgiven the woman.

I roll my eyes and glance down at the vial I'd been siphoning the body fluid into. *Good.* None of the precious liquid has spilled.

But the lid . . .

I disregard the fallen table and the smell that's permeating every fiber of my scarf—and scan the dirty floor. *Where's the vial lid?*

"Rhen, hurry up in there." Seleni's delicate voice muffles through the rear door. "Beryll, tell Rhen to get a move on. We have my parents' party to prepare for."

"Miss Tellur . . ."

I ignore them both and search the floor around the upright table with the dead man. Then around the lady's body still lying stiff with the others on the floor. The old woman's skin matches the storm-grey slate tiles, like the petrified hand of a knight I'd once unearthed.

"Miss Tellur—"

"I heard her, Beryll."

"Good, because I feel the need to inform you—"

"I *know*, Beryll, but I've dropped the lid."

"Not your cousin. The corpse. Something's happening. The stomach's moving again, and—"

"Oh for heaven's sake, if you're that nerved out, just go stand by the—"

A gurgling sound emits from the table above my head.

I grab the glass lid that my boot's just bumped against and slowly rise, lifting my face eye level with the cadaver. One calculated look informs me what's making the noise. Beryll's right.

It's not just another odd twitch of the nerves. The guy's bloated stomach is rippling.

I frown. No, not just rippling. It's . . .

I plunge the lid onto the vial. "Beryll, get to the door."

"What? Why? Is he actually alive? I *told you*—"

I launch for him and pull us both toward the back entrance just as Beryll lets out a horrified whimper.

2

I grab the door handle and yank it open as a popping sound occurs from the dead man's body—right at the place I'd made the first inspecting incision. I must've cut too deep—too near the bowels—because the noise is accompanied by a sudden bursting, and then a haze of gas and fluid erupts from the poor soul's left side like a decrepit volcano. It sends flecks flying across the room to spatter against our skin and hair and faces.

With a hard shove I thrust Beryll out into the shimmering light of the dying afternoon—where we both slam into Seleni in her new lace skirt and take her sprawling to the ground with us.

"What in—? Rhen, I beg your—"

I don't speak, just jump up and pull the two of them with me while gulping in briny ocean air to exorcise the death stench, then turn and propel the undertaker's door shut behind us. *Oops.* I push too fast and the string attached to the bell clapper above the doorway—the string I always pull taut before entering or leaving in order to keep it from ringing—gets tugged, and the thing goes off with a clang.

The sound rings too sharp, too loud, in the narrow stone passage, spiraling up to echo across the rooftops to rouse the constables, and down into the old underground catacombs to wake the ghouls.

Seleni gasps and flips around as her beau, Beryll, turns the color of a late-harvest apple. "Rhen, what in King Francis's—?"

"Nothing. Just go!" I snag her arm and shove her toward Beryll, then click the door's footlock in place before I take off after them down the narrow cobblestone alley that is all filth and stone beneath our feet—and walls of rotting wood on either side of us—with a thin ribbon of sapphire sky peeking through the patchwork of eaves overhead.

The tall, two-story houses slip past, dark and creaky, as we sprint through the winding alleyways. My gloved left hand grips the sealed vial while my right hand tugs my flimsy cloak closer against the specter of cold that haunts every recess and shadow of our otherwise overbaked coastal town.

Behind us, the bell on the inner door starts ringing. *The sexton.*

"Getting sloppy, Rhen," I can almost hear Sam and Will say.

"Overhead!" Seleni squeals.

I look up, then slow down, just as a waterfall of swill lands on the path fifteen steps in front of us. It splatters the ground and walls and our boots as the woman in a shawl tossing it from her window doesn't even bother giving us a second glance.

With a leap and a skip, Seleni and I dance past the mess in the same pattern we did as children when we'd play hop frog along the Tinny River. We wait for Beryll to gingerly step around it before we turn the corner and pick up running the narrow labyrinth of more lanes.

Just above the midway street, which cuts widthwise through the entire sloping hill of cottages and alleys, we reach a clump of steps, which we clear in one jump, to arrive in the middle of the cobblestoned heart of Pinsbury Port. Namely, its teeming and smelly afternoon market.

Seller booths and mingling bodies rush into view, as does a tall, flamboyant flutist trying to earn coin as children dance and giggle. I slam my soles into the ground to avoid hitting them, except my body keeps flying—straight into a man walking in front of the herbalist's booth.

"Look ou—" My strangled yelp retreats down my throat as my face plants into the back of the gentleman's broad frame, right between his massive shoulder blades, just as Beryll and Seleni skid up behind me.

The poor man lurches forward enough for my face to peel off his damp fisherman's coat. "Sorry, sir," I choke out. "I—"

He flips around with dark eyes and a darker countenance, and my words drop away like the damp autumn leaves scattered at our feet.

Oh.

If I could evaporate into the sea-foam air I would. Instead, I stand there, stolen blood in hand, beneath the irritated gaze of Lute Wilkes, best fisherman of the port and school chum who was two grades my senior growing up, until a couple summers ago when I left to be educated at home and he to go support his family on his dead father's trawling boat. His full lips still have that pucker the girls liked to swoon over. The same one I wondered more than a few times if the tissue was actually formed that way, or if he was just perpetually in the mood to kiss things. I once imagined dissecting his face to find out.

A storm behind Lute's eyes suggests we interrupted something. His scowl flickers over my disheveled appearance—my cadaver-stained hands, wrinkled outer coat, and hair that at some point unraveled from its bun into a forest of wild briars. His gaze slowly registers recognition before it moves on to Beryll and Seleni, who are doubled over, gasping.

Two seconds go by and he returns his attention to me. And just like that, his eyes do the nice thing that used to illuminate the earthen cider cellar behind Sarah Gethries's house—the one none of us were supposed to know about, but we all hung out there anyway.

I blink, and the skin on my wrists turns the color of sweet pomegranates. My bloody, gloved fingers suddenly feel very bloody, and my hair very briar-y. And all I can think of is that maybe the whole lip-swooning thing had a point after all because they are rather anatomically balanced.

"Rhen, *what in pantaloons?*" Seleni half laughs, half demands. "You set off the alarm!"

I swallow and nod at her but keep my eyes on Lute, who smells of salt-wood and morning tides and freedom. He's a bit more sun drenched than the last time I ran into him a few months ago when Roy Bellow called my da crazy and my mum an independent woman. At the time, Lute had been helping his mum and brother in the glassmaker's shop where I'd been "borrowing" a particular set of magnifying lenses. Lute frowned at Roy, but I'd already taken it upon myself to suggest that being crazy and independent were far better than being a suckling calf.

Which apparently isn't something one should say.

Roy has tried twice since then to corner me in an alley.

Lute tips his chin down, and a swag of black bangs falls forward as a sprinkle of sun rays catches his dark lashes and scatters thin shadows across his brown cheeks. Like firelight from an evening burn. He raises a single thick brow in a smart look, as if he's remembering the interaction, and slips into an easy smile. "Did you at least hide the body this time, Miss Tellur?"

I bite my cheek and freeze. "Body? I'm sure I don't know what you're talking about, Mr. Wilkes."

He glances behind us, then puckers those well-balanced lips and dips them toward my bloody gloves. "I'm assuming one of your verbal carvings has rid the Port of yet another fool."

Dimples. Deep, genuine, and stupidly distracting while my mind is trying to decipher his words. When it does, I frown and feel my cheeks warm. *Oh.* I sniff. "If such a fool's been rid, Mr. Wilkes, it's by his own doing and likely well deserved."

He chuckles, and the casualness in his tone and grey gaze makes me feel light-headed, as do the cloying market smells assaulting my senses. I frown because I've no interest in feeling that way, particularly not around Beryll and Seleni. So of course I do the only thing I can think of:

I glare.

"Rhen, I asked what happened!" Seleni thumps my arm.

Lute's gaze slides over to her and Beryll.

I blink. *Right. Blood and alarms.*

Clearing my throat, I turn. "It was nothing. Just an accident. I was going too fast and Beryll screamed. Sorry we bumped you, Lute." I reach up to dust off his fishing-coat sleeve, only to leave behind a streak of body fluid. I wince and with a meaningful glance Seleni's way make a *"let's go"* head motion to her. "Nice seeing you again."

My cousin doesn't move. Just sticks a mischievous hand on her hip and points at her beau. "Go? Just look at poor Beryll. He can't go anywhere! You traumatized him!"

What? I turn to assess him. He's not traumatized, he's just . . . I sniff. He does appear to be holding back his lunch. "Okay, so he's traumatized. But *I* didn't traumatize him. The dead man's body was too bloated and I—"

"Dead body?" Lute leans back and crosses his arms. Those dimples deepen.

I stall and hear Mum's voice rush like a tide in my head. *"Rhen, people aren't as impressed by dead bodies as you are. You can't just talk about them in public."*

I pinch my palms and turn to peer back into the alley for

the angry sexton, because this might be a convenient time for him to appear. Instead, I find a group of kids with snot-smeared faces whispering excitedly and pointing toward the northern hillsides where the fancy estates all sit. The highest up of which belongs to Mr. Holm. "Holm'll pluck out your eyeballs with his pointy teeth if you try to sneak in," a girl says.

"And gnaw your fingers off!" another squeals.

"My old man says Holm comes down here at night looking for kids to steal, and when he catches one, he sticks 'em in his Labyrinth. That's what the scholarship test really is—to see how many you can free before he eats 'em."

The smallest of the group nods. "That's what he does to trespassers too. Sticks 'em under his castle and lets the old knights at 'em."

The kid beside him shivers.

"You guys still going tomorrow then?" says the first girl, a suddenly nervous lilt in her voice.

"Of course. I wanna hear who dies first," her friend crows. He casually glances our way, and I catch his eye and offer a smile. He responds by putting on a fierce face and assessing Beryll's fancy, lined surcoat. He points it out to the others and they all start snickering. "Pretty sure *he's* going to be the first to die in there," the youngest says, before his gaze moves on to gawp at Seleni's pretty shoes.

"Care to draw a bet on that?" another asks.

I glance at Beryll just as the baker in the nearby booth growls at the kids. "You rats stop lollygagging and scat! I won't warn you again. Yer scarin' away my customers."

Beryll swallows loudly, straightens his soiled sleeve cuffs, and acts as if he didn't just hear the children's monetization of his impending death. "Miss Tellur, maybe I should explain the predicament you just put me in. Seleni—I mean, Miss Lake—please pardon my current dishevelment, but I feel it my duty to inform you that the horrific event that has just taken place is not what I had in mind when you invited me to attend such an endeavor. And, as such, I hardly want to speak of it, for fear it'll upset your delicate constitution."

Good. Then don't.

Seleni lifts a hand. "Constitution monstitution. One of you dish it before I throttle you."

Not in front of Lute. I glare at Beryll to clamp his mouth shut.

The nineteen-year-old's face falls grave, but he clenches his lips and lifts his narrow chin. "Fine then. In that case, Miss Lake, your cousin here . . ." His tone dips confidentially as he adjusts his sleeve cuffs again and nods at the wide-eyed group of children still observing us from near the baker's. "Your cousin has just exploded a body."

"You did *what*?" Seleni swerves to me.

"Did she really now?" Lute murmurs.

"At first I thought the poor chap was alive." Beryll wipes at his short brown bangs across his forehead. "Which was its own sort of terrifying. I'd rather you not think on it further, lest you faint."

"From the smell of you two, I'm surprised she hasn't already." Lute's amused gaze stays on me as Seleni's cheek suddenly twitches.

"Is there anything left of him?" she demands.

I cough softly into my shoulder.

Beryll lifts a finger to adjust his rumpled collar.

"I'm not sure," I finally admit. "It was like a spew. It even hit a wall."

"As well as your faces apparently." Seleni looks down as if it just struck her that we have actual corpse fluid on our clothes and skin. "Oh dear." Her cheek twitches again. "Oh my."

"Well, in my defense, the stomach gases can build up and—"

Beryll's eyes bulge from their sockets. "*Gases*—really, Miss Tellur? Perhaps you can keep your voice down."

Except there's no need because Seleni has just erupted into a high-pitched peal of laughter that causes the ogling children to stare harder and even a few of the market sellers to turn and look as their customers waver between buying leather shoes or leftovers.

"Miss Lake!" Beryll uses his second-level-of-appalled tone, which is normally reserved for things like exposed elbows, liberal thinking, and every time I talk about undergarments. "I find nothing funny about this or the fluid on our faces. And I'd like to get home to bathe immediately."

"Oh good grief, Beryll." Seleni starts to tug away from the growing stares of interest, except a voice ripples out from the market booths opposite us. "Oh, *Seleniiiii*! I thought that was you over there!"

I freeze. I don't have to see the owner to know who it belongs to. She's married to one of the town's papery owners, with whom my uncle landed me an apprenticeship two summers ago. The woman is squeezed in between two seller stalls with an armful of fresh eggs.

"Did your mother get those cards she ordered, dear? We had our boy drop them off at the estate."

Seleni makes her voice cheerier than usual. "Yes, Mrs. Holder. My mum received them this morning, thank you. So nice to see you."

"Oh good. Well, I'd love to hear if she's pleased with them. If she is, perhaps she could mention it to your father's parliament friends." The woman pauses long enough that I think maybe she's moved on, but I catch her looking at Lute and me. I hold my breath, but her demeanor doesn't alter other than to adjust the load in her arms—as if to suggest we carry it for her. When we don't offer, she apparently thinks better of it and turns away.

I let my shoulders ease, until she stops and something flicks across her countenance as she swerves back our direction. She takes a step nearer and my lungs crawl inside my spine. "Miss Tellur," she says sharply. "I hardly recognized you."

She glances at my clothes, then at our surroundings, and furrows her brow. "Young lady, I'd hate to mention to young Vincent's parents that this is how you spend your time. I can't imagine they would approve." She purses her lips as if she has more to say and believes it would do me a favor to do so. But instead, mercifully, she tightens her arms around her market load and says nothing further. Just turns and strides away, and I am left with embarrassment flaring in my gut and on my face at the mention of Vincent, and at knowing full well what the rest of her words would've been.

That a young woman hanging around the midday market is appropriate if, like Seleni, she has prospects. But for me? It's further proof of why I couldn't hold on to a shop maid apprenticeship at her husband's "fine letters and script" store. "Apathy is unbecoming for a woman of *any* position," she'd told a client within my hearing the day before I was let go.

Seleni flashes me a glance that says she'd speak up if it didn't expose my secret—that it was never a matter of apathy. That words and letters have shifted order in my head for as long as I can remember, and cleaning trays of letter blocks day in and day out was a mix-up waiting to happen. I misplaced the arrangements one too many times and got fired within two weeks.

"No wonder she and her husband drink a lot," Lute says quietly, conscientiously not looking at me.

Seleni snorts.

"As I was *saying*," Beryll interrupts. "I'd like to get home and wash up."

Seleni shoots him a look. "I can't go home with my shoes like this—Mum would fall into fits. And Rhen's house won't have enough water for washing her clothes and hair." She grips me and screeches. "And tonight's party! Mum'll be horrified if we're late, especially with members of parliament there! We need to fix ourselves *now*, Rhen."

I wave toward the wharf. "It'll be fine. We'll take a quick dip in the sea. Fully *dressed*," I add as Beryll turns five shades of berry.

"Because Mrs. Holder's right about one thing." Seleni keeps

talking as if I've not spoken. "Vincent can't see you like this. We have to make you presentable."

"Vincent? As in Vincent King?" Lute peers from Seleni to me.

I grimace and note the wary shift in his countenance.

She nods.

I grip the vial tighter and wish she'd stayed quiet, even though I don't know why it matters or why I care what Lute thinks, but for some reason I do.

"He's pursuing Miss Tellur's hand for courtship," Beryll blurts out.

"Beryll, don't—" But it's too late. My lungs fall as I watch Lute's mood from earlier return and cloud his countenance.

He studies me a moment, as if absorbing this information and analyzing my expression. Whatever he finds there, it's as if the shutters close on his thoughts and his lips pucker in disdain.

He straightens from me and looks to the distance. And when he glances back, his own expression is an ocean away. "That reminds me. If you'll excuse me, I've got some business to get to."

He strides off quickly—almost as if he can't escape fast enough—and I am left staring after him, wondering what about Vincent had upset him. Or was it the fact we're attending Seleni's rich father's party?

Both, probably. The Lowers don't take well to the indulgences of the rich.

I swallow and ignore the squeezing in my chest that says I of all people should know.

"We have to hurry." Seleni yanks my arm as Lute disappears into the crowd.

I push back the urge to go after him—because really, *what would you say, Rhen?*—and, instead, allow her to pull me toward the walkway between the textile maker and millinery booths while Beryll discreetly points out the herbalist nearby. He's got his fingers clamped over his nose and his red cap is askew. He rakes his gaze up and down us as his eyes grow round from his spot in the rickety grey stand that, up until we arrived, probably smelled delightfully of medicinal mint and sweat.

I tuck the vial of stolen blood along with my gloves into my coat's inner pocket—the secret one I sewed into the lining a few months ago after thieves grabbed a bottle from my hand and dropped it on the cobbles whereupon it shattered. They didn't know exposing blood like that is a good way to spread the plague.

"Soldiers, help! Beasts!" A voice roars through the rows of market stalls behind us. "Robbers! Someone tore open a body and—"

We don't wait for the sexton to finish. We plunge down the alley toward the fork that splits the hill, where one side leads up for home and the other leads down to the ocean. Turning onto the latter, we bolt along the shadowed, serpentine stone path that winds past the sloping houses peering out to the sea beyond. More specifically, peering out over our town's livelihood and Lute's dead father's boat.

To the old wharf of Pinsbury Port.

3

There's something about knowing death is on the horizon. About knowing life hangs on a few strands of genetic material, and knowing the only hope for a cure might currently be sitting in a little glass vial inside the toe of my shoe up on the beach, forty paces behind Seleni and her beau. On the shore of the only town I've ever lived in.

According to Da, aside from the abnormal death rate, Pinsbury Port is just like any other place. We have the usual fare of rich and poor, old people and babies, gossipy constables and cat-dressing biddies, all neatly tucked away along the lower tip of a tiny green kingdom called Caldon, also known as King

Francis's Emerald Heart. It sits in the middle of a much larger collection of kingdoms commonly referred to as the Empyral Lands.

Mum says Caldon's greenery wakes with the morning along the Rhine Mountains and spends the day stretching down the valleys and hillsides until it reaches our little town along the Midian Sea, where it likes to lick away the last of the afternoon sun rays and also a few more lives. Because apparently green and death are what we excel at.

Did I mention my mum's a real cheerful sort?

A knot of tears catches in my throat at the image of her saying that, and my chest squeezes as I drift on my back in the ocean among the all-too-real awareness that right now, in this very moment, her life is being licked away along with a host of others. The reality of which just about hollows the breath out of me and keeps me frantically working with Da.

Or hiding out here.

I blink and try to refocus. I don't want to think about it.

A Whitby falcon screeches overhead, and Seleni hollers from the shore, "Rhen, how's your mum feeling today? Did your da figure out anything new?"

The waves froth around and over me, and I let the questions dissolve with the bursting bubbles as the water's foamy arms push me toward shore before they tug me back out to the ocean's glassy surface.

I pretend not to hear her, partly because my answer is always the same—"Not good. Not yet, but we're hopeful. I don't know"—and mainly because I don't know how to explain the insidious fear and grief that come with such questions. They're not the kind of thing you can dip your toes in, then run away from. The emotions crash together in a wave and dash you against the rocks until you're drowning and screaming, and sometimes you just want to dissolve too.

I swallow. If I start down that path today, I won't know how to come back, and I can't afford that.

Instead, I inhale and kick my ankles and float on my back beneath the sun's rays reflecting off the marina, and mentally retreat to the logical steadiness of blood counts and stem cells. I turn the problem over and under in my mind, trying to find the key to what Da and I are missing. How our town can produce such vibrant life—and yet, for the past ten months, can't figure out how to halt a person's crippling death.

"The key is there in the blood cells," he keeps saying. "We've even isolated the strange mutation that's creating this recent disease."

Only every time we think we've clicked a cure into place, another subject dies.

And soon it will be Mum.

Then, he fears, me. Because this new disease seems to hit with no rhyme or reason, other than being centered among the poor of the Port.

"Rhen!" Seleni's voice rings garbled and now irritable in my ears. "For gnat's sakes! I've been talking to you!"

I lift my head and find her in the water up to her ankles, skirt pulled up to her knees. She's frowning and waving me in. "You said you'd hurry! Sun's fading and the party's soon. If you don't dry out, you'll get home wet and your hair will be unbearable to fix!"

I nod and peer across the blue expanse of sky to the sun's spot hedging toward the golden ocean ledge. Then at the falcon diving along the dale that drains into the Tinny River, where the knights of old used to camp during wartime. We have an hour left, but with little heat in my house, dressing will already be miserable—and once night falls, the sea sirens will be awake, and anyone who values her life wouldn't be daft enough to be this far out in the bay.

With a sigh I tip my head backward to let the water lap over my face until only my chin is above salt water and let the cold finish leaching away the smell of cadaver from my nose, my skin, and my clothes. Washing the dead away. Washing everything away for a few precious moments. Then I right myself and, after a last dunk, swim close enough to let the current carry me to where my toes can touch the crunchy sand and I can walk to my cousin and Beryll.

Seleni has just finished wringing out Beryll's waistcoat while the large water spots on his breeches and shirt suggest he's been scrubbing them to avoid immersing his full self in the water. When I stroll up, he glances at Seleni, then blushes like a beet before his gaze shifts to a far-off spot.

I chuckle and flick a handful of water at him. "If wet clothes and bare ankles mortify you, you'd best avoid a mirror, Beryll."

"Don't mock him for being a gentleman," Seleni chides. "Would you rather him look at me like those two men are down the beach? No wonder they've not caught a single fish, with all their ogling."

I glance toward the two cads fishing from the shore not far from us. I frown and refuse the urge to wrap my arms around my flat chest. "Or maybe they could just look at women as if we're regular people," I mutter. *There's a thought. The way Da does. Straight on, as if we're all just his friends.*

Seleni gives a hard shake to the waistcoat and utters the type of fake sigh old Mrs. Mench does when I forget to wear stockings under my skirt. She mimics the woman's high-pitched voice. "Rhen Tellur, your head's so full of man ideas you'll forget your place among the proper ladies. Clearly, your mum and da are to blame for this."

I laugh and grab my rinsed coat from the crook of her arm, then climb up the shore, wringing out my skirt and hair as I go. With a burst of chuckles, Seleni and Beryll follow to the sand beside our pile of shoes, where I double-check that my vial is still tucked away safe. Then pause a moment to soak up the last bit of warmth the scorched beach offers, before I tug on my stockings and slide the vial and scrubbed gloves back into my soaked coat pocket.

Seleni and Beryll's giggling continues, and I stand to leave when my cousin asks, "Did you two finally get your Labyrinth Letters?"

The waves crash and hiss, trickling around her voice. I drape my coat over my arm and move to slide on my shoes. "It came yesterday," I say, and, with a last wringing of my thin skirt, turn toward the busy, steaming wharf and begin to walk.

"My family's arrived two days ago." The white sand crunches beneath Beryll's feet as he and Seleni jump up and fall in behind me. "What about yours, Miss Lake?"

Seleni squeals. "It came last night. I can't imagine what the delay was this year, but it arrived on stamped linen paper with a lovely seal. Mum has already ordered a variation for our winter solstice invites. She says a person's stationery is as important as their fashion—both tell your position, piety, and how well you think of yourself."

I keep my mouth shut.

"Wonderful. Your families will both be attending the event, of course?"

I keep walking toward the landing and let Seleni answer, since Beryll's question is more for her anyway. She's been excited for weeks. My cousin, who is in every way nearly the same as me—same seventeen years, same brown hair and tan skin color—except when it comes to our family stations and interests. She's the socialite and I'm the proletarian scientist. Meaning, she likes to talk about thrilling things happening. I like to experience them.

And now her reply is breathless. "Of course we're attending! We've already plotted our spot to sit out the competition. And Beryll, you'll be a magnificent competitor. Just imagine what it'll be like! Oh, I just know you're going to win."

"So my father hopes."

I stiffen and feel the dull ache of jealousy rise, of what it must be like to compete for such a thing.

"Beryll Jaymes," Seleni crows. "You've got all the smarts to pull it off. You know numbers and equations just as good as anyone. And you're strong too."

"Yes. Except so are the rest in my grade—as my father keeps reminding me."

I fall back to walk beside them, eyeing Beryll. "Maybe. But the fact that you're aware of that will work for you. You'll not go in overly confident. And you're one of the smartest people I know, Beryll. Even if you do scream a lot."

He laughs and gives me a shy, warm nod. "Thank you, Miss Tellur. I suppose it's just the practical experience I fear I lack."

My cousin tips a slender hand at me. "Which is why Rhen took you to the undertaker's today. And why her father gave you his old lecture notes and let you sit in on their experiments last week. Think of all that knowledge no other contestant will have. You even examined a dead body!"

"Miss Lake, you flatter me." But Beryll's countenance lightens with appreciation, and he lifts his hands to tug confidently on his water-spotted waistcoat as we tread through the sand. "I've surely not had enough preparation, although you are correct—I've had more than many my age. And were I to be pursuing a degree in medicine, this would serve me even better. Alas, business studies it is."

I bite my tongue and refuse to let his words keep feeding my hunger. And decline mentioning that if preparation is the measure, I've had at least as much as a good many of the Stemwick scholarship applicants in the science, engineering, technology, and math areas the competition tests for. Instead, I keep trudging and pretend the whole thing doesn't prick at that space inside my chest. The one that can't help wondering what I could do with the type of education Beryll and the young men like him are headed for. What kind of things I could learn. What kind of diseases I might study or cure.

I trail my gaze along the skyline to the boats making port at the wooden docks where Lute's is already moored, gleaming cleaner—as always—than the rest.

"What about your family, Beryll?" Seleni chatters on as a mum with two small children toddles by. My cousin's eyes follow them with a wishful mien. "Will they be attending the Labyrinth examination?"

There's a sudden twinge in her tone, and I don't have to question her to know what it's from—what she's hoping. It's half of what she's talked about the past seven months since she and Beryll have officially been seeing each other, even though he's been a side fixture in our lives since the age of thirteen. Her desire is well known between the three of us—to have his family care enough to spend time with her, and perhaps welcome her like a flower into their fold with open tendril arms.

Sometimes I think being Beryll's wife and having kids is her highest aspiration. But there are certain things even money and status can't buy—like approval of a person or marriage. No matter how high standing one's perfect family is. Especially when in Beryll's father's eyes, apparently no one is high standing enough for his only child.

Beryll's hesitation is so long I finally swerve to glare at him as we step up onto the wide wharf front with its smelly fishing carts and rows of white-curtained shanties stretching on for forever, crossed with the main street leading home. His demeanor is as tight as his voice. "Yes. They'll be attending."

Seleni's sweet, hopeful grin stays, even as a flicker of disappointment and hurt shades her eyes.

I bite my cheek and don an innocent expression. "As will the Schaffer and Newton families," I say casually. "Seleni, your father mentioned they're both keen to get to know you. I hear their boys are hoping to earn more than just your parents' approval."

Beryll coughs and nearly trips over his feet. "Miss Lake—I don't think that's necessary. I doubt—"

"Oh, it's quite necessary if my father wishes it. Just like you do everything your father desires of you, Beryll." Seleni's previous mood dissolves as she flashes gratitude my way, and despite her father never having said any such thing, I feel confident he would've. I smirk as she lifts her chin. "I shall very much enjoy getting to know them better."

A loud shout shuts down whatever Beryll's daft reply is, and a crowd converges along the inclining street ahead of us. A commotion has kicked up between a couple of fancy-dressed financiers and a group of stubble-faced fishermen who've just finished unloading their cargo. By the sound of their voices, neither side is happy.

I quicken my step, but by the time we reach the men, their voices have hushed to murmurs. "No need to upset the town with unproven news," someone says.

"This is a Port matter," another mutters.

"This is rumor is what it is."

I frown and glance back at Seleni and Beryll. *Is it more of the disease?*

"I'll tell you what, though," one of the fishermen growls. "If it's true? I'll kill them."

4

I press against two women to get us nearer as the words float up and over me from the red-faced men whose hair and heavy coats smell of salt and seaweed. The tidbits being talked about are muted so quick I can't catch their context, other than there's no mention of the disease. Whatever it is, it has to do with the wharf.

"See how their families like having to support their kids on so little," the larger of the fishermen says.

I peer around for Lute. Maybe this is what his mood was about earlier.

"There she is!" someone shouts. "Eh, Rhen!"

Will and Sam Finch rattle the air behind us with their boisterous voices. I spin to find them striding up in tight tunics above breeches that are a bit too saggy for propriety and wide-mouthed smiles that promise they've already been up to no good. I snort. Someone in the Upper sector will probably find their cattle tipped over by tomorrow morning.

"We heard there was a ruckus at a certain undertaker's place." Will grins at Seleni and me. His brown hair looks like a peacock fan at the back of his head. "Somethin' about the ghost of bloody King Henry himself explodin' a body and then settin' off the bell—which is when I says to Sam here, 'Sam, that sounds a lot like a certain individual. Why don't we go investigate?' To which Sam here agreed, because he is the agreeable sort. So what, pray tell, have you been up to, and why weren't we invited?"

"Isn't it obvious, William?" Sam indicates Beryll. "They tried to murder someone who threw up on them. Look at the fancy guy."

"In that case, all the better question of why we wasn't invited."

I smile at the two of them who, barely a year apart, might as well be twins, and lower my tone. "*If* Beryll or I had anything to do with a body or bell, it would've been an accident. And I think we've already established neither of you can handle a splinter, let alone the sight of blood."

Sam ignores me and adjusts his too-tight tunic. "So you're saying you did, in fact, commit a murder? Because while it's true *Will* here would've definitely passed out, you know I would've been beneficial." He yanks a fishing blade from who knows where in his loose trousers and wields it deftly with his fingers, as if he's some sort of knife magician. Then winks at Seleni. "Ever seen a blade fight?"

She rolls her eyes and Beryll chokes, but I've moved on to gesturing at the fishermen who are growing more agitated. The crowd is getting bigger and the voices louder. "Either of you know what's going on here?"

Sam wrinkles his forehead and looks around as if suddenly aware there's even a commotion at all. "No idea. Why?"

"Doesn't matter," Seleni interjects. "Because we don't have time, right, Rhen? We've already had enough trouble for one day and don't want to get caught in the middle of whatever this is."

I shake my head. She may not want to get caught in the middle of this, but I do. I want to stay and listen and find out why these faces of men I know are etched with concern and fear.

As if reading my mind, Seleni grabs my hand and whispers, "Rhen, I'm serious. We have to go."

Sam eyes her, then tilts the tip of his knife toward me. "Come find us later and we'll tell you what's what here. Also, we'll tell you what we saw on the east side an hour ago. Seems that crippling death thing has made its way there."

I falter as Seleni keeps tugging. "Wait. You saw evidence of the disease?"

"Stop by tonight, Rhen." Will nods. "We'll talk, and in return, we're gonna need all the explosion details about your latest victim. Also, you can wish Sam and me good luck before we go sacrifice our godlike bodies to the Labyrinth contest tomorrow."

"Rhen would love to, but she has a party this evening." Seleni moves her fingers to clench my shoulder. "But maybe afterward. Now if you'll excuse us." She tries to turn me toward home, but Sam's gaze has focused in on something behind us, and when I follow it, Lute is standing there, fifteen paces away.

"Hey, Wilkes, what's the skinny?" Sam calls to him. "Why the uproar?"

Lute peers our way and his face is a scowl. His eyes hold the same expression they did when at the age of thirteen he caught a group of bullies making fun of his little brother's features and the way he rocked back and forth. Lute had found them in the alley cornering Ben after school and had taken them all on at once. Despite a bloody nose and sliced chin, he'd won.

I'd offered him a cloth, then gotten Da to stitch him up, and while Lute's mum had been none too happy, Da said he was a good kid and those boys had no place teasing a young'un with a special mind.

It's the only time I've ever seen Lute fight.

I try to catch his eye, but he's busy greeting the boys who've headed for him. If Lute notices me, he doesn't acknowledge it, and I don't know why I wish he would, because it's a silly thing. But I do. And then Seleni is dragging me off with the comment that the sun's almost down and her parents' party is waiting, and it occurs to me that the blood vial that's burning a hole in my pocket is waiting too.

"Oh good, you're here, Rhen." A woman steps in front of us as we pull away from the crowd. "You got my order for tomorrow, right? Three buns and five Labyrinth cakes." It's Mrs. Lacey.

"Mine too," her sister adds. "Except I've only the six cakes."

I nod at the women, then cast a glance back at Lute and the boys. "Of course. I'm baking them tonight and will drop them by in the morning." I offer the women a polite smile before Seleni and I take off to follow Beryll up the road toward home.

"Sounds like you've got a full night, Miss Tellur," Beryll says when we catch up.

I absentmindedly acknowledge his Beryll-like attempt at humor and try to ignore my desire to look back at Lute and the crowd again. I'd rather spend the evening with them.

A quarter mile up the walk we arrive at my street, where the air is grimy with a layer of grey floating around the shingled rooftops of our sloped village turning pink in the evening light. Much like the steam gathered in the clefts of the far-off mountains where the rare basilisks breathe fire. The hearths have already been lit, and the smell of smoldering cattle-manure chips stings the nostrils and eyes as the dinners are cooked quickly, before the cheap fuel dies out.

"All right, love. We'll see you in an hour." Seleni gives my hair a hopeful eye and waves, as does Beryll, and the next moment they are gone—hurrying up the hill away from the beat-up houses and broken streets, to the river that cuts like a thread to separate the Lowers from the rich estates. That separates people like Da and Mum and me from those I used to wish we could be: my aunt and uncle, and Mr. Holm of Holm Castle, proprietor of the legendary Labyrinth exams that Beryll and every other eligible young man is set to enter tomorrow. While the children thrill in terror, and the women and girls cheer the young men on with cups of tea and the type of Labyrinth cakes I will bake tonight.

I watch Seleni and Beryll disappear, then slip up to my door before old Mrs. Mench can catch sight of me through her window and rush out with the evening lecture. *"You're awfully noisy at night, Rhen. Who's your father treating now? How's your mum? What have you done all day?"*

I sniff and unlock the latch. *I've been out with boys, showing them my ankles, Mrs. Mench.*

The house is dim when I enter, and the interior smells of leftover yeast and spice from last night's scant baking. I peek into the small kitchen with its washbasin, wood hearth, and tiny round table surrounded by three rough-hewn chairs that only Da and I sit at most days now.

I glance toward his and Mum's room, where she's likely lying down. My lungs and stomach fight the urge to run back outside where the air doesn't feel like a shroud and my dread doesn't sound so loud. Because in here? The grief and fear are a ticking clock that is perpetually winding down on the mantel.

I swallow and pause a moment to listen.

The rustling beneath the floorboards says Da's still working in the cellar.

Good. I head for the stairs.

"And where've you been all day?" he asks upon my descent of the curved, rickety steps to a shelved room lined with alchemy books and medicines, many of his own creation. His pepper-grey hair is sticking up like a puff of smoke, and he's standing between two tables. One we use for cutting up specimens, and the other holds an assembly of his invented equipment and machines—the latest of which has been transformational in our work. He calls it *cell fractionation*.

"Thought you'd be back in bed when I left this morning. Did the deliveries go all right?" He hovers over the nearest table, where he has Pink Lady, the smallest of three rats we've been performing tests on. As a rule I don't name our subjects, but from the moment Da brought her in, I've felt she'd be the one to help unlock the cure. She twitches her rosy nose and bites his thick-gloved finger. She's actually the tame one compared to the other ten in our current possession.

I draw near, watching for the movement of the rat's muscles. Da said if we were going to find a cure, we needed live subjects. I insisted we only use already infected ones—of which, so far, there's been an endless supply.

And so far, she's lasted the longest.

I pat her head, then pull out the few coins my baked goods brought in and set them on the bill shelf. My scant business earns little, but added to Da's income, it helps us live. And it's work I understand—the way the ingredients come together to create a chemical reaction. It's soothing.

"The remaining biscuits came out at four." I stroll back over. "I finished delivering them by ten, but during the course of it I overheard two constables saying a northerner died outside town Tuesday morning. I slipped into the sexton's to get a bit of the corpse for testing before this heat wave reduced it to liquid."

Da nods. "Good thinking. Who was he?"

"The tree oil salesman who came through with that caravan two weeks ago. They all moved on today, except for him."

Da's brow lifts. "The one who swore the oil cured him from a disease?"

I pull the vial of blood from my coat. "Same man." I set it into the metal-looped tray on the equipment table, then turn to slide off my wet jacket and sling it over a hook near the tiny hearth that barely gives off enough heat to warm this room. "There's a bit of abdomen tissue in there as well." I grab a lone log and set it inside the tiny iron stove.

Upon first hearing the man's claim last week, Da and I had tested a bit of the oil right away but found it nothing more than cheap castor cut with floral essence. But the testimony of others from the caravan who'd said that the salesman had indeed come back from certain "life-crippling illness" was something I couldn't overlook.

"*Very* good thinking, Rhen." He lifts a thin silver needle and gently inserts it just beneath the skin on Lady's side. The rat squeaks but calms as soon as Da pulls biscuit crumbs from his pocket and sets them in front of her. She goes about nibbling, none the worse for wear, and he peers up. "So? What'd you find?"

I stand over the stove and let the faint heat warm my cheeks before I answer. What I wouldn't give for a cup of tea right now, except food and drink are forbidden in the lab due to contamination. "I have no idea."

He lifts a brow.

I nod. Exactly. People may die a lot around here, but there's only a handful of causes—and I've learned enough from Da to recognize most all of them.

I walk over to the sterilizing bucket. "I would've done a deeper investigation if I'd had time, but I had Beryll with me. The dead man smelled like liquor and looked twenty-five. His bones were all intact and his skin color was as expected since bloating had already set in. The mouth showed signs of asphyxiation—but from something internal, not man-made. Otherwise, there were no indicators of regular heart failure or choking." I tip a splash of alcohol into my palm and then scrub my hands together quickly as I recall something. "Oh, except there was a bit of clotted *blood* around his mouth."

He frowns and stops his work on Lady. "A blood clot? Like he'd coughed it up?"

I dab my hands dry and eye him. "Maybe it was a virus?"

"Without assessing the body, I can't say, but . . ." Da's frown deepens. "Did you wear gloves while inspecting him?"

"Of course."

He sighs. "Good. Then be sure to sanitize them. And, here, pass me my light." He holds out a hand while clasping the rat with the other and waits for me to find the lantern he's referring to—his favorite one that's on the shelves that span floor to ceiling along the two farthest walls. The wooden ledges are covered with crumbling books and half-empty bottles and pieces of skeletal remains—both human and animal. By the age of four I could name the parts of every single one of them and draw each in exact detail.

I reach past a juvenile basilisk's skull we pulled from a

wetland last year and grab the lamp behind it. The cruel beast's empty eye sockets stare back at me as I turn up the wick before I stride over to light it with a candle and set it in Da's fingers. I beckon to Lady. "How's she doing?"

A cautious smile materializes. "This is the fourth dose of your trial creation I've given her, and her muscles have gotten stronger. Look—" He puts more crumbs on the table—farther in front of the rat this time—at which she squeaks and straightens, then walks to them, barely hobbling as she goes. Da's grin grows wider.

I glance up to meet his gaze, and a flutter of hope erupts in my chest. Not just erupts—explodes. I can't stop the grin that follows it, nor the desperate hunger to hear him say we may have actually done it. That this could be the one. This could be the cure for Mum. Because it's definitely the most promising sign we've seen in any of the subjects.

"I guess we'll wait and see, eh? Speaking of which, have you seen your mum?"

A flare of guilt bubbles up. "I came straight down. Why—is she all right?"

"She's fine. Just more sore today. She ate early so she could lie back down, and I'm headed out in a bit to visit the Strowes. I just know she'd like to see you before the party." He drops his voice to a perceptive tone. "It would lift her spirits, Rhen. And spending time together is good for *both* of you."

I bite my lip. I used to love coming home after a day with Da and his patients. Mum and I would sit out on the front walk, watch the neighbors go by, and make up stories about their lives. Like the time we decided old Mrs. Mench was actually a dragon stuck inside a cat biddy's body, which would explain her temper and obsession with jewelry. And Mr. Camden, her fated savior—which is why he always carries a cane when he has to go near her.

I pick up the glass dish beneath the microscope Da must've been using. The blood droplets on it are dry and brown. I set it aside and keep my voice steady as I fetch a clean one to carefully swab with a bit of the new blood I just brought in, then place it under the scope. "I'll stop in before I go. How's the Strowe girl?"

His reply is so slow I raise my eye from the glass to find his expression clouded. He dips his head in a familiar gesture that says it's better not to ask. Her disease has advanced faster than we've previously seen—she's gone from a healthy, giggly child to bed-bound within a matter of weeks. "It's like the disease is accelerating," he says quietly. Then adds, "How are *you* feeling today?"

"I'm well." I move away from the magnifier and lift my top lip for him to look at my gums, then raise my arm for him to test my joints. When he's done I move to the shelves, where I pull down a tray of vials filled with chemicals and bonding agents.

I unseal one and dip a clean glass stick inside to withdraw a single liquid drop and place it on the glass dish beside the fresh blood sample. "Here, I'll get this next test batch started before I leave."

"No, no. You go get ready for Uncle Nicholae's party. You'll already be late from the looks of you." He lifts up Lady and returns her to her cage.

"It won't matter if I'm late." I smear through the blood on the dish to mix it with the liquid. "The only person who'll care is Seleni."

He chuckles. "You not caring if you're late means you'll forget to show up at all. And this can wait until later. Now go."

I lean closer to stare through the scope at the glass dish. Just like the others, the dead man's blood cells show signs of the disease. And just like the others, there's a faint sense of familiarity about the way they shape themselves around each other. I shake my head. Who cares if I'm late? Pink Lady's progress is tangible, and the reality that we might be onto the cure is something I can't ignore. What if Mum and the Strowe girl could be cured too? "I should stay here with this new blood sample. It looks like he may have had the disease. I'll attend another time."

"Another time you might miss the chance. With the equinox tomorrow, there'll be a horde of people there, and you can't ignore social engagements to sit over microscopes and rudimentary experiments in the dark, Rhen. I'll go over his blood work."

"This is far more important than attending their party. What if this is a real breakthrough, Da?"

"Good point, except now it's just a matter of watching and waiting, and I can do that just as well as you." His tone turns firm. "Mum and Lady will be here when you get back. You can't do anything for them right now. So go do something there."

He's right, of course. Seleni said there would be university and parliament members there.

I nod. "In that case I'll try to explain to the uni and government officials again how bad the illness is getting. Maybe when they hear what we're seeing, they'll reconsider—"

"That's not what I meant. You have to meet people your age, dance, breathe a little."

"I spent time today with people my age."

He snorts and returns Lady to her cage. "From the smell of you, they were all dead. Besides, you know it'll please your mum. Go scrub up, do something with your hair, dance with Vincent King, and make her happy."

"You should've smelled me before I rinsed in the ocean," I mutter. But I don't argue. "I'll try to get them to hear me this time and actually do something."

"Fine." He clears his throat, and suddenly sounds weary. "But try not to get kicked out, yeah?"

With a small sense of purpose and a giant swell of the first hope I've felt in months, I turn to head up the stairs and out to the back, where I take a quick, discreet sponge bath, then come in to shiver and dry my hair in front of the tiny oven in my chemise.

When both are no longer dripping, I comb out my hair and braid the long, brown strands into ropes and bind them at the base of my neck with a string. I slide into one of the two dresses I own that were handed down from Seleni and fancy enough for an Upper party. A midnight taffeta with a slightly-too-loose bodice for my small chest above a puffed skirt that reaches long enough to cover my worn shoes.

I check my reflection in the kitchen window and almost

laugh. Why I expected it would've altered since the last time I wore it is wishful thinking. I look like a fae doll dressed up for a funeral. I drop my gaze and swallow the embarrassment threatening to rise. It'll have to do.

After grabbing one of Mum's shawls from the wall hook, I slip it on, then pause to brace my spine and chest before I set my hand on the door to her room. *You will not cry, you will just breathe.*

I swallow and purse my lips. *Come on—you cut up corpses and run tests on rats. Facing your mum is not unbearable.* But my hands still sweat, and my throat clenches and I want to throw up. Because all I usually feel in these moments is scared and angry and weak. And this time is no exception.

I just want the mum I've always known back. Healthy. Vibrant. Strong enough to steady me when I don't know how to steady myself on certain days. And to hold me when I don't know where I belong—because lately, more than ever, I think I belong nowhere.

Instead, I end up holding her—the slowly fading body of skin and bone that is my mum—and I'm so desperately grateful she's there to hold, yet so desperately terrified that I cannot hold on tight enough. I can't fix her. And when she goes . . . I won't know how to fix Da.

With a deep breath I straighten, choke back a sob, and tap on the door.

Mum is sitting in bed, in the lantern-smoke-stained room, with her head resting on an elevated pillow. Even in her tired state, she looks as lovely as the northern nymphs that come out at full moon. The light from her lamp is low but still strong enough for the flickers to illuminate her soft brown curls and to smooth her sallow face as she breaks into a wide smile.

"You look beautiful." Her voice is an ocean tide trickling over rocks. "Are you headed up to Sara's party?"

I nod and sit on the edge of her rusty metal bed.

"Good. You'll have a marvelous time," she says gently.

I stay quiet so as not to say anything that will make her

homesick to attend. She used to have her own marvelous times, too, when she was younger. She never says so, but I know she misses it. The parties, the dresses, the fancy lights, and the food. As a child of an Upper, Mum grew up in luxury with her sister—my aunt Sara—until Da came along. Never mind he was brilliant and clever, and his university cadaver cleanup position allowed more of an education than the actual students even got. Mum was disinherited the moment she married him. And even Aunt Sara and Uncle Nicholae forbid Da from their home, although they still send Mum and me invites.

In eighteen years of marriage, Mum has never once gone. She does, however, insist that I attend.

I inch closer and give her cold hand a squeeze. She gives a feeble squeeze back, and I refuse my heart to squeeze along with it lest it begin to feel things and then fall apart. "I just wish you were coming."

"And let the lot of them think they're above your da? Hardly. I made my choice, and I'd do it again today," she says, because it's what she always says. She smiles. "Will Kenneth's son be there?"

"He will." I keep my voice even and hold her hand as I casually search her wrist and neck with my gaze. Her fingers are weak in mine, and I can't tell if the skin beneath her left ear is darker. Bruised around her lymph nodes.

"Think he'll fill up your dance card?"

I force a grin even though the idea of such a thing with Vincent nowadays makes me feel like I can't breathe. "I expect so."

"His mother was an old friend." She tries to move her

fingers to pat mine. "Vincent's a good boy. You two have always been compatible." The look on her face says her hopes haven't changed that I'll nab him as a good boy for my own. Before she and Da get too much older. And before she gets too much worse.

I don't have the heart to tell her that we're not quite so compatible these days. Since about fourteen months ago, to be precise. And even if we were . . .

My mind flashes awkwardly to Lute. To the flush he brought to my neck earlier. The way he looked at me as I talked about dead things, and how he *didn't* look at me when Mrs. Holder talked about humiliating things.

Mum lifts a brow and her eyes search mine. "Unless . . . ?"

"There are many good Upper boys," I say quickly, just to see her mind ease—even while I feel the guilt that says I'm probably giving false hope. It's not uncommon for Upper boys to marry Lower girls. Unlike an Upper girl marrying a Lower boy, which is, to quote Mum's father, "utter ruination." Thus, I've tried to find interest in the Uppers for the financial sake of my parents, and specifically in Vincent King, whose passion for science was the same as mine until last year. Only now . . .

I lift my gaze back to Mum's smile and swallow. Only now, I don't know about any of that.

Because here I am. In this moment. In *this* reality. Where a large portion of my heart is dying right here in front of me— and some days I'm not sure there'll be enough of me left to give away to a boy, let alone for a future. Not when my mum's own future is uncertain.

Not when I can continue trying to do something about it.

Not when the test cure we created is actually working on Pink Lady.

I glance across the room toward the direction of the port, as if I can peer through the walls to the people there. To the hunger they feel—like the hunger I have—for the world to be different. I bite my cheek. *You don't need to worry about me finding a husband,* I want to say. *I promise I'll give you something better. I'm finding you a cure instead.* But I don't say it, because I can't promise her that any more than I can hand her the moon. So I just lean down and kiss the top of her head and try not to notice if her frothy hair seems thinner today. "Mum, I have to go. I'll be back as soon as I can."

"Take your time." She chuckles. "I'm not going anywhere."

I close the door softly behind me, but right before it shuts, she whispers, "I love you, Rhen."

I blink nine times and swallow back the tempest in my throat, then yank her shawl around me tighter and stride for the front door.

I love you too, Mum.

A cacophony of noise carries up from the lower streets when I step outside. People are banging on metal drums, and loud voices are hollering amid groups of footsteps running. I frown. Parties for the festival have been going on for days, but the laughter and shouts floating up almost sound angry. What did Will and Sam find out about the commotion earlier?

Forget Aunt Sara, my mind says. *Go see what the problem is.*

But my mind also says, *Seleni will rip your face off and*

Mum will be disappointed if you don't show. The noise is just heightened excitement.

And it probably is. If it'd been anything major, they would've been rioting earlier when I was down there—not talking in whispers. More likely, Sam and Will and a host of others are at Sow's pub challenging each other over drinks, with half the town cheering them on. The Port people are nothing if not proud of their boys, and they've been taking bets for weeks on who'll bring home the win. Even though the Lowers have only won seven years out of the past fifty-four. Tonight is their send-off before it all begins tomorrow.

I chew my lip and, for a moment, debate joining them.

Instead, I turn and start up the road as the lights twinkle across the bridge leading to the Upper district and Aunt Sara and Uncle Nicholae's event of the year.

The beautiful manors and pastures, with their gardens and mini rose forests, sit like crowns overlooking our seaside town and shore. Even in the evening dim, they make a picturesque statement beneath a jewel-crushed sky.

I shake off the familiar fear of what else sits in that dimness and what will happen if its moor ghosts catch scent of me. I can feel their tendrils already—their auras reaching out along the tributaries and roads in search of foolish travelers to pull into the underground cemeteries.

A shrill scream rattles the air and about makes my skin peel off. It's from somewhere out over the ocean—a siren looking for prey. I say a quick prayer for lost sailors and then, with a loud gulp, clutch up my skirts to keep the material from snagging and make my way quick and quiet along the hedge of cattle nettles and berry vines.

Dust stirs up and horses neigh and wheels crunch the gravel as guest after guest drives past me on the road that weaves up to my uncle's mansion, which sits five estates below the towering hill of Mr. Holm and the famed Holm Labyrinth. The coaches' swinging lanterns look like fireflies in the dark, and it's not hard to notice how many more there are than usual.

Seleni says the night before the equinox is the time to host a lavish event—especially if you have a young lady you're hoping to marry off. Let the last impression in the future businessman's mind be of red-stained lips and lilac-scented skin. Because whether the families win or not, they'll remember the way that girl and party made them feel—like they could accomplish anything. Which I hear is a desirable quality in a spouse.

I carefully open the inner gate and tighten the string in my hair before I maneuver through the path in my aunt's underused garden that, as a child, I was enamored with. Seleni and I used to make worm hospitals in the mud and rocks here—dissecting the invertebrates in order to "learn how to save them."

Until her parents found out and recoiled in horror at what kind of children would do such a thing. "Possessed ones," I had whispered, just so we could snicker at my aunt's reaction. From then on they decided my visits would consist of Seleni's nanny teaching us cross-stitch—something far more appropriate for young ladies with clearly too much morbid time on their hands.

I let out a smile at the slip of memory as I round a cluster of elf bushes and overgrown trellises, to arrive at Seleni's back entrance of warmly lit windows and double doors.

The indoor scene is golden. Like something from my aunt's collection of children's fairy books. Candles in crystal chandeliers sparkle through the windows above the space. Tapestries, fireplaces, and bouquets of fresh flowers give the room a rich ambience, as does the assembly of servants carrying silver trays loaded with pastries and drinks. My stomach growls. The guests are filling their plates around food tables and fountains, and the savory smell slipping out promises plenty of rich stews and hot vegetable platters.

I inhale through my nose and smooth my ill-fitted bodice. Then lift a hand to knock.

The door swings open. "I thought I saw you slinking up, you minx!" Seleni crows. "Come save me," she adds in a whisper, and grabs my elbow to drag me through the doorway and into the shiny, marble-floored room.

Light and music splash over us. A waltz is being played on a harpsichord that, from my assessment, sounds as perfectly tuned as the guests' nerves look. I start to smile until I spot her mum, my aunt Sara, standing behind Seleni and peering from beneath a pile of brown curls that seem to be set in some type of hair topiary. I nod, curtsy, and hurry to shut the door to keep in the warmth. "Aunt Sara, thank you for the invitation."

"Of course, dear. How's your mother feeling?" Aunt Sara's features falter as her eyes take in my still-damp hair and crumpled skirt. She leans in and sniffs, then straightens with a frown. "Rhen, dear, did you bathe in the ocean again?" Her voice is intended only for me even as her pale cheeks tinge pink.

"I bathed at home but had to rush. I was working on something with my da, but . . ."

Aunt Sara's gaze falls. She sighs and flips her hand as if to ask why she even tries. "Please take some food home to your mother when you go."

I nod, apologize again, and duck from her before the sense of shame that sometimes plagues my bones when I'm here can flare and leak onto my neck and face. I hustle for the other side of the room, where a fireplace bigger than the five men standing in front of it roars and toasty drinks are being served.

Seleni is right behind me, every hair in place, draped in a cream dress that looks like a cupcake, with a tight waist that's bordering on scandalous in the way it hits just above her ankles. "It's okay. Mum was appalled because I looked 'too winded' when I got home. She had Nanny spend a solid hour fixing my 'atmosphere'—whatever that is."

"She means well," is all I say. Because I believe it's probably true. Or maybe it's just that my aunt believes it's true—that everything she's done has been because she meant well. It's not her fault that most of the world can never be presentable enough to earn her and my uncle's approval.

"I do try," I'd told them once many years ago.

"*Try* and *succeed* are simply degrees between how badly one wants a thing," was my uncle's reply. "We can only provide profitable opportunities for you, child. It's up to you what you make of them."

Which is the same thing he said when he found out Da was pulling me out of classes to homeschool me. Just like my short-lived internship at Mr. Holder's papery, my educational struggle wasn't a matter of trying—it was due to my problem with the letters and numbers shifting places in my head. And even though the schoolteacher agreed that Da's idea of repetitious science and documentation was precisely what was needed, and the two years since had brought about enormous progress, it didn't matter to my uncle. He simply couldn't understand.

Ahead of me, Seleni grabs a glass of mulled tea off a serving tray and offers it, which I down in five gulps as my stomach loudly reminds me I've not eaten all day. "Come on. I'll introduce you around. There's a host of Beryll's friends I'm determined you'll take an interest in. Oh, and some of Daddy's famous political associates are here too," she adds with a soft squeal.

"Did Beryll's parents come?" I glance around for the politicians she referred to.

Seleni gives a sharp laugh in answer, then tucks her arm around mine.

"Well, they're fools then. Because who wouldn't want to spend time with you?"

"Exactly." She sniffs, then pats my hand and leads me toward the group of her friends, a few of whom I recognize from past events.

They're chatting in a circle beneath a vibrant mural of Caldon's royal castle, wearing the same type of fancy outfits and hair grease as the people in the painting. I shyly eye the lace-draped girls perched beside impeccably dressed boys who are surrounded by a fog of cologne. If the parents' preening looks being shot their way are any indicator, at least ten of the boys are going for the Holm scholarship.

"Hello there," a girl in black ringlets and a stiff corset says. "I like your dress. The brown matches your eyes."

I brace and wait for the sarcasm to follow, but it doesn't. She just keeps smiling, and after a second I return the grin. "Thanks. I think the same of yours."

"I'm Moly."

"Rhen."

"I know. Seleni's told me about you."

"Ah, there they are." Beryll clears his throat and holds up a fresh-scrubbed face that gives no indication he was carousing with corpses a few hours ago. "Miss Lake, I was just informing our friends here how you two have never missed a single Labyrinth festivity."

"Not a one. Even when I was deathly ill with fever." Seleni jokingly swipes a hand across her forehead. "Mainly because I've made it my life's work to discover the true identity of Mr. Holm." She releases my arm and slips over to Beryll, where she takes his drink from his hand and sips it. Then nuzzles close to him in a way I recognize as her still feeling insecure about his parents.

"Ah, the elusive Holm. Man of mystery or murder? That is the question," a tall boy to Seleni's left says. I peer over at him and my nerves prick. The guy could probably grow a full beard to match his impeccable dark eyebrows if he wanted, but it's his eyes that make him stand out. They're cold. Detached.

Calculating.

I shiver and decide to avoid any dark corners near him.

"Definitely misery, Germaine. Haven't you heard my brother talk about the contest from two years ago?"

We all cringe at jolly-faced Lawrence and the story he's told both times I've seen him—about how his brother made it into the top three contestants and would've won if he'd remembered the correct equation for harmonic oscillation. But he didn't and instead tried to steal an opponent's place, and when he emerged shrieking from the Labyrinth, the only thing he'd say about it was that a ghoul had climbed inside his head and whispered, "Cheaters eventually meet their maker."

He went on to attend a less expensive university and, from what Beryll's said, has never been dishonest since, for fear his conscience will push him into insanity.

"Which is exactly why I find Holm creepy." Eloise looks up primly from her spot at Lawrence's arm. "My mum says he communes with the dead."

"I've heard he isn't real, but the invented persona of two Stemwick graduates," a boy with a giant plate of cake informs us.

"Well I've heard he's a death wizard." Seleni drops her voice and slowly raises her hands to curl her fingers into claws while the light flickers through them. "He comes out at night on the eve of the autumnal equinox to drink the blood of his victims. And when he's done? He paints his Labyrinth with the screams of their souls. It's how his magic is reborn each year and how he keeps his Labyrinth beasts fed."

I chuckle along with the group. Seleni made that story up

one autumnal eve years ago, and we've scared each other and every child we can with it since.

It wasn't until we got older that we realized there might actually be some truth to it.

Just like the intermittent deaths of scholarship contestants, the rumors of strangers who've wandered near his place at night and never returned aren't just folklore. Sam once told me that his mum heard screams coming from Holm's grounds early one morning.

"She thinks it's his obsession with experimenting," he'd said. "Was probably conducting tests on some poor chap."

"Seleni, you are downright awful." Moly giggles.

"That must be what's killing off so many of the Lowers," Cake Boy adds, in a tone that's attempting to make us laugh. "Their sickness is really spread by Mr. Holm."

The smile dies on my lips. I shift my worn shoes against the marble floor and look away. Clearly he doesn't know anyone with the disease or he wouldn't say such things. But perhaps I should be grateful because it reminds me of why I'm here.

I drift my gaze around the room until—there. My uncle is standing across the hall from us, speaking with a group of men who, if the stiffness of their pocket brocades is any indication, are either politicians or Stemwick University board members. Or both. I study their faces and nicely set hair. Whatever they're talking about seems to mostly involve lighthearted chuckling.

Good.

I check to see if Seleni's distracted—she is, by Beryll—and

am about to break from her circle of friends when a voice says, "Oh, Holm is real, but he's definitely no wizard."

It's the eyebrow boy, and something in his tone is darker than before. I spin to see his eyes scanning our faces.

"And I can assure you he won't be anonymous much longer. Come tomorrow—not only do I intend to beat these chaps at the game—" He looks down his narrow nose at us and curls his lip to complement the cocky way he's standing. Then sniffs and takes a gulp of his drink. "But I intend to beat Mr. Holm at it as well."

6

Seleni giggles. "And how, may we ask, do you plan on doing that, Germaine?"

"Quite simply. By breaking the rules and exposing Mr. Holm for the cheap-trick charlatan he is."

Half the circle bursts into laughter and the rest resort to eye rolling. "Not this again," Lawrence says. Except, Eyebrow Boy's arrogant expression says he's quite sincere.

Moly lifts a hand. "Holm has single-handedly funded numerous university educations over the years. At least give him that."

"Money-schmoney, I'm talking the game itself." Germaine strokes his left brow and slides his dark gaze around. "The 'magical illusions' he uses in his Labyrinth are an insult. If he's so anxious to give his money away to charity, why not have a normal process? Instead, he amuses himself by creating inappropriate ploys that any street magician could do. And he endangers all of us in the process. The man has the blood of at least five contestants on his hands."

"Fair enough," a boy I don't know says. "But according to the estate's official declaration, those deaths were all due to those boys not following the competition's regulations."

"Were they?" Germaine looks at his drink. "Or was that just what he needed to say in order to keep operating? Because, ask yourself, what kind of academic scholarship competition actually allows for young men to die? Let alone the *way* they died."

As if someone opened a window and let the moor wind in, a chill ripples through the group. Even my own skin gets goose bumps at the recollection of the stories. The most recent— from four years ago when the body was so badly damaged they couldn't perform a proper funeral. The whispered suspicion was that whatever had gotten hold of the lad had made teeth marks the size of a fist.

"Whoever's fault those were, I believe Miss Lake here asked how you plan to beat him."

Germaine takes a second-long sip of his drink, and for a moment I think he's not heard Beryll. Until a short, broadshouldered guy I'd not noticed before steps out from behind Germaine and answers for him by leaning over and slapping Beryll on the back. "Aw, poor chap—you scared? Well, you should be. You best just accept this competition will be highly *volatile*—if you know what I mean—and make your peace with Miss Lake here. Because you boys might as well pull your brains out and toss them to us now." He crosses his arms and mimics Germaine's smirk. "That or we'll be ripping them out one at a time."

I lift a brow. Beryll might be a ridiculous person, but only Seleni and I can be condescending to him. I snort and turn to the twit. "Perhaps that's why Mr. Holm hosts his competition the way he does. To ensure it accounts for more than just one-sided intellect."

The broad-shouldered boy and Germaine look around until their eyes land on me. "Explain," Germaine demands.

I glance at Seleni and Beryll and try to come up with more. "From what I've heard, the test is as intuitive and physical as mental. Maybe Holm understands not everyone's had the same interests—or educational opportunities, for that matter—so he's being fair."

"I assume you're referring to the contestants from the Lower district, Miss . . . *Tellur*, is it?" Germaine's gaze narrows. "And that's precisely what makes the test nonsensical. It circumvents the correct process by making it achievable for anyone, rather than those who'll benefit the most. Why waste an education on someone with less ability?"

My nerves flare. "Less *ability*?"

"Less aptitude—less motivation. I'm referring to those who could elevate their status if they applied themselves harder. There's a reason those in the Lower district live there, Miss Tellur. And while they should absolutely be allowed to earn a scholarship, putting them in the same league as us only under-mines the effectiveness of the process."

My mouth drops open but no words come out. They've been lost somewhere between my head and my rippling, infuriated spine.

"Well, I believe it's only fair to give everyone a chance," Seleni says, in a tone warning he'd be wise to watch his mouth.

Germaine shakes his head. "Not when money would be wasted. We all know there's no way an Upper's education can be bested by someone who's barely passed year eight in school. Thus, fully funding their future learning for beating a sub-standard contest? Promotes a substandard system."

"And yet you're entering," I say quietly.

"But even *if* a contestant wins," Moly hurriedly butts in, "they still have to pass Stemwick University's entrance exams."

"Has anyone with the scholarship ever *not* been allowed in?" Germaine challenges. "And money is money, Miss Tellur. If I need to play a game to win it, fine. Doesn't mean I have to agree with everyone else he's allowing to play it."

I swallow and place a hand on my hip. "If that's how you feel, then perhaps the scholarship contest should be open to women as well." I look coolly around at the group. "At least that way your friends might have actual competition."

The words. They spill out like a spurt of blood, and the moment I utter them I wish I could take them back. His expres-sion says I *should* wish as much.

Germaine flicks his gaze down my body to slowly scan my chest before he slithers it toward my hips. He smiles suggestively and lifts his eyes to meet my glare. Even as he addresses Seleni. "Miss Lake, I'd heard your cousin would be a fun one, but I'd no idea just how pleasurable. You must bring her around more often. I think I'd enjoy getting to know more of her . . . *spirit*."

My cheeks warm. I hold his gaze and straighten my shoulders in the midst of this high-ceilinged room with its fancy dresses and fresh faces that suddenly feels suffocating. I lower my voice and flick my gaze down *his* body. "Mr. Germaine, I assure you—were you given the opportunity to know more of my *spirit*, I believe I'd find the experience wholly unsatisfying."

If there was a gasp at my comment before, this time there's an explosion of laughter mixed with a few eye daggers.

"Annnnd it's time for more cake," someone says.

"I think Seleni's mum is beckoning," crows another.

Germaine narrows his jaw and dips his head at me. And says quietly, "Perhaps you'd like to test that theory out, Miss Tellur."

I open my mouth to respond, but his broad-shouldered friend picks up a plate from the fireplace mantel and lifts a piece of Labyrinth cake off of it. His expression flashes furtive. Cruel almost. He looks down at the pastry and takes a bite before he holds the plate above his head. Staring straight at me, he says in a low voice, "Careful, Miss Tellur. Women who don't know their place have a habit of losing their place, just like your mum did. You keep on with that attitude of hers, and you'll stay just like her—begging people to buy your cakes and living with a crackpot husband who murders his patients."

I freeze. Twenty different emotions bubble up and threaten

to compress my lungs. I steady my gaze and refuse to let the mixed waves of fury and shame play out across my face, even as I feel my cheeks turn the color of our port town sunsets.

"Rubin and Germaine," Seleni snarls. "That's quite enough. Your remarks reek of insecurity, and your offensive manners have tainted the evening as well as my cousin's opinions of you. I expect—"

"Seleni, dear." My aunt's voice rings out from across the room like fork tines clinking on her china. "Bring your friends into the great room. We're doing a waltz." She claps rapidly as if to break things up and move us along.

"Oh, and Rhen." My aunt's trilling voice calls even louder. "I've asked Mr. King there to accompany you in the first dance."

She claps again, then moves to usher her friends in, and I turn to where she's pointed—to Vincent, Kenneth's son, who is standing casually in a cream waistcoat and jacket on the far side of the now-dispersing group. I frown. Was he standing there the whole time? Had he heard the conversation?

"Miss Tellur." He extends a hand my direction, followed by the same type of wide smile I've seen his father give constituents. The smile Vincent used to hate because "it looks hungry" but now imitates so perfectly that I cringe. "It's nice to see you again. It seems you've made the rounds of my friends." He nods at Germaine and takes my arm, then leads me into the great hall and onto the center of the dance floor. Where he slips my hand into his.

The music tinkles and floats through the blue-and-white wallpapered room, and Vincent lifts his arm to begin. His feet are far more astute than mine, as are his hands, which are cupped around my stiff waist as we step to match the movements of the thirty other couples filling the glittery space. Can he feel my skin squirming beneath his hot fingers?

"Miss Tellur, your cheeks are positively glowing," he says in a warm voice. His blond hair swags across his forehead in a boyish style that complements his roguish chin and finely chiseled features, all of which mimic his father's, and all of which he's had since we were children. He once cut a lock of that blond hair so we could perform genetic experiments on it to better hone our skills. And those chiseled features now have the ladies sneaking glances at him—especially in light of his recently declared intention to forgo science in pursuit of Upper government.

He drops his voice as he leans in. "I know your aunt suggested I claim this dance, but I freely admit my parents and I were hoping you'd be here."

I nod and try to smile back courteously and don't mention that, while his parents' attentiveness is very kind, my flush has nothing to do with them. Rather, it's me trying to assess which version of Vincent I'm getting tonight—the one who'll soon ignore me or the one who wants something from me. While also shielding the disgust still burning through my bones for Germaine's and Rubin's insults. My body's trembling from it, and I've a good mind to go over to where they're standing at the far wall, tracking the other competitors, the room, and me with their eyes—and give both boys another tongue-lashing.

They're like hunters tracking prey, my gut whispers.

But I don't. I stay and behave and sway to the trilling music as Vincent spins me against him. When he twirls me out, he follows my eyes, then tips his chin in Germaine's direction. "You were a little hard on him back there, don't you think?"

I blink. And frown—as he bestows on me the other kind of smile. The one Da gives when I've skewed an experiment.

"Germaine was just stating his opinion, and it's not his fault if there's some accuracy to it. You needn't have embarrassed him," he continues quietly. Then pulls me around to place my hand tighter inside his and winks. "At least not *quite* so badly."

"Mr. Wells insulted my neighbors and was inappropriate toward me."

The persona cracks and Vincent shrugs in the way he used to. Simple. Boyish. "I completely agree. But I've known him for most of my life, and I don't think he intended to imply anything. If he overstepped, you'll have to forgive his somewhat intense social skills. After all, his father's a politician, so what can you do?"

So is yours, I almost point out. *So are you. Or at least you will be.*

Instead, I study his confident blue eyes and feel mine waver as my mind reels back through the conversation with his friends. *Was I too hard?*

I don't know. My head feels muddled. I thought the remarks about the Lowers were unfair, and Germaine's comments regarding me improper. And I'd think someone who used to be my friend would feel the same. Even though these days Vincent's acquaintance seems to be more about his myriad moods, or what I can do, than any echo of what we've been. Which just makes it all the more jumbled. I furrow my brow in confusion and awkwardly note the skin on my arms is reddening. Perhaps I *am* being a bit too sensitive.

Vincent laughs. "No need for mortification, my dear. Just thought the woman I intend to court should know for future reference." He tilts his head kindly and lets the light catch his eye, before playfully adding, "Although you look positively lovely when you blush."

I feel my flush deepen at the perplexing mix of what feels like calculated flattery and correction, and unwanted declared intentions. I don't know if any of those is even accurate—but then Seleni is twirling past us in time to the music and whispers, "Are you all right?"

Yes. No. I don't know.

I feel like a trapped animal that maybe should run.

I peek at Vincent, then up at the gold spire clock hanging like a globe from the ceiling. Sam and Will and the other boys are probably still down at the pub, tucking into their fourth ciders. My chest gives an odd flutter—is Lute there too?

"Of course." I lie to her, amid the dancers' shoes *click click click*ing to the tune of Variety in C.

But then, maybe it's not a lie. I firm my spine and focus on the fact that Mum would be thrilled to see me doing this. I picture her happy expression in place of Germaine's, which is currently boring into the back of Beryll's neck as he reclaims Seleni, who grins and giggles and fits perfectly in his arms. I ease my breath and try to smile at Vincent like a decent person. "How is your father's job these days?"

"Excellent. He's influencing the House of Lords to make real changes for Caldon."

"And your own aspirations?" I say it quietly, without malice or any insinuation of the mutual camaraderie we used to have versus the lonely distance that's settled in its place.

But it doesn't matter. His expression cools, and that stiffness that presented fourteen months ago when he changed career focus clicks cleanly over his face.

"My father has begun taking me to parliament as an assistant, which, as you can imagine, has opened a glut of connections. Once my education is finished, my position will be assured."

He sounds like a machine the way he says it. I shiver and want to ask more. To ask what happened to him and to remind him of the fact that he used to not want his father's life. He wanted to study anatomy and cellular abilities and create cures just like me and Da and his friend Lawrence.

"And what about you?" His tone stays just as taut. "How's your research on the disease coming along? Have you found anything more on it yet?"

It's the same thing he's asked every time he's decided to speak to me in the last year. Like it's the one nod to the past he'll allow. *Have you figured it out? Do you know how it started? Did you find a cure?* I frown and answer honestly. "Not yet, but I think we might be close. If the medical community or politicians could take it on and fund more actual research—or even take an interest—"

It's his turn to frown as he reclaims my waist with his hands. "They've got other things to focus on, and they'll just get caught up researching how it originated rather than fixing it."

I start to argue, but he lowers his voice into a sense of urgency that's familiar to the team we used to be. "Keep working at it. I know you can find the cure. And when you do, my constituents will adore you for it. They may not even mind that tongue of yours," he adds with a chuckle, then twirls me past three older gentlemen before he returns to lock arms with me.

Finally, the dance is over and everyone is clapping, except for Vincent, who hasn't yet released me. Instead, he leans in. "Now that that's settled, let's talk of better things—such as *you*. Because I confess to having another reason for hoping you'd be here."

My body stalls. I gulp and catch the glances of a group of women emerging into view over his shoulder. They're swathed from head to toe in the latest fashions, low-cut bodices and bustled skirts, and they're all watching us. The curve of their lips say they'd be proud to have their daughters where I am—wrapped in Vincent's arms, his gaze looking at mine with so much favor. I swallow down my nerves and allow a nudge of guilt. Uncle Nicholae would also be proud.

Vincent peers around as if he, too, can feel the ladies' attention. He grabs my hand and leads me from the room of flushed faces and out into a side hall. "My parents were hoping your family might like to join them for the opening picnic tomorrow."

"I'm sure they would like that, Mr. King, but—"

"Good. And on a more intimate level, Miss Tellur . . ." He pulls me into a small recess, away from prying eyes, and looms his face close to mine with a look of presumption. "I believe it'd be most honoring of you to lend me a token to carry into the contest."

A token? Honoring *him*? I furrow my brow. I've heard of girls giving such things to the entrants before, but I've never been asked. My stomach twists as that feeling of being a trapped animal squeezes tighter.

"Perhaps a kerchief or hair ribbon?" he prompts.

I don't know how to respond, so I just nod and give an awkward, "Thank you. Maybe I can think of one and let you know once I arrive?"

"Of course." His grin comes as smooth as his warm breath on my neck, and for a moment I'm tempted to stop this nonsense. To beg him to go back to who he was before—a friend I miss, exclaiming over a mutual discovery—rather than whatever this new role is that he's playing. But the last time I did so, he irritably informed me that he'd grown up and perhaps it was time I did too.

I firm my jaw and peer around him—to get away—and spot a group of men slipping up the stairwell at the end of the hall with my uncle, toward the floor that holds his study. The next moment they're gone and Vincent's gaze flashes to where I'm looking.

He frowns and looks back at me—and suddenly his fingers are beneath my chin, tipping it up toward him. "I'd very much like to hear more about your experiments. You said you're getting close?"

"Yes, I—"

He puts a finger to my lips and slouches in at an awkward angle, and oh-hallowed-Francis, I think he's intending to kiss me. I yank back. "Mr. King, what are you *doing*?"

He drops his finger and retreats with a look of surprise. Then nods. "My apologies for coming off a bit too forward. It's easy to do with you." He holds out his hand. "But as penance, might I invite you to join me in another dance?"

I don't want to dance anymore. I don't want to do this with Vincent. Whatever *this* is he's doing. I want to make my stomach stop shaking and get this weight off my shoulders—this pounding pressure that says something is wrong with me, and Vincent, and his friends, and this place, and that any other girl in my shoes would be flattered while I simply want to leave.

"I think one is all I'm good for. Besides, I just realized I haven't yet paid my respects to my uncle. If you'll excuse me?"

He stiffens a moment, then just as quickly relaxes and bows. "Of course. I look forward to your return."

I pull away, hoping he'll see fit to invite another girl, and leave him to make my way toward the arched staircase as a loud laugh goes up from a group surrounding my aunt. They're talking of holiday trips they'll be taking this year. I swallow and press through the bodies of guests who smell of soap and perfume and apparently enjoy this type of thing. Is this really the life of comfort Mum and Da hope I'll have?

Because everything about it makes me feel *un*comfortable.

I pick up my pace and shove through the archway that leads to the study.

The staircase and landing are empty. Not even a speck of dust on the shiny balsam wood beneath my quiet footsteps or fingers as I hurriedly trace the paneled walls up to the lavishly carpeted second story. A wide hall with three doors on either side greets me at the top, and shadows of male figures extending from the second room on the right match up with the voices emitting. This is Uncle Nicholae's section of the house.

I tug my shawl higher on my shoulders and head toward the voices just as my uncle's fills the air. "Do they know yet?"

"It was announced this evening in the Port. We wanted to give the fishing boats time before the regulations go into effect next month."

My steps slow.

"It had to be done to protect the future of the port and shoreline. The population's grown too much to sustain the current intake."

"That's going to be rough on those who make their livelihood from it." My uncle emits a low whistle.

I narrow my gaze. *Fishing boats? The port?* I stride the last few steps to the open doorway and peer in to find ten men, drinks in hand, speaking in official tones. "Well, you know," one of them says, "there's only so much we can do. It's our responsibility to make hard choices for the benefit of everyone—not favor a few." His eyes flicker up and land on me, and abruptly the room falls silent.

7

Excuse me," I mutter. "I was asked to pay respects to my mum's brother-in-law."

I wait for Uncle Nicholae to say something as my heart beats so loud I'm certain everyone can hear it as they stare at me from beneath the wire cages containing stuffed exotic birds hung from the ceiling. My uncle bought and posed them years ago to look in midflight or midsong, but even for someone fascinated by the science of life and death, I have always found them morbid.

After what might be forever, Uncle Nicholae smiles and beckons me into the bright room. "Ah, Rhen, glad you could join us." But his eyes don't change expression as they flash down to assess my dress and presentation.

I lift my hand for him to take. "Thank you for having me, sir."

"Of course, of course." If he thinks less of my nearly dry hair or too-loose dress, he doesn't show it. Just turns to the men with him. "Gentlemen, this is my niece, Miss Tellur. We've taken it upon ourselves to entertain her when we can. Rhen, these men are from the board of Stemwick University and Caldon's esteemed parliament."

Of the ten men standing there, one is Vincent's father, and I suspect five may be with the university where my father used to be employed, because their faces seem to register recognition at my last name. Before they can comment, I quickly add, "Charming to meet you. Thank you for the work you do. I'm certain it's quite valuable." I'm not sure if I'm supposed to curtsy or not, so I end up giving a half dip, which comes off more as a stumble.

Their expressions turn pleased. "It's quite rewarding," says one, who I think Uncle Nicholae referred to as Millner. "We're happy to work for the benefit of our constituents."

"Tellur. As in the local alchemist?"

I freeze and my neck goes cold. I glance at Uncle Nicholae, but the board member continues without a hitch. "How is he? Is he still seeing patients and testing rat cellulitis?"

"He's seeing patients, yes. And his recent work involves research on a cure for the crippling disease."

"Ah, yes." The elderly man turns to his counterparts. "The

recently emerged crippling disease. It comes on slowly and attacks the nervous system, leaving the individual paralyzed until their heart and lungs seize up. It's an interesting phenomenon—one that, alas, only seems to affect the poorer of Caldon's communities."

"Due to a lack of clean sanitation habits, no doubt," one of the parliament men says, and Vincent's father nods as if this is common. "Has the university begun studying it?"

"Only to ascertain that it's a low-threat status."

"But it's a growing threat," I say. "We're seeing it more frequently, and its symptoms now present within weeks instead of months."

"Yes, well, there are always idiosyncrasies. But compared to the long list of other concerns we see regularly, it's rather minimal." The university board member smiles gently at me, then turns back to the others.

My mouth falls open. How can they be so casual about it? "People are dying. My *mum* is dying from it."

Vincent's father looks over to offer a sad smile, but he stays quiet while the board member turns and says, "I'm very sorry to hear that, my dear. Our university is discussing an educational initiative to teach the port people better sanitation next spring. I hope that will give you some solace."

I stare at him. Is he serious? I start forward. "You don't understand—"

But Uncle Nicholae's brow dips in sharp irritation. "Which is why we've taken on poor Rhen," he says calmly. "To see her properly educated in higher society and clean living. Isn't that right, dear?" He bestows me with the tight grin that's really a hint that it's time for me to run off and find Seleni.

My head and chest are exploding. I want to argue—to say the disease has little to do with sanitation, considering it's at a cellular and nerve level. To say they don't know enough about it because it's too new, and if they truly *had* studied it, they'd at least know that while it may have originated in the Lower Port, it has the potential to spread. In fact, a recent house call Da made in the Upper district suggests it's already begun.

I scowl. Maybe if we posed my mum in a cage like those stuffed birds, these men would pay better attention. Maybe they'd see her.

But I stay silent because if I say more, I will end up raising my voice and bursting into tears, and their intellectual dismissal will only turn to embarrassment for me.

"You're a good man, Nicholae. And you're a lucky girl, Miss Tellur," one of the men says heartily. "Not everyone has such an opportunity. I expect to see good things come from it."

I stare back at him. Then simply firm my shoulders and softly reply, "Oh, don't worry. You will."

After forcing another curtsy, I exit the doorway before my shaking knees give way, and take a deep inhale to brace myself so I can go find Seleni and tell her "Thank you for the evening, and I'm heading home now."

Except one of the board members murmurs, "I find it surprising anyone would allow her father to treat them after his pseudo-experiment with the university equipment killed that one woman."

I stall beside the wall in the dim hallway—and blink twice to rebuff the heat furiously flooding my eyes and the quick words flying up my throat. My father didn't kill anyone. Mrs. Sims was going to die anyway. Da simply allowed her the hope of trying an experiment he'd already told her was unlikely to work. But at least she died feeling she'd had a choice—and that someone was willing to keep fighting for her. Even if it was the cadaver room caretaker. And even if he was wrong to have done it.

"Your niece is quite inspired, though," Mr. King murmurs.

"Yes," my uncle says. "It's just a pity the apple fell too near her mother and father's trees. If she were more inclined to certain things, she'd make a solid catch."

I bite my lip and refuse to wince. And start walking. I don't want to hear what Mr. King has to say to that.

I've gone exactly five steps when the door to my uncle's study swings shut behind me with a soft, decisive thud. I clench my jaw and continue walking as one of the doors up ahead gives a quiet squeak and pops open from the shift in air pressure. It swings ajar enough to emit a slit of dull light along with a new set of voices emerging.

I slow. These are my uncle's rooms—no one else should be up here. Perhaps it's Seleni? I quietly step to the slatted opening, set my hand on the knob, and listen for her or my aunt.

It's neither. A blend of male voices are whispering excitedly about the Labyrinth competition. One of them laughs, and it's chilled enough that the warmth leaves the walls for a moment. "We'll take each one down fast so they won't have time to warn the other players."

"But if we take out too many, won't that look a bit obvious, Germaine?"

Germaine? I freeze and pull my hand away. What are they doing in there?

Edging closer, I peer through the narrow slat into the room. Only three boys are visible—Germaine, Rubin, and one other I recognize from earlier but have no idea as to his name. The latter two's faces are flushed and giddy. Germaine's is stale and smart.

"It's a competition," he mutters. "If Holm doesn't like the way we play, then he shouldn't host it. But he can't sift for the smartest minds in Caldon and expect they'll be the ones playing within the regulations."

"But what you're suggesting can get us in trouble," the nameless boy hisses. "You do realize we might actually *kill* people."

My spine ripples. *Kill people.* I peer harder through the crack only to see Germaine sneer at the speaker, then at the person beyond my view. "Welcome to the new game, boys. It is what it is. You want to win? You have to risk. Just make sure that if anything does happen, it looks like an accident."

Every nerve ending I own goes paralyzed. This is bizarre. It's way beyond besting Holm at his own game. It's taking things to a whole other level—one where they're willing to do harm.

A rustling behind me makes me jump so fast I have to catch my hand from flapping against the door as I spin around. A voice tinkles out like clock chimes. "Such naughty chaps who delight in sinful traps. Can you imagine being in competition against them?"

My lungs catch in my throat as I scoot away from the room and scan the corridor, but all I see is an empty hall. Until my gaze lands on a wall inset twelve feet away where an elderly man is hiding, steeped in shadow, watching me. From his secretive expression, I've an odd suspicion I've just interrupted some sort of romantic, geriatric meet-up. I try not to imagine such a thing but glance around to see if he's got a lady nearby.

Thankfully, no.

He waves at my uncle's closed study door and continues talking as if we're in midconversation. "Or even being in parliament with those older men, for that matter." He tips his head. "'The problem, my dear, must be sanitation.'" His voice is a perfect mimic of the politicians as he flicks his fingers, then gives a tinkly laugh. "Good grief, so much opinion from opinionated humans." He lifts a pipe to his lips and takes a puff, except no smoke curls up.

I eye the pipe, then his lavender eyes. The thing's unlit. Is he a friend of Uncle Nicholae's? And how long has he been up here? I note the man's wrinkled face and clumped grey whiskers that hint at mischief beneath a pair of rather magnificent eyebrows that look almost unreal. Above those, a giant tuft of silver hair is enhanced by his colorful suit, which blends rather impressively into the tapestries on each side of the inlet he's standing in.

I ease my shoulders.

He stops his snickering and taps on his pipe before he scrutinizes me with curiosity. "You got a name, girl?"

"Maybe." I glance at the door Germaine and the others are

behind, then look back at the giant blue buttons on the elderly man's vest. "Do you?"

"Of course—everyone has to have a name. I'm Kellen." He blinks at me in expectation.

Fine. "Rhen. Rhen Tellur."

"And I take it you were just on your way out, Rhen Tellur?"

"I was."

"Well, that makes one of us. Me? I leave when I'm inclined or when my presence is declined," he rhymes. Then puffs his unlit pipe again and leans back against the wall as he cheerfully grins. "But before you go, tell me, whence exactly do you hail, Rhen Tellur?"

I stare at his pipe. What exactly has he been smoking in it? Normally I'd enjoy chatting with an old guy off his nutter— but not when boys in the next room are talking about killing people. "I live across the bridge, on the port side. This is my uncle's house. Speaking of which, I'm not sure why you're up here, but I don't think he'd like it."

"Neither should those boys in there, I wager. And yet—" Kellen spreads his arms. "Here we all are."

I half snort, half chuckle, as Germaine's and Rubin's voices waft out from the cracked door. *Fair point.* "So it appears. And where are you from?"

"Oh, from all over and nowhere and everywhere at once."

Yes, he should definitely lay off whatever herbalist's blend is in that pipe. I move my gaze back to the room where the boys' whispers have reached a fever pitch, and I shift my posture to return to the door, but the man continues, "Forgive me for noting it, but you appeared quite bothered at those men in your uncle's study."

He heard? Of course he heard. "It's nothing. I'm regularly put out with them. Aren't most people?"

His brow goes up. "They are? How fascinating. And why, may I ask, is that?"

"Because they're out-of-touch Uppers who don't know the first thing about living in the real world." I wave my hand. "Now if you'll excuse—"

"You think so, do you?" The man stops with the pipe midway to his mouth and peers hard at me, as if curious whether I'm serious. Then he nods. "I see. And what exactly would you have them do differently, Tellur?"

I shift impatiently. *I don't know.* I don't even know why I'm wasting time talking to him or why he even cares about any of this. But he's standing here waiting for some kind of answer, so I finally shrug and say, "I guess I'd want them to listen to the people they're making decisions for. Maybe a variety of voices rather than that monolith of middle-aged men." I clear my throat politely. "Now if you'll excuse me, I really must go. And not to be rude, but I think most people wouldn't like the idea of you spying on them. Even if—"

"Spying? Ah, but isn't that what *you're* currently doing too, Miss Tellur? Besides, I don't spy or lie. I simply listen in as conversations swirl. If people forget I'm here and say things they shouldn't, that's hardly my fault. For instance, do you know what they're plotting in there?" He points his pipe toward the room Germaine's in and clicks his tongue, then bends forward confidential-like. "Seems rather unsportsmanlike, if you ask me. Distasteful even."

He shakes his head, clamps his teeth around his pipe stem with a click, and dusts off his grey-and-lavender sleeve. Then pushes off from his spot and walks toward me. "And for the record, Miss Tellur, I rather believe you about the need for varied voices. Keep trying."

He strides past me and heads down the stairs. I narrow my gaze and turn. "Mr. Kellen," I whisper after him. "Mr. Kellen?" But the old man's only reply is to pick up humming a tune as he reaches the bottom and strolls away.

I shake my head and stare at the back of his fancy suit, with no idea what to think—until my senses kick in and I return to the door through which I can still hear the boys mumbling, and Rubin says, "Isn't that right, Germaine?"

Germaine's tone is so low I have to tilt forward not to miss it. "You boys just take care of it. The two of us will make sure you're paid."

"Good, then it's settled. The other contestants won't know what hit them. Tomorrow when they've all—"

"There you are. I wondered what was keeping you." Vincent's deep voice makes me jump for the second time tonight. I slide backward to the middle of the hall, but he is already stepping onto the landing near me. Vincent glances down to my uncle's study where the door is clearly closed and then at the crack of space in front of me, from which the light is peeking forth. He scans the opening as Germaine's voice creeps through, then lifts a brow and eyes me and says with a reproachful tone, "You know, eavesdropping is not very lady-like, my dear."

I swallow as he studies me, before his features morph into interest. "So what are you overhearing? Anything I should know?"

I should tell him what they're planning. Vincent's going in the competition tomorrow and deserves to know. But I don't because Seleni is calling loudly from the bottom of the stairwell, "Oh, Rhen, there you are!"

We both look over as she comes skipping up the stairs with Beryll on her heels, and in the back of my mind I note the boys' voices have fallen silent through the door even as Seleni's grows louder. "We're about to play a game of Tell or Fail. Are you in? Where are the others?"

I lift a finger to my lips, except it's too late because the door in front of me yanks open and four faces look straight at us as Germaine's broad shoulders fill the space.

His cheek curves up along with the edges of his lips as he stares at me, then moves his gaze on to Vincent. "Vincent. Rhen. What a nifty surprise."

From the corner of my eye, I see Seleni and Beryll frown at the assembly who've trespassed in Seleni's father's room. Germaine glances at them, then turns to where the other boys are standing with their arms crossed. "Looks like we're missing out on a party in the hall, gentlemen." He forces a smile. "Perhaps it's something we should get in on."

Vincent slides his arm across my shoulder. "I think Rhen and I are going to get a little fresh air. We'll catch up with you shortly. Excuse us, Miss Lake."

I look at Seleni. My stomach's suddenly flipping and my nerves are buzzing because I don't want to get air with him. "I'm sorry," I whisper, shaking my head. "I—I have to go." I shove past Vincent and hurry for the stairs. Seleni's startled gasp follows me as I push between her and Beryll and scurry down to the lower level.

I don't glance back—just head for the door and out to the garden—away from them—from the party. From the lights and Vincent and Germaine, and the type of future that would be financially stable and wise and supposedly comfortable. My head pounds and all I know is that I really should warn Sam and Will and the others that something is being plotted surrounding Mr. Holm's Labyrinth tomorrow. And I can't shake the feeling that Vincent is plotting something too—in regard to his hopes for me.

8

I run through the garden. Past the charmingly cottage-like carriage house and stables. Past the milking cows and down the
estate hill to the road where the night mist is emerging over the
moor like a ghost spreading out her long, white wedding train.

I shiver and tug Mum's shawl tighter through the murky
damp that's come on thick—and keep going despite the fact I
can hear Vincent's voice calling after me and a crackling in the
air that signals it's not just the ghosts who are out hunting now.
The ghouls of the knights whose bodies are buried beneath
Holm Castle like to emerge when the moon is hidden. They
hunt for lost travelers along King's Crossing on Tinny River.

I rush across the wooden bridge to the port side, with its misty, narrow walkways that feel as familiar as my own skin, and barely slow for breath when something rustles and snaps, like a stick breaking underfoot, in the nearby fenced graveyard. The subtle scent of sulfur emerges to tickle its way down my nose and singe my throat.

I don't wait to investigate. I know precisely what it is, and I've no interest in having my chest cavity excavated tonight. I fly down the winding cobblestones toward the pub—sticking to the main street to avoid the side alleys—until the miasma drifts dotting the ground are so thick I can no longer see more than a few feet in front of me. The fog has grown dense and the lanes louder as more and more people begin to appear from the shadows. *Safety in numbers.*

But my frown deepens as the nervous tick in my stomach expands. Why are they all out tonight? I peer through the haze just as a crowd swarms out and rushes around me, nearly toppling me over as their voices fill with bewilderment and rage.

"What's going on?" I ask a woman hurrying by.

She doesn't look at me—just shouts something about parliament and pushes on. I ask again, this time of a man who says, "They're shutting down the port."

"What does that mean?" I yell after him. The conversation in Uncle Nicholae's study flashes to mind. I pick up my pace and follow the man and the others with him on a road now just as cluttered with port people as it is with squashed fruit and discarded papers.

A noise cracks the air and I jerk as a group of youths

emerge, hurtling bottles and tossing threats into the night. I skirt around them and keep up with the flood surging down the sloped path toward Sow's pub.

"Pardon me. I'm sorry," I say repeatedly. I duck beneath old men's elbows and ladies' arms that wave like bony branches.

"Hey, watch it!"

"Move, girl!"

I sidestep out of the way before I realize it's not only me the voices are snapping at. Everyone is lashing at each other in tones suggesting they're hungry for a target to unleash on. I slink lower and make my way between them to the front of the creaky old pub, with its weathered, low-hanging sign that announces:

SOW'S FINE SPIRITS & FOOD
TALK IS FREE, ADVICE IS NOT.
IF YOU NEED SOME, GO ASK YOUR MUM.

The doors are open, but the ten feet in front of it are a swamp of people. I push through the bodies and squeeze my way inside to the space that's as large as my entire house and yet hardly holds enough air to breathe. The place is like a greasy tin of sardines. Oily faced people line the walls, tables, and stairs, and the smells of pipe tobacco and sour beer saturate the air with a stain that never leaves one's clothes. The enraged shouts outside are nothing compared to the deafening noise in here.

I aim for the tall left wall behind a row of young, sunburnt boat hands whose agitated movements warn they're ready for a fight. It's like a carnival mirror reflection of the party I just came from, where everything's a bit off and the tinkling laughter that flowed around silk suits and powdered cheeks has turned rife with ragged, hungry faces and unguarded frustration.

The occupants are yelling at a fisherman standing on the counter amid the smoke-filled air. I haul myself up to stand on a rickety chair in the corner from which I can scan the room long enough to study the crowd for Will and Sam.

There. Near the front. The guys are huddled around a hefty blackwood table on the same side as me, with a host of other boys. At least five of whom are from fishing families. In fact . . . I scan the room again and my chest constricts. Most everyone here is a fisherman—even if the bitter, overlapping voices make it impossible to pick out individual speakers.

Not that it'd matter much, because they're all saying the same thing.

"If they want to decide things for our livelihoods, then they should reap the consequences just like the rest of us!"

"The ocean belongs to everyone! It's how we make a wage!"

Their words prick my skin like needles. This is what Uncle Nicholae's conversation was referring to. It's what the fishermen and businessmen had been discussing in town earlier today. Why they'd seemed so upset. Rumor of whatever this is had already been trickling down.

Gripping my skirt, I slip off the chair and edge my way along the wall toward Will and Sam, keeping my head low so I don't accidentally get backhanded by some raging sailor. As soon as I reach them, I hunch behind their stools. "Psst!"

Both glance my way with keyed-up faces and unbrushed hair as Jake, Tindall, and the other boys shout agreement to something the local butcher just yelled.

"Was wonderin' when you'd get here." Will scoots his long legs over to let me wedge between him and Sam. "Did you hear they're shuttin' us down?"

Sam grins at my dress. "Looking fancy there, Rhen. Almost as good as me." His brown hair swags over one eye as he leans over. "How were the rich kids?"

"Terrible. What's going on?"

"Your uncle's friends are putting restrictions on the Port's fishing industry. They say it's to protect the port and our future."

Jake peers back at us, his eyes like daggers. "Of course that's what they'd say—it's not *their* businesses at stake."

"Gentlemen, please!" The fisherman on the pub counter puts his hands up for quiet. "We'll still be allowed to fish. They've just limited where and how much can be caught per day. It's not perfect, but they're trying to preserve the coastline."

"Limited catches, my hind end!" someone yells. "How much are we talking?"

"They're saying they used multiple sources to calculate it," the man on the counter answers. "But it should be enough to feed our families and still sell some on the side."

"Sell some on the side?"

"What do they mean, it should be enough? How would *they* know?"

"No one ever asked us!"

I look at Sam and Will and Jake who are yelling right along

with them, and my breath thins at the realization. No one in that room of my uncle's had any idea what this decision would do, because it won't ever directly affect them. But for one-third of the men and families in our Lower Pinsbury Port?

It's their entire livelihood.

My stomach turns. Where's Lute?

I scan the crowd, but from where I'm crouched, his black hair and thick blue jacket are not among the two hundred other thick blue fishing jackets clogging the room. Does he know yet?

"They threaten us with this every few years," Jake says angrily, returning his gaze to me and Sam. "The House of Lords likes to talk of putting restrictions on fisheries, but they've never actually done it." He suddenly does a double take at me, as if just now realizing I'm here, and his deep-green gaze promptly drops to my dress. He tips his head at it and lowers his voice. "Better not let anyone know you just came from there, Rhen, or they'll tear you limb from limb with the way this crowd's worked up."

"Right. Thanks." My neck warms because I hadn't thought of that. I hadn't thought of anything other than getting away from the party. I yank my shawl closer and try to look smaller, even as I tell myself these people here know me. I am one of them. Hopefully they'll remember that fact and not blindly take offense to a silly dress. *Although*—I peek around—*looking at their faces, they're in the mood for offense tonight.*

"By the way, you get any further on that cripplin' disease thing?" Will leans in and speaks low so only Sam and I can hear.

The disease. I shake my head. "Why? What'd you see that you needed to tell me about?"

Will looks at Sam. Both hesitate, and Sam finally says, "It might be nothin', but there was a community outside town we passed today, and a good fourth of 'em couldn't walk and hardly eat. Some were coughing up blood. Said it'd come on less than a month ago."

My spine bristles.

"We didn't know if it's related or just some sickness, but they showed us a couple graves and said the people just got paralyzed, then died." Will swallows. "Scared us pretty good. We hightailed it out of there and reported it to the constable but . . . figured we'd mention it to you and your da too."

I bite my lip. I don't know if it's related either. But the coughed-up blood sounds like the guy I saw today. "Thanks. I'll look into it."

My words are drowned out by another shout from the men around us, and then the fisherman on the pub counter lifts his hand to try to regain control of the room. "Listen! We've lived through change before and we'll live through it again. The important thing is—"

"The important thing is we've just been handed a death sentence!" someone shouts.

"Now hold on there." The man tries again. "Let's just keep our heads—"

"Keep our heads?" Jake's father yells from his spot in front of us. "This isn't the time for calm—this is the time for action!"

Jake turns, and his green eyes have darkened beneath his stiff red hair that sticks up like straw thanks to its constant exposure to salt spray on the boats. "He's right. We need to push back on this to show them we're not weak. They need to feel what we feel."

Sam and Will nod vigorously, and I follow suit. It's like the crippling disease. If the politicians actually knew what their decisions were doing—what they *are* doing—in the midst of the needs already plaguing our town, maybe they'd understand. We just need to find a way to *make* them understand.

Except when I peek up at Will and Jake, something in their faces suggests they're not talking about starting a letter campaign and sending representatives on our behalf.

I lick my lips and start to ask what they have in mind, but they've already jumped up with the crowd to cheer, and after a moment they're not just cheering. They're banging fists on the tables and lifting glass bottles over their heads, and I'm suddenly aware I'm one of only a few women in a room full of rather agitated men. And if tempers grow higher or one of those lagers gets dropped . . .

Sam and Will and the boys have now climbed on their stools. They're waving their arms above their heads. I slip back to get some distance lest they tumble off, but from their flushed cheeks and shiny eyes, it's clear they're not coming down for a while. I scoot for the wall and almost reach it when a gentleman launches from his chair to join in the yelling, and the next thing I know, his giant bear of a body trips over me. He hardly glances my way before straightening and raising his empty mug as he bellows, "Are we going to let this stand?"

I duck to move away from his swinging arm, but my dress stays. *What in—?* I turn to find the gentleman's foot standing on part of my skirt. I can't move without it ripping a waist seam or pulling off completely. "Excuse me, sir." I nudge him and try to push his boot off, but he's too busy hollering.

"Fellow friends, our fight is not with each other, but with the men who made this decision!" he yells. "They may not have wanted our input then, but I suggest we give it to them now!"

A roar goes up so loud it shakes the wood planks beneath my feet, rumbling all the way into my nerves. I try to move again, and this time there's a small tearing sound, but I don't care. The shouts have turned into an earthquake inside the lungs of every person in this place, and it's vibrating the entire room. With a last fierce tug, my dress rips loose enough for me to scramble the rest of the way to the wall, where I press my back and inch for the door as the crowd's energy grows higher and their faces redder.

This is what Beryll was referring to in the undertaker's cellar—why the constables would have better things to worry about than us siphoning blood. Because they're about to have a blasted riot on their hands. And of course Beryll had known. His father is in parliament. His father helped make this decision. I frown. The least Beryll could've done is give us a little warning.

Jake's father shouts, "So let's take the fight to *them*! Let's see how they feel when it's *their* children who go hungry!"

"Take the fight to them!" another voice crows.

I stoop beneath a man's arm and attempt to twist around the front of him, except I miscalculate and his elbow comes crashing down. I can't get away fast enough to avoid the coming impact—but suddenly a second arm is there to interfere. The hand reaches out and grabs my shoulder, and I swerve just as the person abruptly plasters himself against my body in a manner that, given any other time, would be considered far too forward. I recoil and spin around.

And come face-to-face with Lute's piercing eyes, unruly black hair, and tight mouth.

"What are you doing here?" he hisses. He keeps his arm on my shoulders and pushes me toward the door.

"Lute." Despite where we are and the vexed look on his face, a silly flush of heat flutters across my cheeks.

He ignores me and half shoves, half ducks us around a unit of men who are jumping up and down, getting louder and more brazen as they bump into us. I trip over floorboards and shoes and finally have to grab his wrist to keep from falling.

"Mr. Wilkes! You can stop pushing me. I'll exit when I see fit, thank you very much." I manage to lock my legs in place enough to turn and force him to stop.

He stares at me like I'm mad, then leans over and jerks his chin at the room. "Have you seen what you're wearing, Rhen? You can't be here. You need to leave."

I cock a brow to hide my embarrassment. "I have just as much right to be here as anyone else. They know who I am." I don't tell him I was already leaving.

His bold eyes slip to my dress, then return to mine with an alarmed glare. "These men are about to tear this room apart, and they're going to tear you apart with it because you look just like one of *them*."

"One of whom? An *Upper*? Except I'm not, and everyone here knows it."

His jaws clamp so tight, the sound snaps in my ear. "And that'll mean exactly nothing in ten seconds when the people in here notice you. They won't care. You came from there tonight. And dressed like that, you're not one of *this* group right now either."

I flinch and clench my fist at the small sting his words give. *I came down here because I care. Because I live here.* The bias is ridiculous, and Lute of all people should know it. He doesn't fit in with people any better than I do.

I scowl toward the front of the room where the boys are all standing on their table now, and the crowd surrounding them has their hands and hats in the air. And yet Lute is right. Coming from the Upper party without knowing the town was triggered may have been accidental—but it won't matter. The atmospheric shift is clear. The energy and rage in here are a furnace about to blow.

Lute's gaze softens and he leans in long enough to murmur, "It's not you, Rhen, it's them. Just . . . please."

A sizzle in the air is followed by a snap, and the next moment a man near the counter lifts up a stool, and something inside me starts yelling that we all need to go. We need to go *now*.

And then a bottle is flying across the room and hits someone near the pub counter. And the place explodes into chaos.

9

I swerve back to Lute, but he's already yanked off his jacket to toss over my shoulders. He tugs it around me to hide my dress, then throws his arm over my head and presses me toward the door.

The sound of breaking bottles and angry fists hitting bone fills my ears as Lute shoves us through the doorway and out onto the jammed street, where he slips his arm from my shoulders and grabs my hand as I gasp. "What in Caldon's name is wrong with them?"

"They're angry. Everyone is. Look around, Rhen."

"I know they're angry! But they're taking it out on each

other instead of the people they're mad at. They're not even thinking."

"Exactly." His grey eyes flash as he pulls me from the midst of the throng of bodies to the other side of the street, then yanks us against a wall as a new flood of marchers goes running by. The moment they pass, he veers us into a side alley and releases my hand.

Keeping his vantage point to the pub, he gives a quick scan of me—from my fingers clenching his loaned coat, down to my dress hem that's sweeping the stones at our feet. My hands are shaking, and I grip the jacket tighter in hopes he won't notice. The next second he's apparently concluded I'm fine because he tilts his head to the alley as his black hair slips over one cheekbone. "Let's get you home before this whole place—"

"Oi! What've we got here? Fancy dress for a fancy lady, eh?"

A rough gentleman I don't recognize looms toward us from the crowded street. Two men slip up behind the man, and the stench of alcohol and anger rush my senses as he jerks his thumb back at the pub. "Thought we wouldn't see you sneaking out of Sow's?"

Lute shifts his stance. "We're not seeking trouble. She's just headed home."

"Is she now?" The man takes two steps forward while his eyes assess my body too slowly. "Heading back to her place in high society, from the looks of it. Maybe she can explain why her kind is having parties right now while we're left with the bill."

I feel Lute's body ripple as he slides his hand beneath my elbow. "She had nothing to do with it. If you want to pick a fight,

Booth, the pub's all yours. Now if you'll excuse us—the fog's thick enough to draw in predators tonight. I suggest you be on the lookout."

I glance up. The ocean mist has condensed so rich we can barely see six feet in front of us, but either the man's new to town or is too drunk to care what a thick night mist means, because rather than react, he just peers at his companions. "You defending her association with those fancy folk, Lute?" A leer edges his lips. "Or maybe you're just busy associatin' with her in your own way?"

"I'm defending your right to keep your throat in one piece." Lute's voice is low. He nudges me to walk behind him, farther into the alley.

Except before I've moved a step he's released me, and the heckler's fist flies through the air in a drunken lunge. I twist and duck at the same moment Lute lifts his own fist to clock the man right in the chin. The assailant's knuckles barely scrape my cheek before Lute pitches the man backward into his friends, who stumble apart and let the man hit the ground.

"What the?"

"Now you've done it, Wilkes."

All three of them raise their faces to us, and my lungs lodge in my throat as my cheek throbs like the dickens. *Ah, hulls.*

Lute's hand slides around my back and urges me to go, but it's unneeded—I'm already running. He stays right behind me up the miasma-cloaked alley before we cut in on another side street, while the men pursue us with curses through the dark. Until the air gives a sudden crackle and a low clicking sound picks up, followed by the sulfuric scent from earlier that bleeds toward us through the fog.

Lute slows, then drops his hand from my back and flips around just as I reach out to shove us both into the nearest wall. He crowds in, facing me, and uses his back like a shield to hide us from the dull, glowing eye sockets we both know are accompanying that sound.

The clicking turns into the long, low moan of a ghoul's telltale cry, and Lute's body freezes with my own. The thing is searching for us. The light from some street oil lantern must've glinted off us and drawn it in.

I shut my eyelids to make us harder to find and begin to count my heartbeats to keep my nerves focused. Except the salt-breeze infusing Lute's heated skin and hair fills my head and lungs, and pretty soon the scent is making my head spin. Because I'm suddenly aware of his heartbeat picking up beneath chest muscles that've been honed from years at sea.

My own heartpulse quickens to match his until I can't distinguish between them. Just like his soft breath that's so close it's tangling with my inhale.

I open my eyes and peek up.

His gaze is locked onto mine.

I stall. The flicker in his expression isn't scared—it's conflicted. He looks as if a weather system he wasn't prepared for just appeared, and he's trying to decide how thunderous it'll get before handling it.

I open my mouth and his gaze drops to my lips, then promptly retreats to my eyes. Where it stays.

Until the look expands into something more. Something bewildered and rattled and captivated.

The three men's voices heighten and I jerk as the ghoul's moan suddenly alters. The ruffians must hear it because they erupt in shouts and their footsteps pick up pace, but this time heading away from us.

Neither Lute nor I move as we listen to the grotesque moaning just before the sound stutters and veers in the direction of the men's boots hitting the stone cobbles. The sick sulfuric smell dissipates as quickly as it came. Lute's arms relax against mine, and the next second he drops them and steps away so quick it's like I've scalded him.

"You okay?" he asks.

I nod and try to catch my breath that for some reason has thinned. "My cheek'll bruise, nothing more."

Lute makes a choice comment about having a "chat" with Booth tomorrow, then, as if remembering the company he's in, closes his mouth and scrutinizes me. He rubs a hand through his hair. "You sure?"

I shrug and start to assure him that yes, I'm perfectly fine, but his unsettling gaze fastens so tight onto mine it occurs to me he's not just asking about the run-in with those men. He's asking if in the midst of everything surrounding tonight, I'm honestly all right.

My mind darts to the pub, the drunks, the ghoul. Then to my aunt's house—with Germaine and Vincent. My throat tightens. A flicker of nausea emerges with the uncomfortable realization that, for whatever reason, I've felt safer down here in the midst of a riotous pub and sinister alleys than I did up there. I've felt safer being with *him*.

I swallow and I don't know how to answer him because all I can think of is how foreign but also pleasant that feels. So I just say, "I'm fine. Are you?" Without waiting for a reply, I add, "You know ghouls don't actually eat people. They just cut open their chest cavities in search of souls."

His brow goes up and he stares at me with an unreadable expression. Suddenly his dimpled mouth twitches into a puckered smile. "I . . . did not know that."

And because I'm not finished making a fool of myself yet, I nod. "They're looking for a home."

He clears his throat and keeps eyeing me, but thankfully his expression recedes before I can wax more on the nightlife of ghouls or say anything about how anatomically perfect his lips look right now. He stops rubbing the back of his head and turns, and when he pulls his hand away there's blood on his fingers.

I frown. "Lute—"

He glances at it and shakes his head. "It happened a few days ago—from a hook on the boat. Must've got bumped at the pub and reopened. I'll be fine. Let's just get you home."

"I can get myself there. You go take care of that and your family." I point at the blood on his palm.

"My family's fine, but your da would never forgive me for letting you walk home alone in this." He indicates the fog.

My da.

He's walking me home for my parents' sakes.

That realization shouldn't prick, but it does. I should appreciate his thoughtfulness, but instead a mad desire flashes through
me. I can't help wishing he was walking me home for his own
enjoyment. For whatever it was I saw on his face back there
against the wall, when he stood closer than any man has stood
with me and offered up his breath and space and protective body
without requiring anything in return. My neck grows warm
and I shove away the strange desire that brings. *You're just tired,
Rhen. Get a move on.*

Before he can see the blush on my face, I pivot toward
home—but the side of my shoe brushes against something firm
beneath the mist swirling around my knees. I glance down and
an uncouth word tumbles from my lips.

Lute follows my reaction to the ground where a body is
splayed out beside me, barely visible through the fog.

A dead body.

What the? I reach down.

"Rhen, wait." Lute grabs my sleeve and points to the man's
eyes, which are wide open, staring up at us.

I already know the man's deceased. I also know he's possibly
contagious from illness. I just wish I had my gloves. Squatting
low enough to see the corpse better, I carefully place my right
hand on his leg to feel his muscles. They're cool. Then, as I peer
over the rest of his body, a blossom of unease unfurls in my
stomach.

He's not just dead—he's freshly dead. And like the tree oil
guy in the undertaker's and the people Sam and Will described,
the man's lips are speckled with a couple of blood clots.

"He used to come to the wharf to beg fish," Lute says. "I haven't seen him in a few weeks." Lute surveys the ground, then points out drag marks leading from the body to somewhere beyond the fog. "Question is—which of tonight's rioters did it?"

"None of them." I force down the lump in my throat. "I think sickness took him." I rise and step away from the body. "And I think someone set him here because they didn't know what else to do."

Lute looks at me. I don't tell him I know this because of the blood around the mouth, or the way the body's muscles felt atrophied beneath my touch—and he doesn't ask. He just nods. "I'll carry him to your da's lab for you."

"Not without gloves." I look at the fog and then at the Upper hilltop ahead where the party lights from the estates shine faint. "And by the time we get back, something else will have taken him."

As if in confirmation, the smell of sulfur trickles through the gloom.

I purse my lips and peer at Lute, and his eyes communicate the same thing—we need to go. But instead he says, "Hold on," and disappears for thirty seconds into the fog in the direction we just walked from. When he returns he's carrying a dirty, half-shredded blanket he gently lays over the dead man's chest and face. "Saw it snagged on a post back there. Probably one of the rioter's, but still—" He straightens and without looking at me says, "Everyone should be allowed a bit of dignity. I'll let the constable know about him on my way back."

I blink and stare at him—at this person who isn't scared to

be around death and dead bodies and ghouls. And who doesn't flinch even at honoring the dead.

I wait for him to look up and nod that he's ready, and then, without a word, I turn and we continue up the alley toward my house.

His strides are twice as long as mine and soon we're far away from the body, and I'm hurrying my pace to match the boy with tempestuous grey eyes and a gradually preoccupied tension. Even as I can still hear the crowds below chanting protests and declaring every pox in existence upon the parliament members and their families.

The alley turns into a lane and a few people jog by, but their lantern-lit faces are filled with just as much fear as rage. "Do you think they'll go after the parliament men in the Upper district?" I ask.

Lute glances over, then shakes his head. "They'll likely destroy a few of the port businesses and then go to bed. Especially when they realize the predators are out. They're only doing it because they feel trapped and need to be heard, but they won't go so far as to ruin the equinox festival. They'll wait until it's over to show any real resistance—although parliament would've been wise to delay the ruling until after, just in case."

"And what about you? What are you going to do about it?"

"The restrictions?" His mouth flinches as he keeps his attention on the cobblestone street ahead. "From the paper I saw, it's pretty severe. I don't know that anyone can provide for their families on what they're allowing."

He won't be able to provide for his family? I stare at him. "Are your mum and brother okay?"

His eyes indicate surprise. "They don't know about it yet," he says softly, and keeps walking.

"The truth is," he adds after a moment, "Ben's taken a few steps back after a bad ankle sprain last month. Most sleeved clothing's been bothering his skin, which means he and Mum are stuck at home much of the time."

I wince for him. For all three of them. His brother was born with a mind that works different than most—he's like a five-year-old in a fourteen-year-old body. But it means he has a lot of sensitivities that require their mum's full-time care.

"I'll ask my da to come around and check on him."

Lute's reply is so gentle it barely registers before it dissolves into the night. "Thanks."

When we reach the house, he doesn't come up the broken stone walk. Just stops and waits with his hands tucked in his pockets and his disconcerting gaze on everything but my face as I stand seven inches away in the mist so milky that the noises and lights and everything outside of us falls away. And for a moment the world is made up of only him and me, and our breath and pregnant silence. He keeps his hands in his pockets and his interest on his shoes, as if they've suddenly become very absorbing.

I slide off his jacket and offer it back. He takes it without a word. Then nods. "Good night, Miss Tellur." And turns back to the road for the long walk home.

"Lute."

He stops six feet from me. Glances back with those ocean-deep eyes. And calmly waits while I sort through my words.

And suddenly I'm aware I'm standing here in a torn dress and shaky skin in front of a fisher boy who is nothing like Vincent or Germaine or any of them, and everything like the sea, with his wild disheveled hair and torrid grey gaze in a not-wholly-unattractive face. "You'll be okay tonight—in the mist?"

He gives a slight smile. "Always."

I swallow. "In that case, I know you'll figure it out. The fishing thing, I mean. But thanks. For helping me tonight."

He opens his mouth as if to say something more. Maybe to communicate the thing from earlier that's suddenly reemerged in his expression. It elicits an odd hunger in me—one that seems to be growing around him today.

Instead, he simply tips his head and turns again to leave, but the sound of horse hooves and carriage wheels interrupts his departure. A coach is pulling onto my street, rumbling loud over the rocks and pebbles and potholes. Two horses emerge into view, followed by a beautiful black carriage. I frown. It's not Seleni's, but what other Upper would come down here tonight?

"Whoa," the driver calls to the mounts, and the coach pulls up right in front of me as Lute returns to stand behind me, and then a curtain slides back from the window.

Mr. King's face is staring at us. Vincent is just behind him. I catch the surprise and flash of irritation in Vincent's eyes at the same time I sense Lute's body go rigid. My gut drops. I wrap my arms around my chest and give a breathless, "Good evening, Mr. King."

"Miss Tellur," Vincent's father says. His expression is stiff as he assesses the scene. What he thinks of it, I can easily imagine. "My son was concerned with your swift exit this evening and desired to ensure you arrived home safely." His eyes flit to Lute. "It would appear you have."

I lick my lips. "There's been some disturbance tonight in the Port," I say, as if adding some reasonable explanation will calm the suspicion clouding both his tone and Vincent's face. "Mr. Wilkes lent me his assistance against a group of ruffians."

"I see." He sniffs in a way that suggests he's gauging if I'm lying. "Vincent said you'd left early to continue your studies regarding your mother's disease. I know he believes in the work you're helping your father do, and I simply hope his progressive stance does not turn regrettable. Now, it's a cold night, and seeing as there are a good many uncouth characters about . . ." He narrows his tone, and though he doesn't look at Lute, he might as well be. "I suggest you head inside, young lady."

"Father, I think it wise to—"

Vincent's father shakes his head to silence his son's opinion, then taps the coach and lets the curtain fall.

As soon as they rumble off, I spin to Lute. "Lute, I—"

"Mr. King is right, Miss Tellur. You shouldn't do anything that you or your friend there will regret."

I blink. His tone and demeanor have completely altered to an aloofness that borders on frigid. I glance around, then back at him. *What just happened?*

Before I can explain that Vincent's not exactly my friend—and not that kind of friend—and, for that matter, I don't even know what kind of regrets they're all speaking of—old Mrs. Mench's light flicks on and her head peeks out her window.

Lute turns on his heel. "Good night, Rhen." And strides off into the murky dark.

10

I unlock the door and dart inside so as not to wake my sleeping parents within, or incite more of Mrs. Mench's attention without. My head is a blur over whatever just happened out there. Lute's discomfort with Mr. King was warranted—he's one of the politicians who signed the fishing restrictions. But Lute's altered behavior and comment as if he were—what? Lumping me in with them?

I run back over the scene in my mind. Did I do something to indicate such a thing? But the only point that sticks out is Mr. King's insinuation that my work was regrettable even as he seemed to be suggesting his support of Vincent's interest in me.

I try not to let either nip at my pride and, grabbing the lantern by the door, I strike a match to light it, then jot a note for Da to check on Lute's brother when he gets a chance. Then I slip to my parents' door to peek in on them. Da has his body wrapped around Mum's, who looks twice as old as her thirty-eight years. Her breathing is labored and uneven. Da's is rough and heavy, hinting at the hours he's spent leaning over the medical tables and patients during the past twenty years.

I tiptoe across the floor and kiss both their heads, then turn to go when a discoloration on Mum's upper chest catches my eye. I lean closer. It's a bruise. Deep purple and black.

It happens. Everyone gets them. It doesn't mean her sickness is advancing.

All the same, I skim her neck and face—only to land on a speck of blood on her pillow. I hold the lamp as near as possible without disturbing her and study the dark spot that's no bigger than the size of a tiny merrymarch flower petal. Then trace it up to another matching speck beside her lips.

I pull back and try to hold my breath so the cry launching up my throat can't emerge. Then scour her skin for any other spots. There are none.

There don't need to be. Because my mind is already explaining away any similarities between her situation and the dead people I've seen and heard about today.

She has bruising, but the others didn't. Her disease is different. Slower. I carefully back out of the room and shut the door behind me. And lean against it until my shaking chest can breathe evenly. Then head for the cellar stairs.

At the bottom I turn the lantern wick up and let my eyes adjust to the light before I stride over to the shelf where the rat cages are lined up against the left wall. The rats rustle and squeak as I walk past, until I reach the end, where Lady is kept. The metal pen is quiet. I tap it. No movement.

I hold the lamp up and peer through the tiny bars. Lady's small body lays stiff as a board with a tiny dribble of blood dried around her mouth. This time I don't hold in the cry. I let it rip up my throat in a quiet tearing of earth and soul as I slip on a pair of gloves and reach in to pull her out. I check her. Her limbs, her gums, her eyes that are staring lifelessly up at me. She's dead.

Not just dead—she's bleeding from the mouth dead. Meaning, not only was our cure worthless, but something's very wrong. In the past ten months, the disease has never presented with the blood before.

It's a coincidence. Or maybe there's another virus going around that just happened to hit here too.

Or . . . the crippling disease could be changing.

Shutting my eyes, I stick Lady's body back into the cage, then pull away to stare at the room. My own blood begins to boil at the implications.

After a moment I walk to the microscope Da and I were using earlier. He's set new glass dishes beside it, each with what appear to be fresh blood droplets and labels. I select the one Da marked as Lady's, taken from a new draw two hours ago, and place it on the tray, then hone in the lens on it. I frown and switch it out for the dish labeled as my mum's, also dated two hours ago, as a sick sensation rises in my stomach.

Something is off. These samples look different. I shove down the fear and, after a moment, replace her dish with the one containing the tree oil man's blood from this morning. But I already know what it shows.

I zero the scope in until the cells come into focus. Then again. Then again as horror fills my chest.

According to this, Mum's and Lady's diseased blood hasn't just been accelerating.

It now matches the dead man's.

Their illness is morphing.

I glance up at the cages, then at the overhead ceiling boards— one of which creaks right where Mum and Da's room is. And bite back the vomit rising in my throat as the soaring hope I'd felt just hours ago crashes to the floor. I rip off the gloves as my mind spins and the weight of what this means sets in.

It means we've failed.

It means the cure I'd hoped we'd finally found was nothing all along.

I turn back to the cage to stare at Lady's stiff body as the realization hits me. This will be Mum's fate too. To die quickly. Trapped in an immobile body, suffocated by her own lungs, without the ability to escape.

Trapped.

Just like Lady.

"They're only doing it because they feel trapped and need to be heard." Lute's words flare in the back of my mind.

The fishermen. The rioters.

My mum.

My eyes fly open. I reach for the shelf above the cage and, with a quick shove, swipe its contents on the floor—the books and tins and bones. Then turn around and glare at what else I can destroy, because suddenly I know why the pub's men were lashing out so recklessly tonight. They're scared of choices being made for them that will sentence their families to a life—or death—they have no control over.

It's the same reason I got angry at the Uppers in Uncle Nicholae's study.

"You're a lucky girl, Miss Tellur. Not everyone has such an opportunity. I expect to see good things come from it."

What opportunity? What choices? What life?

We can't even get anyone to listen to us voicing our needs.

"I rather believe you about the need for varied voices," that strange Mr. Kellen had said. Then he asked, *"And what exactly would you have them do differently?"*

I glance at the slab we use to examine the dead. What would I do differently?

I'd stop pretending Da and I will find a cure down here using our rudimentary equipment and my inexperienced skills.

I'd make them listen to our town's need.

I'd heal my mum.

I'd pursue the real future I want—a future that isn't just including me in someone else's plan, but that is for me. *I'd—*

My gaze catches on the Labyrinth Letter that's floated lifelessly to the floor from the shelf I shoved the books off of. I pick up the piece of parchment and scan it, even though I've had every word memorized since the age of five.

All gentlepersons of university age (respectively seventeen to nineteen) are cordially invited to test for the esteemed annual scholarship given by Mr. Holm toward one full-ride fellowship at Stemwick Men's University. Aptitude contenders will appear at nine o'clock in front of Holm Castle's entrance above the seaside town of Pinsbury Port on the evening of 22 September, during the Festival of the Autumnal Equinox.

For Observers: Party refreshments will be provided at intermittent times. Watering facilities available at all times. Gratitude and genial amusement are expected. (Those who fail to comply will be tossed out at *our* amusement.)

For Contestants: Those who never risk are doomed never to risk. And those who've risked previously will be ousted should they try again.

For All: Mr. Holm and Holm Manor bear no responsibility, liability, or legal obligation for any harm, death, or partial decapitation that may result from entering the examination Labyrinth.

Sincerely,
Holm

My mind pricks. Something about the letter niggles at me as I return to the opening sentence. *"All gentlepersons of university age."*

Not gentle*men*?

Gentle*persons.*

"Rhen?"

I jump and drop the letter on the table as the door creaks and a light illuminates the steps as well as the entirety of Da's face. He rubs a hand across his eye. "Thought you'd be home later."

I shake my head. "I went to Sow's pub to see the boys."

He frowns and tilts his head. "You went into town? You're all right though, yes?"

"They put restrictions on the fishing industry." I set my fingers on the table in front of the letter. "They're limiting how much the men can fish."

"I heard." He's still analyzing me with his gaze that's ensuring I'm okay as well as taking in the fact that I've not even changed or begun baking. "It was all anyone was talking about when I went to see the Strowes."

"How can they do it, though? Just—*decide* something like that for everyone. Especially when it won't even affect them." I glance around. "And—and *Lady*." I turn toward her cage. "Da, Lady's dead."

He descends the stairs and sets the lantern on the table beside mine. "I know."

"So what about the Strowe girl? Is she still alive?"

In the lamplight his eyes glisten and turn damp. "She became incapacitated today."

Exactly. Of course she did. I press my fingers harder into the table until I can feel the sting of my blood pulsing—until I can feel the life that is wasting away here—and whisper, "And that's okay with everyone? We're just supposed to live with that?" I jerk a hand toward the stairs and whisper, "And what about Mum? Did you see the blood on her pillow tonight? Did you hear her breathing? What is wrong with the medical community that they can just let this happen?"

Da's face goes two shades of pale and his gaze flits to the stairs. He obviously didn't see Mum's blood. My heart implodes, and I throw both hands in the air. "Da, what are we doing?"

He still hasn't moved. "We'll get it figured out, Rhen. I promise."

"No, we won't! Or at least not soon enough." I gesture at the vials and dishes on the floor around us, then at the tiny room. "Not with this rudimentary setup!" And I'm yelling, and I don't even know why I'm yelling at him because it's not his fault. He's not causing this, but I can't stop.

"No offense, but you've been telling me for years we don't have the supplies to test the methods like we need to. To even try to create new medicines for simple infections. We can't even get the dead tissues we need without breaking the law!"

He blinks and studies me, then sits down on the low stool, and his body suddenly looks old. More than that, it's his stance. Weary. Defeated. I can see it in his eyes. "I definitely don't think we should give up, but I agree that we may be at the mercy of the state-supported researchers on this one, Rhen."

"Wait . . ." My voice falls. "Are you serious?" A rush of warmth fills my vision, and I blink it away. "Da, what are you saying?"

He looks sadly at me. "I saw Lady when I got home. I just hadn't got around to moving her."

"Okay, and?"

"I assume you saw the blood samples I took this evening," he says quietly. "The salesman was fine a week ago." Da's tone goes scratchy. "And your mum's blood has altered to look more like his. Rhen, the disease is morphing, and I . . . I think I'm out of ideas on this one."

What is he saying? Oh hulls, what the bleeding fury is he saying? That he's given up hope? That he doesn't believe we'll find a cure? Did he ever believe? Or was he just letting me think I could become something more—and that we were actually making a difference?

I look around as hot tears fill my eyes. This has all been a joke—one in which we've been playing make-believe and pseudoscience. I'm not a scientist in training. I'm a child entertaining fancies about who we are and what we can do.

His eyes are soulful. "I know what you're fearing, and it's not true. I still believe someone will eventually get there. I just don't know that it'll be us. But I don't want you to give up hope."

"Hope for what? That Mum will miraculously recover? That enough people will die so the researchers will finally look into it? Or maybe that parliament will fund them? None of that is *hope*—it's dependency, and it's pathetic."

"I know, but other than keep trying there's nothing else we *can* do. Someday this disease will reach their doors, and we'll hopefully have something to show them. At that point they'll pay attention. Right now it's just too new. Too unknown. So until then we keep doing what we know. We've already created an antibiotic for the weak fever, and you've almost cracked the vaccine for the lung-fluid illness. Even if . . ." His voice fades off, as does the hope I've built our entire past six months around. Hope that he and I could save Mum. That we were doing something bigger—something more worthwhile with our time than simply watching people slip away into a sickness we don't even have a proper name for.

I grit my teeth and sound like Jake and his father and all the men down at Sow's. "Maybe we should *bring* it to their doors."

His head jerks up so fast I realize I'd forgotten for a moment he's still in his late thirties. "Young lady, that is completely out—"

I'm already shaking my head. "I'm not talking of *infecting* them, Da. I'm not insane."

He slows. Eyes me. "I think you'd better explain then."

I don't know how to explain. Because I don't even know what I'm thinking exactly. I look around. "I just—I'm saying, maybe we need their clout and position."

He stares at me blankly, as if my insinuation is not getting through.

"We need the Uppers' benefits, Da."

"You're going to pursue matrimony with Vincent then."

"No. I'm saying we need their positions more than we need them. I'm saying we need to *become them*." My words erupt faster along with my breath as the idea takes root. "Last week you said that if you had even half their supplies and technology, you'd be able to figure this thing out. Well, if I attended one of the universities, I'd have access to the labs like you once did.

I could help Mum and become a *real* scientist. You've always said I was cut out for this. So what if I am? What if I can attend university like the men do? What if—?"

"Oh, my dear Rhen." He stands up and walks toward me as one does a wounded puppy or an angry morning bird, then smiles down with all the love I think one person can probably have for a child. "If your mum and I could want anything for you, it would be to see such a thing in my lifetime. But as much as I applaud where your mind is, you and I both know it can't happen. They'd never let you in. And as much as it hurts me to admit it, we could never afford it, even if they did."

"But if I could pass the qualifying exams, they'd have to consider it at least."

"I don't just mean they won't let you in. I mean they would *never* allow you to even test for it. Society isn't quite ready for such strides, my girl."

"But what if they didn't know it was me? What if—?" I wave a hand. "What if I went in as a boy?"

He chuckles. "Your lack of conventional thought is what would make you a great scientist." He pats my cheek and chuckles. "And if anyone could pull off such a thing, my vote would be on you. But it wouldn't work. They check every name, every family, every detail of an applicant's life—as they should— before they allow them to take the examinations."

My fingers fall to the Labyrinth Letter along with my gaze. "Unless there was a different test altogether I could enter."

He puts his hands on the sides of my head and snorts before he presses my ears and releases me. "You are a specific kind of species, my girl. A strange and terrifying beauty of mind." He kisses my forehead and pats my cheek again. Then blinks quickly and tries to clear his throat. "But I need to go check on your mother." He glances toward Lady's cage, and with a heavy sigh heads for the stairs.

I watch him go.

He's just reached the bottom ledge when I quietly ask, "Do you think she's getting worse? Mum, I mean."

He clears his throat again but doesn't answer—and he doesn't have to. His slumped shoulders and tired step are clear as anything. He starts up the stairs and doesn't turn around, doesn't look back, and something tells me that if he did, his face would be wet. So I leave him to his dignity and watch him slowly ascend the steps as my face dampens with my own grief-stricken tears.

When he is gone, I turn back to the Labyrinth Letter and stand tapping it for a full three minutes.

"You're a lucky girl, Miss Tellur. Not everyone has such an opportunity. I expect to see good things come from it."

I shake my head clear, then check the letter again. *"All gentle-persons . . ."*

I pick up the bone-cutting shears and turn them over exactly four times in my hands.

Then clench my jaw and lift the blades to my loosened, braided bun. And make one snip. Then another.

And watch my locks of hair begin to fall around me onto the ground.

11

The morning of the autumnal equinox dawns, not with the normal bustle of creaking carts but with the sound of a rooster's strangled crow piercing my thin glass windowpane.

An omen, Mrs. Mench would call it. *A sign that more death is on the horizon.*

I squint. *Of course it is—death occurs every day.* And yet an unwelcome shiver scuttles across my skin anyway.

I close my eyes and let the dim grey light creep through my dirty windows and across my eyelids and the thin, frayed quilt cocooned around me, waiting for the golden rays to emerge with their warm courage. Instead, a *tap tap tap* on the roof right above my head picks up, and I peel one lid open to glare at the glass—only to find a drizzle has begun. Another bad sign. I shiver again and shove my head beneath the blankets until a soft squeak on my bedroom floorboard jerks me from the covers.

"*Rhen,*" someone hisses.

A ghost cloaked in shadow stands at the foot of my bed.

"Are you awake?" the voice chirps.

I peer through the grey haze, then bite down on my tongue as the outline of Seleni's nose and chin emerges into view.

Oh for Caldon's sake—"What are you doing here, Sel?"

"Scoot over before I freeze to death." She shoves me over to make room to slide in beside me. I yelp. Her body is so cold and damp that by the time she's done situating herself among the blankets, I'm frozen.

"Sorry," she mutters, ducking low to tremble under the covers. "It's frigid outside, and I barely slept a wink last night. Where'd you go? You abandoned me to everyone! Also, I tried one of your cakes in the kitchen—they're lovely and still warm. Good job."

"I went to Sow's pub." I rub my eyes and wonder what the town looks like after last night.

"Sow's?" She frowns. "You left my party to hit up the pub? No wonder Vincent and his father went to check on you. You could've been hurt just from fraternizing with those boys! I heard there were riots! It's all the men were talking about after you left."

"It was fine. Lute walked me home and—"

"Lute?" She lifts her head and looks at me through the dark. "Lute Wilkes? *Walked you home?*"

I don't answer.

"And?"

"And what?"

She scoffs and punches my arm. "Rhen Tellur, you've been sweet on Lute since age ten. And I saw you blush yesterday—so don't *'what?'* me. Does Vincent know?"

"It's not like that. He was just ensuring I got home safe. And it was for my parents' sake, so I really don't see how that's Vincent's business."

She laughs and falls into her gossipy tone. "Um, maybe because Vincent keeps hinting that he's planning to court you? And because—as I mentioned before, *you may recall*—you've been pining for Lute since forever."

"I have not. We barely even speak."

"Did you honestly just lie to me? Because liars go to the underworld, and I'd hate for you to spend your eternity with Germaine and Rubin." Seleni's brown eyes stare at me, daring me to disagree again.

Fine. I clear my throat. "He walked me home because he is nice. I may or may not find him enjoyable, but it's a non-issue because he doesn't feel the same."

She gives a soft squeal. "I *knew* you liked him! Although—" She swerves to me. "What about Vincent? I heard he tried to kiss you last night."

My tongue sours. "He did."

She giggles again, then utters a sigh. "A rich boy pursuing

you, and yet your heart is for the poor one. That's Tinning's poetry right there, is what it is." She puts a hand on her forehead. "I wish Beryll would try to kiss *me*. And then we could get married and—"

I roll my eyes. *Ew.* "If this is what you came down at the crack of dawn to talk about, I'm kicking you out. And then I'm telling Beryll you stuff the top lip of your corset."

She launches up. "You wouldn't! I'd die! Swear to me you won't!"

"Then keep your Beryll fantasies to yourself. Now what do you want?"

Her mood sobers. "It's *about* Beryll, actually. Rhen, I'm scared for him. That stuff Germaine and Rubin were saying in front of everyone—" She drops her voice. "I know the Labyrinth contest is as much a mind game as anything, but what if they were serious? What if they really *are* going to pull out the other players' brains? You know—metaphorically?"

"I suspect they'll try."

"Wait, you think *they are*?" Her voice pitches as she shoves her face near mine. "Why? What do you know? Because when I brought it up to Beryll, he blew it off. But he's nervous—you should've seen him playing darts with the group after you left. I thought someone was going to get impaled. And Beryll's not like them, Rhen. He's tender. If they do something, he'll be the first to get injured, I just know it."

I'm glad it's still dark so she can't see my face. Poor Beryll. And yet—she probably should be worried. We all should. It's not just Beryll who could get injured. It's all of them. All of *us*. Including me.

My thoughts stall.

Me.

Because I'll be right there with them.

Seleni pulls back and glares through the dim. "You're not saying anything, which means you don't think Beryll will be okay either!"

I rub my face again and don't know what to tell her. I need to make my cake deliveries and get back in time to prepare. I need to find man clothes. I need to figure out what Germaine might have in store, because she's right—Germaine is an oaf and Beryll's in trouble, just like me and Will and Sam. I choose my words carefully. "I don't know what Germaine and Rubin are planning, but I overheard them talking of taking out the competition in a less-than-tasteful way."

She grabs my shoulder. "I *knew* it. What exactly did you hear?"

"Nothing other than that. But we'll warn them. Beryll and the others are smart—they'll know what to do." I squeeze her hand even as my mind races ahead to what we'll need to look out for. How could Germaine target the contestants and Holm—but without Holm suspecting?

Her throat makes a choking sound. "I despise Germaine and his friends."

"Me too. But it'll be okay," I promise. And I mean it.

She keeps one hand in mine and falls quiet except for the nervous tapping of her fingers against her stomach. I listen and watch the room gradually lighten along with the dull, wet skies and set my thoughts toward preparations. Not only do I need boy clothing, I need a way to disguise my face. And is there anything I'm allowed to bring with me? I frown. Every year at least one person attempts to sneak in a blade or notes, and every year that person comes flying back out through the giant hedge to land in the crowd.

Which begs the question of Germaine's plans and what they'll be able to use if they can't take anything in.

It also begs the question of whether the Labyrinth itself will recognize me as a girl and throw me out before I've gotten through the gates. Just like it recognizes other items that don't belong.

My gut tightens. I hadn't thought of that. What if Holm has a way to tell?

A burst of thunder rattles the window and makes me and Seleni both jump. I roll over to the glass pane to see how bad it's coming down and whether the town got burnt to the ground last night. Nope. Everything looks the same, just a lot wetter.

I sigh and sit up. I need to make my deliveries. I look at Sel. "I'm going to rush through my rounds and then I'll be—"

She puts a hand up. "Stop. *What the stars?* Turn your head."

I raise a brow and turn, only to hear her screech, "Rhen, your hair! What'd you do?"

My hand goes up to touch the locks now barely longer than my ears. I forgot. I flip around as if I can hide it. "Nothing. I cut it, that's all."

"You didn't just cut it—you murdered it!"

"Shh! Mum and Da will hear—"

"But why?" she squeaks again, climbing onto her knees.

"And what were you thinking? I mean, have you *seen it*? You look . . . you look . . ." Her horrified gaze moves from my hair to my face, then back to my hair. "Like a . . ."

"Like a boy, I hope."

"What?" Her tone is now full volume.

"Shh! Seleni, *please*! No one can know. Not even Mum and Da. At least not yet."

"Except they're all going to know the second they see you!" She presses a hand to my forehead. "Are you ill? Did you swallow something? Look at me."

I pull away. "I'm not sick—I'm fine."

She sits back aghast and studies me. "I think you'd better explain. Thoroughly."

I take a breath, hold it—then let it out as fast as I can. But my voice still cracks. "Last night I tried to talk to the university and parliament men about my mum. Not only did they not care, Sel, they made it perfectly clear they won't do anything." I look down as my throat goes thick. "But my mum really isn't doing well. She's getting a lot worse a lot faster, and this week she's having a hard time even moving from bed."

I stop before a sob slips out—except one already has, and it matches the strangled sound of the blasted rooster that's resumed his crowing.

"Oh, Rhen." Seleni's face falls with her voice. "But what about your latest cure? You said it was so promising."

"It was." I wipe my thumb and forefinger over my eyes to press away the threatening dampness, and don't explain further lest I erupt in cursing or tears. I need to leave. To run. Hide. If

I'm going to enter the competition, I can't have this conversation. I need my emotions clear and focused.

"Sooooo, what does that have to do with your hair?"

I lick my lips. Then lick them again and try not to sound ridiculous. "I've decided to try and enter Mr. Holm's scholarship contest today."

Her face scrunches up. "You're what?"

I strengthen my tone. "I'm entering Mr. Holm's contest."

"The Labyrinth? Why? What for?"

"Shh! For hull's sakes, Sel—I'm entering to see if I can do it. And because I'm just as good as the boys at most things, so why not?" I push off the bed and head for my single, small wardrobe where I yank out a blouse a tad harder than necessary.

"I mean, I may not have a good shot at winning, you know, but what if I did? Maybe it'd get people to listen to me and Da. Maybe they'd actually consider letting me in a university."

"But what about your parents? What'll happen if you get caught? You could get court-martialed or something."

"I'm not breaking the law. I'm joining a private citizen's event. If they allow me to play, whether they know it's me or not, then it's on them. I'll be in and out, and I'll do whatever my parents want. And for all I know, the Labyrinth won't let me compete anyway."

She crosses her arms. "You're pulling my leg, right?"

"I'm not."

"I'm not jesting, Rhen. This is bizarre. Even for you."

"I cut my hair for it."

She acknowledges this fact with a nod and continues eyeing

me from her spot on the bed. "Well then, you know this is the worst idea you've ever had, right? And no offense, but that's saying a lot."

"I know." I tug the blouse over my head.

"It's stupid."

"I know."

She stands up and swallows so loud I can't tell if she's choking back tears or vomit, but when I glance up there's a small spark of fear in her eye as her shoulders straighten and her hand clenches.

I frown. "You're not going to tell anyone, are you? Because I'm not doing anything wrong. I'm just tired of feeling like the way things are is the only way they can ever be."

She watches me pull on a bonnet that I know looks ridiculous but will keep people from wondering what's underneath. A second later she walks over to my armoire where she tugs out clothes and starts to change into them, as she quietly says, "I'm not going to tell on you. Because I'm coming with you."

"You don't have to. I'll be back in a couple hours—we can talk more—"

"Not just the deliveries, fool. I'm coming with you into the Labyrinth."

It's my turn to slow, and turn, and stare. *She's jesting.*

Her expression is serious.

I shake my head. "No way. If there are two of us, it'll be easier to get caught. Plus, no offense, Sel, but this type of thing isn't exactly your cup of tea."

"Says who?" She tugs on her stockings. "I've been involved

in every episode you've gotten us into since birth, Rhen. And I've held my own in doing it. I may not be as scholarly, but I've got a lot more savvy than half the boys in there, and more intuition than you. And even if you don't need either, Beryll will, because I'll not have you looking after him for my sake. And I'm not about to have both my best friend and the future father of my children get their heads ripped off without me."

I stare at her.

She's dead serious.

She slips on her shoes. "Of course, I'll not cut my hair, but I'll pin it tight and we'll find me a kettle boy's cap. Now . . ." She stops and looks up. "How do we get man clothes without drawing attention? Because if we try to steal from our fathers, we'll get locked in our rooms until the contest's over."

I squint at her and chew the inside of my cheek. This could be an okay idea, or it could be the worst one ever. I'm leaning toward the latter.

She arcs a single brow. "I've made my decision, so stop acting like you have the right to make it for me. Now answer the daft question."

I ease back and, after a moment, give her a nod and half grin. "All right, fair enough. Except as far as the clothes go . . ." I shrug. "I was planning on hitting up the grave digger's place to borrow some off a body."

She snorts. "Of course you were." But because she is Seleni, she doesn't even argue.

We're quiet as we load up the baskets of baked goods and slip out the door before Mum and Da can hear us.

It's pouring rain as Seleni and I make the deliveries—biscuits and scones to the regulars, Labyrinth cakes to those who can afford the extra splurge for a festival breakfast. At every house we visit, the upcoming party is all anyone wants to talk about. We listen as we shiver politely in front of their stoves or on their porch steps while water drips off our clothes in rivulets and puddles.

"You going up to Holm Manor this evening, ladies?" the fathers ask.

"Yes," we say.

"I hope you have something fancy to wear—I hear the party will be extravagant." The wives smile. "Rumor has it, Mr. Holm brought down fruit and meats all the way from the Rhine Mountains. Maybe we'll even have basilisk steaks."

"Basilisk meat is poison," I politely say, because I think they should know in case they are ever offered some.

"Any young men you specifically hope will win, Rhen?" the old cat biddies ask.

"No." Because Seleni and I aren't men.

By the time all the goods have been delivered, our clothes and hair are soaked to the skin and our flesh is frozen to the bone. We tug the baskets higher on our arms and duck down the alleys to the old Port church, then across the yard to the back, where Mrs. Mench claims her dead husband walks periodically. Which is unfortunate seeing as he went to the grave wearing nothing but his birthday suit, and that's more trauma than anyone needs to see these days.

Seleni and I step softly around the gravestones and up to

the grave digger's cottage located at the far end of the church-yard. I pull out the two cakes I saved, then knock on the narrow door. "I need two sets of boy clothes," I say, when Old Timmy answers. I shove the cakes under his nose. "About my size, if you have them."

"Boy clothes?" He eyes me, then the cakes, then Seleni, before he nods and disappears. A minute later he returns and shoves the clothes into Seleni's hands before he takes the cakes from mine. "Tell your da I hope your mum's gettin' better."

"Thanks," is all I say, and then the door shuts and Seleni and I turn and hurry for my house.

We've just put the baskets away and finished changing into party dresses for the festival—her into the dress she wore this morning that's now dry from the oven, and me into her sec-ond hand-me-down I own, a yellow cotton that makes my eyes look gold. I've just topped it off with a hat that's floppy enough to make my hair looked pinned up rather than cut, when Da comes through the door in a rush of cold air. He's winded from head to foot and looking a bit wild, even as I note the rain has stopped. I pat the wide-brimmed hat set low on my head. "Everything all right there, Da?"

"Fine, yes—just checking on the Strowe girl again." He pulls off his coat. "How's your mum?"

I pause halfway to Mum's room with a cup of steaming tea as if in explanation. He nods and follows me to their room, where he takes the tea and sets it onto her nightstand. "Rhen's here to see you," he says, and I frown because she can obviously see that.

Mum smiles and lifts her head. She beckons me over to where she's been looking out the window at the housetops that lead all the way down to the sea, where the sun is peeking through the dissipating rain clouds.

"How you feeling?"

She nods and pulls me into a weak hug, and I refuse to look at the blood spot still on her pillow. Her hair and skin smell of lilac and illness and home, and it's all I can do not to squeeze too tightly because the dread and grief are surging with the reminder of last night's revelation that this is all going much quicker than it should, and I have just borrowed clothes from dead people, even as everything in me is screaming that death isn't too far from our own door.

I can feel her ribs and spine through her thick nightdress.

I look down at her, and a sudden sense of shame at my Labyrinth scheme fills my throat. *What am I thinking?* This is where I should be. I'm needed here, with her, in what might be her last few days or weeks. And yet—I'd also give anything not to be here.

I force a smile. "I'll skip the festival and just stay here with you, Mum. Seleni can go, and—"

"Come now, we'll have none of that," Da says from behind me. "You and Seleni will get ready and go enjoy yourselves. Your mum and I'll be just fine here without you. Happier even without all the noise." He winks. "We'll both be here when you get back."

Ignoring him, I pull Mum tighter and rest my cheek against her warm one. "What do *you* want, Mum?"

"I want you to be brave," she whispers.

"Of course. That's not—"

Her fingers find my arm and hold me in place, while her other hand lifts to pat my hat covering my head. Her cheek moves against mine into a weak smile, and she pats my head again and murmurs, "In the Labyrinth, I mean."

Every nerve ending goes numb.

"I heard you and Seleni upstairs," she says in my ear, in a voice too low for Da to hear. "And if you're going in, then you do it bravely and show this world who you are. And when you're done, you come back to me."

The next thing I know, she's released me and shut her eyes and moved her head to the pillow. When I look up at Da, he gives a small, clueless nod. "Enjoy the party for the three of us, sweetie."

"But Mum—"

She gives my hand a quick squeeze as if to say she may be weak but she's still the person who birthed me, so I'd better obey.

My tread is slow as I count the steps to the door, but I wait until I've left the room to let my throat choke and eyes well up. I wipe my cheeks with my wrist, straighten my shoulders, and turn to climb to the loft where Seleni will be.

"Everything all right?" she asks from her spot plopped across my bed.

I shrug and put on dry socks and booties, because if I do anything else, like actually speak, I will do something daft like cry. Once they're on, I pull out a second pair of shoes that Seleni will need and shove them into a woven bag along with the dead boys' shirts and trousers and caps we will take with us for the Labyrinth. Next, I find the case of pins in my drawer that Mum used to do my hair with and help flatten Seleni's long, brown curls against her head in a way that looks purposeful but can also double as a boy's cut beneath a hat. When I'm finished, I stand back and eye us both.

Seleni tips her head and studies us in the mirror, then strides over to the oil wick on my lantern and trims off a part of it. She drops it in the bag. "For our faces," she says at my questioning expression.

Good thinking.

Careful to stay quiet so as not to disturb my parents, I retrieve the Labyrinth Letter from the cellar, where I notice Da has removed Lady's carcass from the cage. I turn away and try not to think on it, then shove the paper into my pocket, in case it's needed as proof of—of what? My right to enter? To be there? I don't actually know how Holm decides who is allowed and who isn't. An attack of nerves roils my stomach, and I have to brace for a minute to calm my breathing. *The worst they'll do is kick you out, and people will laugh or scorn, Rhen. Both are things you know how to live with.*

With a deep inhale I return upstairs where Seleni is waiting by the door. I peek over at my parents' room. Should I say something? But I don't know what it would be, so instead I step out the front door with Seleni and walk across the four stone markers that connect our house to the cobbled street. Just as the rooster gives another strangled crow.

12

Holm Castle sits on the tallest hill in Pinsbury Port, on an estate gracing the far side of the Upper end that stretches all the way down to touch the sea a full mile from the wharf. From Seleni's and my view on the road, the tops of the century-old stone and shingled roofs catch the late-afternoon sun and gleam like pinpoint pearls, shimmering above the vast green hills and hedges that tumble away from the mostly hidden home.

Legend has it, King Francis's great-grandfather, King Edmundton, deeded it to Holm's great-grandfather for his use of magic that turned the tide of the great Oceanic War. And while the subsequent Holm and royal descendants' relational arrangement is unknown, in times of national crisis a carriage bearing King Francis's crest has been rumored to show up in the dead of night at Holm Manor.

I inhale the smell of damp earth and leaves and wonder what King Francis thinks of the Labyrinth contest—or whether any of his family has ever privately attended.

Seleni and I start up the walk as a breeze rustles from the wharf and floats over us on its way up the river. It's pushing back the thick blankets of rain and fog, like a dragon rolling back its breath, until they recede into the tiniest nooks of the Rhine. The rush of salt spray latches like perfume onto our hair and skin, carrying with it the sound of excited voices—shouts that rise a little louder, and laughter that uncoils a little looser. And when I glance around, even some of the faces from the pub last night look a little lighter.

The hill soon becomes steep and my feet slide inside my shoes as the soggy gravel crunches beneath them. *Crunch crunch crunch*—the sound is muted by the voices and hollers of the families up ahead, who are clearly enjoying the day's climate change. If the water was a gift to cool off tempers, the setting sun has now locked in to warm us all back up. The people we walk by greet us with bright eyes that say they are choosing to celebrate the fact that even if parliament is against us today, the weather is on our side. And so is the host of boys we're sending into one man's crazy maze.

Beside me, Seleni chuckles at the kids running back and forth. They keep taking off toward the river while their mums call them back. "Not too far! The basilisks will eat you if we can't find you!"

I laugh along with her, but it's sharper than usual as my nerves bleed through. A bead of sweat trickles down my back. I scan everyone's faces for Lute or Will or Sam, but all I find are more parents and kids and elderly as we start up the final part of the slope.

Seleni leans over. "You're walking like a girl, Rhen. We should practice acting like males."

I am? I glance to see how she's walking and try not to burst into real laughter because she looks like a cross between a swaggering monkey and a pregnant mouse. I peer around at the men and boys trekking along beside us—*how do they walk?*—and after a moment adjust my gait to a longer distance that doesn't have to care whether one's skirt floats up or if one's hips swing too much to attract inappropriate attention. I grin and nudge her, like I've seen Will and Sam do to each other. "Like this?"

"Yes, that's better." She straightens her shoulders and dons a bored expression before she juts her chin at me like Beryll does when he walks by other guys. She keeps doing it until we both erupt into giggles. "Although I still think it might've been smarter if we'd just dressed at your house and come in disguise. It would've given us more time to practice."

I shake my head as a group of rowdy ten-year-old hooligans from my neighborhood runs by us, their bare feet grinding over the rocks as they hoot and holler. "It'd raise the chances of people seeing through our disguises. This way there's little time to suspect."

"You'd better hope so, because if they do suspect and we're caught, you know Mum would never allow me to speak to you again." She pretends to imitate my aunt Sara. "Seleni, this is the last straw. Rhen will be the ruination of any reputation you have left. I forbid you from seeing her."

Another laugh bubbles up my throat, partly because the reality of that is painful and partly because the look on my aunt's pointed face might actually be worth it.

Someone bumps my bag containing our boy clothing and I instinctively yank it closer. Seleni waits until the woman hurries past before she whispers, "But seriously. If we do get recognized, what's the plan?"

"We say we spilled something on our dresses at the festival and hadn't any other clothes, so we borrowed from the crowd." I check the thickening throng again. Their faces are shiny with perspiration and their pace is slowing the nearer we've gotten to the top of the hill where the estate's entrance lies. "But like I said, we won't be recognized because no one's looking for us to be dressed like that. We'll just seem like two boys in a host of fifty others. I think the bigger concern is remembering to use different names."

"Renford," she mutters.

"Sedgwick," I say.

She nods. "That, and I hope I can remember to use a deep voice."

"I'm more worried you'll cuddle up to Beryll or kiss him while in disguise."

Alarm fills her eyes. "Oh, Rhen, can you imagine? Poor Beryll would drop dead in surprise."

"*After* he gets appalled."

We both break into giggles again as we reach the cusp of the hill that is really a mountain, and the humor turns to gasps as we come face-to-face with the tall hedges and wide entrance that lead to Mr. Holm's manor and estate grounds.

Seleni and I have made this trek for seventeen years, and each time the thrill is just the same. For as extravagant and mysterious as Mr. Holm and Holm Castle have always been, there's a reason very few people have ever made it onto his property and come back to tell of it. Namely, it's nigh impossible.

If the rumors of disappearances and brain-eating banshees guarding the space won't keep a person out, the thirty-foot-tall thorn hedges surrounding the entire perimeter will. One prick from those and, best case, you'll be vomiting for a week. Worst case, you'll be dead. And not only do they encase the estate, but they're arranged inside of it to guard the castle itself—as well as the Labyrinth.

"*Mr. Holm likes his privacy,*" I'd once said to Sam. "*Wonder what he does with it.*"

"*I know what I'd do,*" Will had said, grinning at us both. To which I'd promptly informed him no one else wanted to know.

But even now, as close as we are, the only thing visible aside from those twelve castle rooftops is the thirty-foot-wide gap where the gates stand open to usher the crowd onto the glittering driveway that's edged with a rich green lawn.

The small girl walking beside us squeals and points up as her mum tries to keep hold of her hand. I follow her gaze to seven patchwork balloons that come into sight through the entrance, and suddenly Seleni squeals too. They float like giant bubbles of sea foam above the inner hedges and lawns, and baskets are attached beneath them with people inside.

The child flaps her arm at two women looking down. They wave back, and her eyes grow as round as sand dollars. "Mum, can I ride in one?"

"Those are for brave people, not babies," her brother teases. "You have to be older."

She shoots him a glare. "I am brave. And I'm going to ride in one when I'm two inches taller." She jumps up as if to stretch her height, and Seleni catches my eye before the little girl pries free of her mum's hand and skips ahead to the wide metal gates. Within moments we arrive as well—only to be pressed in on all sides as the festival-goers merge to squeeze through.

I glance up at those thorn hedges reaching for the sky on each side. How many people have actually died because of them?

I grab the back of Seleni's sleeve to keep us from getting separated as the crowd's anticipation grows. "Do we need to find your father and mum?"

She shakes her head and leans back to yell in my ear, "They came up with their friends. I told them I'd be with you or Beryll . . ."

Whatever else she says is drowned out as we're carried through the gate with the crowd, then emerge on the other side at a wide stone driveway that is so smooth the thing looks like gold in the sunset light. Which is when I feel it. The atmospheric ripple.

Even for someone who believes in the science of what I can

tangibly see and hold and explain, I've always known the unexplainable is possible here. The air is tinged with a magic that quivers around my skin.

Ahead of us, the drive veers to the right—to another gate set into an arched set of bushes—and beyond that the massive, hundred-room castle rises like a crown above the thorns and dense foliage. As far as I know, the only Port people ever to have seen inside the building itself are the contestants—none of whom will speak of it, whether due to fear or a signed agreement, I don't know. But Lawrence once told us his brother said the castle's intricate halls give the impression of being in a spider's lair and that Mr. Holm's extensive riddles make your mind feel full of webs.

Seleni tugs my hand and points toward the front of the estate, which is spread out to the left of us in blankets of green lawns and stone terraces—each one cascading in levels away from the house, until they reach a flat meadow down below. And beyond that, sloping hillsides that run for miles down to the sea. Dotted across the terraces and lawns are groupings of parties sharing blankets or tents, with gangs of children running beneath white lanterns strung in zigzag abandon from pole to pole. They're bouncing in the breeze.

Except they aren't really lanterns, but something referred to as electric suns. It's a new technology this year, and one of Holm's own invention from what I've heard. I've yet to get close enough to study one, but even the university knows little of their makeup, which Mum says is just another in a host of reasons he's so catered to as a benefactor. Contrary to Germaine's assessment last night, Holm's inventions *are* more than simple illusions. I've even studied a few—enough to have attempted re-creating them. The majority, however, are beyond me or even Da.

Although, standing here, I can understand why most people think of Holm as an illusionist. The white lights certainly look like illusions. Like thousands of stars set above glowing faces, to offer warmth and safety and illumination.

They look like magic.

Seleni tugs my hand harder and her voice sounds shaky. "Let's find food and Beryll."

I nod. The nerves are setting in. I lead us toward the first terrace that sits in front of the Labyrinth hedge and house where a collection of musicians are playing an evening waltz. "Where's Beryll's family supposed to be sitting?"

"With his mum's aunt." She points at a lawn to the right of the staggered levels where some Upper attendees have already erected beautiful white linen tents that look more like small cottages than simple overnight bedding.

I wrinkle my nose. Of course the Uppers brought half their homes. Probably their servants too.

I turn toward the normal folk and sift through the faces— many of whom were full of hurt and fury last night but are now filled with laughter. The kind that comes as a distraction from grief and the internal ache that will still be there tomorrow. I bite my lip and ignore the thought that I recognize it all too well.

"No one here seems overly upset about the fishing restrictions," Seleni whispers.

"They are—they're just refusing to let it ruin their festival." I pull her down the stone stairway leading to the second patio, which is filled with long, golden banquet tables covered in fountains of bubbly drinks splashing into goblets. We dodge the swarms of people and move on to the third patio, where fire pits are assembled, for toasting desserts from the smell of it. My stomach rumbles and I realize I am famished.

We wander from terrace to terrace, slipping bites from tables covered in more kinds of meat than even Seleni will see all year, to giant spreads of breads and puddings and Labyrinth cakes, to entire galleries set up just for wine. It's a feast for the senses, including the choice of music soaring above us in a perfect complement to the smells and sights and sounds.

The crowds around us are filling their pockets and plates now, and I follow Seleni to grab a few more delicacies—and hope I don't promptly throw them back up from the anxiety that's taken full root. I shift the bag on my shoulder and take a couple hunks of cheese and bread, then turn to focus on the task at hand. I need to find Sam and Will and tell them about Germaine. I need to make sure I know how to shadow them into the Labyrinth.

It takes a minute of scanning the lawns to find the crowds of local folk. And then another moment to spot Sam and Will's family at the bottom of one of the terraces. They've set up a small sleeping tent and seem to be settling into their place next to one of the larger fire pits for the long haul. I look around, but I don't see Sam or Will. All the same, their family's laughter and tones of anticipation carry over, and something in me wishes I could join in with them for a while.

That thought brings an ache to my chest with the awareness that without Mum and Da here, the festival is not quite the same. Unlike past years, there's no specific place for me—no spot I belong. The twinge of that realization surges and I wait for it to settle. Then eat my bread and cheese and meander a bit more before Seleni turns and grabs my shoulder. "Come on. I see the boys."

The "boys" means Beryll and friends. They're seated up top with their backs to the hedges that make up the Labyrinth—as if claiming their spot to be first inside. Or maybe they're using it for a full view of the festivities, because Beryll waves at us the moment we start making our way up. He and Lawrence are with a host of boys I've never met. Plus a few I wish I hadn't.

"My dear Miss Lake, where have you been?" Beryll rises from his seat.

"We have a half hour," I whisper to Seleni, before she saunters over to join him. I turn to see if Sam or Will is anywhere around.

"Nice hat, Rhen," a male voice calls from a spot between two girls. I peer over at Germaine as the girls with him giggle and take sips of some type of bubbly drink.

"Looks like your plan to stay an old maid is on target."

"That'll make two of us then," I say, and keep searching for the boys.

Germaine chuckles. He stands and brushes off the girls and then approaches me with a thick-eyebrowed expression of something between amusement and disdain. He reaches his hand out to tap the brim of my hat, and his black eyes flicker. "I can see why Vincent likes you. You're something to tame."

My hand instinctively goes up to push his fingers away from my hat—except he's already dropped them, and his calculated expression turns cool as he looks behind me, then takes a step back.

I feel Vincent's presence before I hear him. "Miss Tellur, I've been searching all over for you. I'm glad you're here. After last night, I admit my mind began to wonder a bit."

I frown and Germaine's eyes glint at my obvious confusion. *Wonder what?*

Vincent moves to stand in front of me with his perfectly coiffed hair and smile. Which expands before it falters at my hat and clothes. He keeps his mouth shut, but the impression is clear that he's not pleased with my choice of outfit. I smirk. The next moment his grin is back and he pulls me aside from Germaine and drops his voice. "I know your walk with Mr. Wilkes last evening was out of innocence, but may I suggest you be more cautious? My father, specifically, was rather concerned with the appearance of it."

I raise a brow. "You'll pardon me, Mr. King, but I believe—"

He presses a forefinger to my lips. "Shh. We'll speak of it no further. Only please know the occurrence pushed me to make a decision. I had a long talk with my father, and I told him what incredible incentive you have and what an asset your brilliant mind can be to us. To me. And while hesitant, he has acquiesced." He puts a hand to his neck to loosen his collar.

My frown expands. *Acquiesced to what? What is going on? What does he want?*

"Miss Tellur, all that's to say—I am prepared to officially

request permission from your father to court you after the equinox festival." He breaks into a smile that is odd, and even a bit proud, while his cheeks turn the color of a beet.

I stare at him.

"I'll take your silence as joy." He lifts my hand and places a quick peck on the back of it. "And please know I've not forgotten your idea to finish your research on the lung illness. I plan to ensure you have access to all the lab equipment you need. In the privacy of our home, of course." His breath speeds up as he continues—as if the very idea excites him. "Imagine how people will respond if you can offer them health. They will love us, Rhen."

I shake my head. The lung-fluid illness? That research was from over a year ago. It took me two years to develop it only to find out it didn't work. Something went wrong in the process and the cure began attacking itself. I heft my bag up and try to focus on what he's been saying.

"So? What do you think?"

What do I think about the fact that he believes he's officially going to court me?

My words stick in my throat. I think this is too strange and too fast. Or maybe it's a year too late. Maybe I would've been thrilled even two years ago. But now?

I feel nothing but the world closing in.

His gaze has fallen on my bag. "Am I right in hoping you've brought me a token?"

I grip the satchel. "Actually, I think I left it with my aunt and uncle. I'll have to go find it." With that I whirl and hurry off—down the stairs that lead away from him and toward the space where the air and people and mindsets are clear enough for me to catch my breath again as I try to stop the spinning of an evening and event that just went off-kilter.

My future is my own, I repeat in my head as I run. *I didn't say yes. My future is still my own.*

I don't slow until I've made it down to the outer lawns where the port people are gathered beneath the white lights that ignite the dark and offer illumination while allowing me to hide. There's a carnival here, with giant swings suspended from the trees as trapeze artists spin circles on them.

I wander through and watch the children ooh and aah, and the men walk around on stilts with a collection of peacocks and zebras. In one spot people are dancing—in another, waiters are serving while a theater is being acted out in a garden nook. The air is rich with the smell of sugar strings being made in hot spinning bowls. The artisans are handing them out along with popped corn and toasted chestnuts.

My shoulders relax. This is better. I can think here.

I pass a group of boys I don't recognize who are getting lectured on last-minute equations by a collection of parents. I chuckle and push down my nerves. If they aren't prepared by now, a few last-minute tips are doubtfully going to help.

"Rhen!"

Seleni and Beryll trip down the sloped lawn toward me. "We came to get sugar strings!" When they draw close, Seleni drops her voice. "I told Beryll what you overheard Germaine and Rubin say last night."

Oh. I glance at Beryll.

"Do you have any specifics?" he asks.

I shake my head. "I don't."

"Well, in that case, I'd really like to—"

I drift my gaze across the grass as he keeps talking.

Except, I've stopped listening.

Because my eyes have landed on Lute.

13

Lute is with his mum and brother sitting a good distance from the crowds beside another woman with a boy who looks about half the age of Lute's brother. Ben is fully dressed and Lute's mum almost looks relaxed—both of which, I suspect, must feel like a victory these days. I elbow Seleni. "Hey, I'll catch up with you in a minute."

She follows my gaze, then glances at me.

"Otherwise, come find me in ten," I say, striding away. I leave her to Beryll who is still chattering and slip across the lawn and through the partiers toward the small group.

Lute hands each lady a plate of food before he takes one

over to Ben. "Hey, James," he says to his brother's friend. "Your mum has your dinner. Ben, bud. You hungry?"

"Lute, you eat too."

Lute ruffles the boy's brown hair, then grabs the grape his brother holds up and tosses it in the air to catch in his mouth. His brother laughs. "Good job, Lute."

"Thanks." Lute grins and glances over, and his gaze lands on me. His eyes light up with what looks like surprise, or maybe even pleasure, or maybe that's just my own sudden sense of hopefulness after the conversation with Vincent. Lute knocks knuckles with Ben before he straightens and offers me a wink. "Miss Tellur. Enjoying the evening?"

"I am. What about you both?" I wave at Ben, who puts a grape in his mouth and stares at me. He turns to Lute. "Who's that?"

"It's Rhen. You remember—she came and played with you when you had the falcon spots. Her da sometimes brings you medicine."

I stop in my tracks. I didn't realize Lute even remembered that, it was so long ago.

"Oh." Ben wrinkles his nose. "You like her, Lute?"

Lute smiles. "Yeah. I like her, Ben. She's good people."

"What about Mum? Mum like her?"

I grin as Lute laughs. "Yep, Mum likes her too."

"Okay. Then I like her too."

I grin even wider and take a seat on the grass in front of the two of them. "Nice to see you, Ben."

"Rhen, watch. Watch me catch it." Ben tries to toss a grape in the air like Lute did, but it lands on his lap. He picks it up and tries again, this time a few inches from his mouth. The fruit makes it in and Ben lifts his hands. "Ta-da!"

I clap and chuckle because it's the nicest, most beautiful thing I've seen all day. Actually, it's the most delightful moment I've had all week.

The realization of which hits me.

It's the most delightful moment I've had all week.

I pause, mid-smile and mid-delight, and stare this moment in the face. Minus Vincent's strangeness. Minus my mum's illness. Just Ben's joy in impressing himself and Lute and accepting me without qualm—as the three of us sit here close to each other on the dewy grass beneath white-lit trees and a starlit sky. Amid an atmosphere drenched in music and laughter and Ben saying, "Watch me, Rhen! Watch me again!"

"She's watching, bud." Lute's eyes have softened along with his demeanor into what seems like contentment. He pokes Ben's arm. "And you didn't answer me earlier—are you going to be good for Mum while I'm gone?"

His brother quits trying to amuse me and promptly shoves a bite of food in his mouth, then looks away as if he's not heard.

"Ben?"

He sighs. "Yeah, I be good. Where you going?"

"I told you—just for a day, then I'll be back."

I, too, want to ask where he's going, but I don't because it's obvious he didn't answer Ben for a reason.

"Is Rhen going?" Ben asks.

"You going to introduce us to your friend, Lute?"

I twist to see their mum. She's seated ten paces away and

her expression transforms from interest to recognition in a heartbeat. "Oh, Rhen! I didn't recognize you in that hat. How are you, love? How's your mum doing?"

I start to offer a quick reply of, "She's fine," but the look in her eyes stops the words in my mouth. I swallow and feel a desire to tell the truth to this woman whose very tone gives the sense of warmth of holding your hand until the world is all right again.

I blink back the heat from my eyes, lift my chin, and say softly, "We don't know how long she has, but thank you for asking."

"I'm sorry to hear that." Her face falls and she glances worriedly at Lute. "Is there anything we can do?"

"I don't think so, but thank you, Mrs. Wilkes." I wince and look away before the guilt from earlier can flare around what is so obvious in this moment—that I am here at a party while my mum is dying at home.

As if reading my mind, Lute's mum gently says, "Well, I'm glad you're here, Rhen. I want my children to grab life's joyful moments when they can—and I'm sure your mum feels the same."

I blink harder and nod in gratitude, and Lute clears his throat. "Speaking of grabbing a moment, Mum. I've got Ben and James. You ladies go grab another slice of pheasant."

His mother starts to argue, then winks at me and acquiesces. "As long as you act like a gentleman and invite Miss Tellur to dance, son."

I start. What? Then notice the waltzing tune is carrying more loudly across the lawns. It's the signal they're getting ready to officially start the evening. I turn to Lute, and my reaction is the same as what's on his face.

"Yes, Rhen, dance!" Ben claps and jumps up to do a jig, until Lute and I ease back and laugh.

"Only since you asked, Ben." Lute hops up and extends his hand. "Miss Tellur?"

He pulls me up and places his large, rough hand around mine while fitting the other gently against my waist, and I am instantly a bundle of self-conscious nerves.

I try to focus on the music. On my feet. Then on his, because apparently he's just as awful at dancing as I am. He bumps my shoe, then bursts into a chuckle as Ben cheers us on. "I should've warned you first. I'm kind of terrible at this sort of thing."

"That makes two of us."

"I'll take that as an achievement then."

When I lift a brow, he smirks. "You've apparently quite the skill for blowing up dead bodies. Since I've no such talent, I'm at least appeased that our waltzing abilities are equal." His black bangs swag down as his gaze flashes to my warm cheeks, then lips, and stays there for a full count of dance steps before he looks back up to lock his eyes on mine.

And I doubt he intends to, but what he reveals there feels like I've just waded too far into a sea that's about to crash over me. All I know is that Lute is better than half the politicians and people of this world, and no amount of money can make him or his entire family richer than they already are.

I try to think of something to say. Of anything that will keep my heartbeat from breaking through my rib cage and my head from drowning. Because suddenly the feelings inside me don't compare to whatever this is in front of me.

The next moment he blinks, and that hint of last night emerges and makes my lungs catch. It also makes my lips wonder what his might feel like against them, and then I'm wondering if he's wondering the same thing too.

If his expression is any indication, he is.

My breath gets a whole lot shallower until my head is a hazy mess.

One . . .

Two . . .

Three dance steps I don't take . . .

Move, Rhen. Or at least say something.

"Mr. Wilkes," I finally choke out. "I could show you a dead body one of these days if you'd like."

"Lute."

"I think I'd like that very much, Miss Tellur," Lute says, before turning to Ben.

"Lute." Ben's tapping his brother's leg. "Someone's—"

"Well, this is becoming quite a concern," a voice rings out behind us. "Pardon for interrupting. But Mr. Wilkes, I believe this is the *second* time in a day I've happened upon you behaving questionably toward Miss Tellur."

I drop Lute's hand and turn to find Vincent three paces away. His scowl is deeper than the one last night, as is his tone. He briefly drops his gaze on me, then lifts it back to Lute, whose mouth has curved down in disapproval.

"Mind if we have a word, mate?"

Neither of them moves their eyes from each other as Lute appraises Vincent and, after a second, points him over to a spot far enough away from Ben to be discreet. He keeps his voice low as he strides over. "On the wrong side of the estate, aren't you, Mr. King?"

I sit near Ben who's just grabbed the cake his mum brought back to him. She looks at me and smiles. "Thanks for hanging out for a bit, Rhen."

"Thank *you*, Mrs. Wilkes," I say, then grimace as Vincent snarls, "From the looks of things, you're crossing into *my* estate, Wilkes. I'll ask you once, politely, to back off, please."

"You'll have to pardon my confusion." Lute snorts. "Are we, in fact, waxing about your grand estate or something else? Perhaps you can be clearer."

Vincent leans in and lifts a hand my direction. "I believe it's obvious what I'm talking about. And as one gentleman to a . . . fisherman, I'm requesting you honor my intentions. Miss Tellur is an old friend who is of particular interest to me."

"I think we should let Miss Tellur decide who her friends and interests are. But if that's what you're concerned about—trust me, I am quite committed to Miss Tellur's honor."

"I disagree."

"On which part? Her decisive abilities or her honor?"

Vincent's hands curl into fists. "All I'm saying is stay away from her, Wilkes. Or the next time I ask, it won't be as a gentleman. I've made my intentions clear and she's accepted. Are we understood?"

Lute goes still.

I bristle. What is he talking about? I did no such thing. I go to say as much, but one look at Ben's concerned face peering up at me and I check my outburst.

Lute stares at Vincent before he flicks me a questioning look, then tightens his jaw. When he speaks again, he simply says, "Perfectly."

Vincent steps back in what appears to be relief. "Good. Let's keep it that way." Then, louder, adds, "Miss Tellur, I believe the contest is about to start. My parents are expecting you to sit with them. I told them you'd be right up."

My neck crawls at his words and tone. If Ben and Mrs. Wilkes weren't here, I'd have sharp words for both men, but I refuse to be a source of further stress on the boy or his family. I rise as if I was just going anyway—when a horn blows across the terraces and lawns, calling everyone's attention. Vincent nods at Lute and then hurries off to climb the hill toward the Labyrinth's entrance.

As soon as he's gone, Lute strides over and, without looking at me, says coolly, "Miss Tellur, thank you for the chat. I hope you enjoy your time with Mr. King's family."

I scoff. "Mr. Wilkes. Mr. King is misinformed. As was your conversation about me—seeing as it didn't actually include me, which I highly resent—" Except my words have been drowned out by a kid yelling across the lawn. "They're about to get started!"

I peer up at the stars to check the time—drat. They really are about to start. I look around for Seleni, but she's already running toward me when a voice booms out from the terrace at the top of the hill.

"Gentlepersons of all ages, please welcome yourselves to the Festival of the Autumnal Equinox and Mr. Holm's Labyrinth. We have a few regulations, rules, and festivity announcements to go over, so please lend us your ear. If you don't, you're liable to lose that ear due to any number of dangers you're about to experience here."

14

Hurry!" Seleni hisses. "They're making the festival announcements."

"Hold your panties—it's *fine*. They always take forever. Now stand still!" I nudge her. "If we don't get this right, it won't matter how quick we get up there—your hair will give us away. What in Caldon were you doing with it anyway? Rolling on the grass?"

She blushes as I stab another pin into her curl to flatten it back in place before she shoves her bare legs into the pair of threadbare breeches behind the row of thistle bushes where we're changing. She ties a string through the belt loops and tightens them around her waist, same as I did mine, then straightens so we can observe our work. I pat her head. It'll hold. I hand her a boy's serving cap, then reach for my own to pull on like a sock over my short hair and ears.

Seleni wrinkles her face at me. "I have *never* worn something so appalling in my life. These clothes give me the creeps. Did the men die *in* them or *because* of them?"

I'm tempted to tell her she actually looks good, but that'd only offend her. "Okay, but do we look like girls?" Screwing my brow into a doubtful expression, I step back. "Because from the neck down, you're good, but your face still looks too much like *you*."

She snaps her fingers, then rustles through the bag and pulls out the trimmed oil wick we brought. Smearing her fingers with the blackened grease, she proceeds to wipe it in the creases of our faces and beneath our eyes until my skin feels both smooth and itchy and nothing like I imagine most boys or men feel. When she's done, she assesses me and nods in satisfaction. "*Now* you're a boy, albeit a rather sad and unclean one. Just be careful not to rub it off."

I walk around her in a circle, and when we're face-to-face again, I grin. If I look anything like her, I'm an unrecognizable ragamuffin who lives on the streets of a nameless town. "You ready?"

She nods, even though she looks like she's going to throw up. Suddenly I'm wondering if I will too. I'm scared, and I have no idea what to expect other than that at any moment someone in the Labyrinth or out here could recognize us.

What if Lute and his mum find out? What if Vincent or Germaine discovers us?

Stop, Rhen. Focus.

You're not doing anything different than Sam or Will or Beryll. If they can do this, so can you.

I force my shoulders to relax and my lungs to exhale, then shove our other clothes and the lamp wick back into the bag and tie it tight. I stuff it inside the row of thistle bushes we've just changed behind, then stand to eye the terraces where the crowds are assembling.

Deep breath.

Here we go.

"You good?" Seleni whispers.

"No. You?"

"Nope."

"All right then. Let's do it."

We do our best to mimic the men as we trek the tall hill toward the Labyrinth above, which no one but contestants has ever seen inside of. Mr. Holm's setup doesn't allow for spectators. Just the use of his lawns, food, and entertainment as the partiers wait for intermittent updates from either the announcer or the boys who reappear from the maze once they've been disqualified.

The boys are always met with a combination of disappointment over the fact they lost and excitement over whatever minimal details they're allowed to give. Like who's ahead, who's behind, and who's likely to end up dead.

Any more sharing of what the Labyrinth is like and those

boys will supposedly end up in the sudden employ of King Francis's army.

The voice of the announcer, whom some believe to be Holm himself, carries across the estate. "Now that you've been briefed regarding your participation, we hope you'll settle in to relish the rest of your stay with us. Please enjoy the food, drink, bonfires, and facilities, and please refrain from losing your children, lest the werehounds find them for you."

"Bobbles! Bobbles for ya!" a woman yells just as we reach the halfway point on the hill. It's old Mrs. Mench, who's apparently been assigned the job of giving out celebration necklaces for the event.

I tip my head, and we stop right in front of her. I smile and hold out my hand, and the neighbor woman looks me up and down, then narrows a brow at first mine, then Seleni's clothing. I brace and wait for her to lose her calm when she recognizes me—but she just nods and hands us each a necklace.

"Thank you," I say, practicing a deep tone.

"You're quite welcome, young men. Go find some pretty chums to give them to. Now move along."

We slip around her and keep walking, and I can feel Seleni's momentary relief.

"Now for the real test." She lifts her gaze toward where Beryl and the other boys are waiting for the announcer's droning to end.

"Be sure to check the handwritten schedule posted at each terrace entrance for all times and events—including ballooning, theater, air aerobics, bread pudding toss, and petting the legendary basilisk. But be careful—they rather enjoy the taste of port flesh. The older the chewier."

The crowd's laugh ripples out in waves as we slip through the masses of people—most of whom let us through with comments of "Good luck, boys," and "It's as much about character as it is brains."

When we arrive at the hilltop, we make our way along the thirty-feet-tall hedges to the Labyrinth's single, gated entrance, which is said to be the only way in or out of the place. In front of it are fifty or so boys, all of whom look to be near the same age as us and just as nervous as the crowd.

"There." I point to Beryll, who's standing with Lawrence behind Sam and Will.

"I told him to find and warn them about Germaine."

As we press toward the four, a few faces turn our way, as if curious what level of competition we'll be. The rest pass right over the visual assessment I'm used to and simply nod as if accepting us as one of them—then go back to throwing glances at the nearby group of girls cheering for them. The boys casually nudge each other and grin.

"Has anyone seen Miss Lake? Is she around?" Beryll shouts over their heads.

"Over here," Seleni says, then claps a hand across her mouth and shoots me a look of panic. She pulls her hat lower over her eyes as he turns, and adds in a low voice, "Sorry, thought you were asking about someone else."

He marches over anyway, and I can feel Seleni's blood pounding through her arm pressed against mine—but then

Beryll smiles. "No worries. You going in there?" He juts his chin at the Labyrinth gate.

She nods. "You looking for your girl?"

I discreetly kick her with my boot.

"I am. Well, best of luck to you." Beryll sticks his hand out.

I thrust mine to meet it and give it a firm shake, and the next second he's scanning the crowd again. "If you chaps will excuse me . . ." He tilts his hat and moves off, and I breathe out relief as Seleni slumps against my shoulder.

"I'm going to get us caught, aren't I?" she whispers.

"You're going to get *you* caught. You blow it, and you're on your own. Same as me."

She starts to reply, but a sudden flare goes up and a firework explodes with a bang over the party. More cheers are followed by more fireworks. One looks like a basilisk shooting across the sky, his wide mouth and scales a myriad of colors and his long tail waving. Another resembles a school of fish swimming through a reef, like those we have off the coastline. The oohs and aahs grow with each explosion, until the crackers finish in a hail of sparkles so bright, it almost seems like daylight where Seleni and I are standing.

"Ladies and Gents, now welcome yourselves to the highlight of this equinox festivity—the fifty-fifth annual scholarship for a full-ride education to Stemwick University!"

The crowd roars and Seleni and I roar with it, because that truly is something to roar about.

"Contestants, please give us your attention for a few moments while we go over the specific rules with you. As always, the event will take place over a number of hours. Within that time, only contestants will be allowed inside the Labyrinth, the castle, and the lair. If you are found trespassing, you will be possibly torn apart by our resident beasts and definitely handed over to the authorities. In which case, your entire belongings—including food, clothes, and grandmothers—that are left on these grounds shall be confiscated. Grandmothers will be dealt with according to their baking skills, assuming they have any."

The assembly erupts into laughter again, but this time there's an uncertain edge to it.

"Now . . . if you are not one of the contestants, we ask you to please step back at this time."

I grab Seleni's elbow sleeve to secure us both in place as the boys around us jostle closer, and the spectators scoot back to give a wider berth.

"Young university hopefuls, Mr. Holm would like to congratulate you on your bravery to enter his contest. Please be aware, once again, that you do so at your own risk and that Holm and the Holm estate bear no responsibility for what happens once you're inside the Labyrinth. How you choose to play will determine how you survive and in what shape you emerge upon finishing. Mr. Holm strongly encourages you to back out now if you are weak of heart, stomach, or spine."

I feel Seleni look at me. I clench my jaw and keep my eyes straight ahead on the gate. *Just get through the gate and into the maze, Rhen. Once in, you can figure out the rest.*

"The rules are as follows:

- *"One:* The only accessories allowed inside the Labyrinth are the clothes you are wearing. If you're not wearing clothes, please simply be warned that all, er, loose *objects* may be at greater risk of injury. Also, should you encounter any moving devices while inside, you'd be wise to keep all appendages as close as possible.
- *"Two:* The test is broken into multiple parts, and it is up to you how much time you spend on each one. While they pertain to different sections of the Stemwick educational standard, including maths, technology, sciences, and engineering, they are also a fairly reliable judge of character. Again, it is your choice how you play. However, fall behind in any one of them and you'll wish you hadn't.
- *"Three:* You are highly encouraged to think outside the normal, and in fact will not pass otherwise.
- *"Four:* Upon entering the first section of the contest, you will have precisely eighteen hours to complete it or be eliminated.
- *"Five:* Interference with the contest itself or injury to other players will be cause for immediate dismissal, prison, and/or public harpooning, depending on the level of infraction.

"Consider yourselves fairly warned. And now"—the voice gets louder and deeper all at the same time—"are you prepared to compete for entrance to the top university in our fair King Francis's kingdom? Then step forward now or forever hold your peace." There's a metallic creaking sound of gates shifting, and a cheer goes up. The boys press in, even as their teary-eyed mums try to catch and hug them.

"Only players at this time, please," the announcer repeats. "Only players at this time. All else move back."

"I'm a player." I say it softly. Quietly. Like a ghost leaf rustling in the air. Firming my resolve.

I stand next to Seleni amid a host of bodies crowding in as they become keyed up with excitement to the point the anticipation is dripping in sweat off their skin. She utters a grunt of disgust, and I give a shrug that says, *"Guess we better get used to it,"* before I lift up to bounce on the balls of my feet like the rest of them are doing.

Until something catches my eye, and I peer over to see Lute also bouncing. I frown. *What the?* He's standing on the other side of Will and Sam in the midst of the fray just like Seleni and me. What's he doing in here? Why isn't he on the sidelines with his mum and Ben?

I swerve to Seleni and point to him. She looks surprised, then whispers, "Maybe it's the fishing restrictions. I wonder if he needs it."

I swallow. Of course he does. He said the fishing couldn't support his family anymore. I bounce and holler louder even as the thought that he's here for such a reason rubs against the grain of my gut. He's only ever wanted to be a fisherman. Now, because of a law, he's being forced down a different path.

"You boys ready to be slaughtered?" Germaine shouts from in front of Lute. Sneers are plastered securely on his and Rubin's mouths as they face the group.

I peer at Lute again. *He doesn't know about Germaine's plans.* I grab the side of Seleni's tunic and tug her his direction. We have to at least get close enough so I can warn him.

"Contestants, you may now enter," the announcer says.

The gates stop creaking. Then, with a clang, they swing inward.

The bodies around me jolt into movement—shoving and jostling and clawing their shoes into the dirt to give them any slight advantage. I grip Seleni's tunic and shove us into position behind Beryll, Sam, Will, and Lute.

Seleni looks at me, and I nod.

The boys in front of us yell and lunge forward.

We jump in.

15

The moment we step through the gates, the boys behind us shove and press us into the bodies ahead, until male hips and elbows and hands are plastered against every minute curve of my frame. I might cringe if I could breathe, but I'm too busy trying to stay upright to think of anything more than finding air and avoiding being trampled in the sweaty stampede.

A hand grabs tight to mine, and from the corner of my eye, I see that Seleni looks like she's drowning. I pull her over and push her ahead, and the next second the boys in front have broken free, and we erupt into a square garden barely wide enough to hold three carriages.

It's a box. Made of grass at our feet and hedges reaching almost as high as the castle, with only the sky above and a few of those hanging white bulbs for light. And no exit other than the one we just came through.

The sound of grating metal pricks the air and, with another clang, the gates swing shut.

I blink and glance around along with everyone else to see who made it in and who didn't. Silence falls around our breathing—which becomes slower and heavier the longer we wait. One minute turns into an uncomfortable two.

Then into three.

"What is this?" a boy behind Seleni mutters.

"We're like trapped cattle," another says.

"Maybe he really does feed contestants to his beasts."

"Not funny, Rubin," Lawrence growls.

A movement shakes one of the hedges and is accompanied by what sounds like the hiss of a snake. It's followed by a thump and then a scream, and Seleni and I jerk together just as I note an empty space where a boy to the left of us just stood. Another slithering noise emits on my right, and I look over just as another cry goes up. Then another. The rustling grows louder and suddenly it's close and the boy next to me is plucked up and dragged through the air into the hedge. It closes around him like a mouth eating its prey, and the next second he's disappeared.

"Duck!" someone yells just as a thin, trailing vine snaps out and grabs one of Will's friends by his arms. Quick as lightning it drags him into the foliage.

My eyes widen. The vines are everywhere—hovering above and around us, slithering this way and that, as if tasting the air. In spite of the fact they're a scientific impossibility.

I squeeze Seleni's hand, shut my eyes, and wait for one to take us because we shouldn't be here. But it doesn't. And as quickly as it started, the rustling stops, the vines recede, and the hedge goes back to normal. Whatever normal is.

"What in Caldon's name was that?" Lawrence yells.

"Tsk, tsk, the rules are clear—only first-time contestants are allowed. And no contraband." Like the chimes of a clock, the words ripple on all sides, until they echo through my bones and skin. I frown.

"But now that we've dealt with them fairly—hurry, hurry, find your way. No stopping now, come what may."

The tone and musical flow are unmistakable. It's Mr. Kellen, the odd, elderly gentleman from my uncle's party. One moment he's speaking, and the next he's standing in front of us, clapping amid a chorus of gasps and cursing. Except instead of his pipe, he now holds a cup of something steaming, which he lifts and sips as he waits for our silence.

I stare at him. *Is Kellen Mr. Holm?* I inch behind Beryll and Sam and tug Seleni to follow because I have no idea if he can see us or his magic can sense us. Why hasn't it already?

"Good evening, gents," he says, when the boys have calmed. "In the wall behind me you'll find four doors." He grins, then takes another sip of tea as the hedge he's standing in front of rustles and four silver doors appear, each one three feet from the other.

An utterance of "ah" goes through the crowd.

"Behind those doors is the beginning of your future." Kellen holds out one delicate hand—and from it falls a key attached to a chain that's attached to his forefinger. "Follow the path and the voice of Mr. Holm, and you might make it through the first task." He gives a sly smile that looks oddly mesmerizing on his merry face. "If you make it through, you'll move on to the next obstacle. Fail, however, and you'll be at my mercy."

He swings the key out in front of him—like a hypnotist does with a watch. And for a moment I swear that's exactly what he's doing—hypnotizing us—because for the life of me I can't look away. Can't look anywhere but there—at Kellen, and his lavender eyes, and that precise pendulum-moving key.

"Your quest is a key. The first one who finds and uses it correctly will escape the Labyrinth. Alive." He jerks the key up and into his palm in one swift motion, making me blink. Then steps back. "Find the key and open the door to your future," he says again, as a mist begins seeping from the ground and rippling around his feet. Soon it's swirling up his legs, then his arms and face and that silver hair, and a murmur picks up among the boys in front of us.

His voice cracks the air again. "Pick a door, any door—but those players you go in with will be the team you're stuck with. Until they are whittled away one by one and the last person standing will be the one who won. But for now, the question becomes—how well do you know your maths?" His words fade and a swell of music tinkles and the mist surrounding him thickens. Until there's a poof, and the space where he stood is empty.

"Here is your first clue." His voice reverberates in my head. And in the spot where he'd been standing, four words are etched into the ground.

WHAT ARE YOUR FEARS?

The boys are blinking and looking around, same as Seleni and me.

"So . . . we pick a door?" someone whispers.

"But which door? How do we choose?"

"Is there a difference?"

"Who cares? He just said to hurry." Germaine strides for the farthest door on the right, yanks the handle, and hurls himself through. Two seconds later, Rubin follows suit, and as if a spell has been broken, the place erupts into chaos.

I dodge to the side to avoid getting shoved and grab a handful of Beryll's shirt to pull him and Seleni with me toward Will and Sam and Lute. If Beryll notices, he doesn't seem to care—probably because everyone else in here is doing the same.

"Which door?" Beryll yells to Lawrence.

"Follow Germaine," I reply in a deep voice.

He obeys and tags after three kids who are going for it too, and Seleni and I trail the lot of them until suddenly it's my turn, and I'm charging through the doorway into Caldon-knows-what.

The moment we enter, the hedge shivers and ripples, and I don't have to spin around to know that the door behind us has just dissipated. I look anyway and find I'm correct. There's no exit—only forward. The feasibility of such a thing is beyond me, but it doesn't matter—there's no time. I turn back and see Lute stopped on a narrow path that shoots thirteen feet ahead before it splits into a cross-section going two opposite directions. The back of Rubin's blue tunic is just disappearing around the left curve, and the three boys we followed through are heading for the right.

Lawrence grabs Beryll's sleeve. "Wait!" He points at the bushes the tall hedges are created from.

They're Sleeping Man-Traps, one touch of which will leave a grown man passed out cold for a solid five hours. Da and I regularly use the poison in sleeping aids for patients—but having it here? I look around. This isn't just about getting through this section the fastest—it's about getting through it *at all*.

"Sleeping weeds," Lawrence says. "They'll knock you out."

Lute nods as his face flashes recognition. "Don't touch the sides, boys." Then points at Lawrence. "Want to lead the way, kid?"

Lawrence firms his jaw and starts forward on the path just as three more boys erupt from the disappearing door behind us. With little more than a shout of "Move!" they hustle through and head for where Rubin disappeared. Except the moment they turn the corner to enter that path, the hedge shifts and closes around them and another section opens to our right. As if growing and shriveling.

"What the?" Sam looks at Will.

Lawrence ignores them and hurries us to the only path now available. But the moment we take it, the hedge closes behind us, same as it did to the others.

Two more paths promptly open, and Lawrence looks at the group.

"Go left this time." Beryll takes the lead, but before we reach the path, the vines cave in and force us to go right again.

"I think we're making a circle," Sam shouts.

"We need to move faster then." Will steps into one of three openings that have just appeared, and the rest of us barely make it in before it regrows.

"There's too many options!" Lawrence says.

"Just keep moving!" Seleni shoves Lawrence onto a path in front of us, but something's niggling at me. It's not just that there are too many options . . .

The poisoned hedges are starting to shift faster. I look up at the starry night sky. Then back at the path as a new opening emerges. The niggling gets stronger.

I watch another route sprout open at the same time the entire hedge in front of us ripples and seems to grow larger. Which is when I see it.

The paths are growing narrower.

I yell at the group—to tell them it's shrinking—to say we only have a short time to figure this out. But it's unnecessary. The moment we turn the new corner, the hedge narrows again, and the boys' expressions say they see it too.

Beryll looks at Lute. "Any ideas? What if—?" His voice cuts

off as his eyes grow round at something to the right of us. He lets out a soft whimper.

Lute and I turn just as a series of shrieks starts up through the Labyrinth, beyond our hedge corridor. But it's the thing Beryll's staring at that about rips my spine from my skin.

An impossible mirage materializes to the side of us—it's of Beryll's father. Beside him stands what appears to be Beryll as a small child trying to get the man's attention. Except the mirage alters, and Beryll's father suddenly becomes a basilisk monster that stalks toward us—toward Beryll in real life. In the maze.

I jump back as Seleni gasps and Lawrence lets out a scream. Except the air now ripples around *me*, and suddenly my mum is in front of me, lying dead in a grave with dirt being thrown on top of her. I retreat and shake my head. What is going on? Why am I seeing this? Except just like Beryll's, the image is changing and I am the one in a grave, with an older version of Vincent standing over me, and he's mumbling something about me having become the pliable wife who got him to the positions of fame he needed.

My eyes water as the scene alters—even as I'm aware that more screams have picked up—not just from Beryll but from others in my group also as maybe they're seeing their own horrors. The vision in front of me changes to a scene where I'm waiting with dinner in hand as Vincent tells our children to stop stressing him out. He comes over and puts his hands on my face, and right before he kisses me, his face and eyes turn into those of a ghoul.

I lean over and vomit onto the grass at my feet.

When I look up, no one else is watching. Seleni is screaming at her vision of Beryll kissing another woman. Lute is weeping as a mirage in front of him shows Ben standing alone at Lute's and his mum's graves. I can't see what Sam and Will are looking at, but from their gaping expressions, they're drowning at sea.

What did Holm do to us? Maybe the fog he disappeared into had a mind-altering compound. Either way . . .

I force my gaze past the boys—through their visions to the shrubs. We have to get out of here. We have to *move*.

I seize Seleni's arm and start shoving at the rest of them. "Guys, we have to go!"

Maybe a different part of the maze will bring relief.

The motion brings Lute around. He shakes his head and blinks, then glances back at me and my vision of Vincent that's following even as I desperately try to block it out. He frowns and tilts his head, then grits his jaw and jerks his gaze up at the sky. He grabs my shoulder and calls for us to go to the right, then the left. Then straight. Then peers up at the sky again and points us to another left.

He's using the stars to lead us east, away from the Labyrinth gate entrance.

We follow down one path, then another, and with each turn we make, the nine-foot-high foliage regrows. But at least we're heading in the right direction.

I think.

The next time the hedge opens up, Lute pushes to the left again, then curses and trips as we run smack straight into Germaine, Rubin, and Vincent who are standing frozen in front of their own visions. From the corner of my eye, I see Vincent's nightmare. It's of his own face as a roomful of dead people sit up and begin to come for him. They look diseased.

Something lands at my feet and the next second I'm smacking Will, who's slumped to the ground. "It's not real," I snap at him. "Follow Lute." I grab his shirt and hoist him up, then sprint forward.

The maze keeps shifting and we keep falling, getting up, and running—single file now—until it feels like time is lost and escaping from these visions is the only thing I've ever done, and we are stuck in an endless loop of a nightmare sequence.

A sequence.

Like in math.

I stop so fast both Sam and Seleni plow into me. I shut my eyes and try to remember Kellen's voice. What did he ask? *"How well do you know your maths?"*

I spin my mind back over the number of turns we've come through and approximate number of steps I've run for each. It takes a minute of counting until I land on what is one of the latter maths I learned in my studies with Da. But Lute's right—it has to do with the stars. The maze is an equation.

"It's a Foradian equation," I yell.

"What?" Lute and Vincent both blink through their visions and stare at me.

"A Foradian equation. Count the moves according to the stars—add them up—and follow the formula to find the correct path out."

Beryll nods even as his mouth stays open in a continuous

scream, and Sam shakes his head because he never went that far in school. But Lute and Vincent are already eyeing the sky and calculating the formula same as me.

Count the steps, Rhen. And move.

I start forward but my nightmare's suddenly in front of me—that image of the ghoul screaming, with its hands on my face.

Ignore it, Rhen.

The scream grows louder and so gut-wrenching, it tears at my blood.

Don't blink. Don't alter your gaze. The equation is simple— five left hedges forward, plus three closed behind—

I begin counting off aloud as Lute and Vincent do it with me, and soon Germaine and Seleni are doing it too, until there's a sudden opening in front of us.

We step through and a flash of something silver wrinkles in the greenery ahead. A door. I have no idea whether it's back the way we came or forward to the next obstacle. I don't care. I just want out of here.

Lute presses my shoulder toward it, then turns and grabs Seleni's, then Sam's, as Rubin and Vincent and Germaine bolt for what I swear is solidifying into a tangible piece of metal. "Let's go, Beryll," Lute yells.

But Beryll's not coming—he's staring at the shifting hedges we just erupted from. "Where's Lawrence?" he's asking. "Where's Lawrence?"

"You need to move, mate," Lute yells. Seleni turns and her eyes go wide, but Lute's already jumped backward to grab him, and I am reaching for the door Germaine's just gone through in an effort to keep it open.

"Here—help me!" I shout at Seleni. The thing is far heavier than it should be.

Seleni obeys, then lets out a screech as a green-eyed ghoul plows from the hedge right for us. I shove the door open as hard as I can—and it's enough for Lute to clear the threshold with Beryll before Seleni and I tumble inside after them.

The door slams shut, and Seleni, Vincent, and I shove our entire weight against it until we hear a click.

Which is when the lights go out.

Y ou guys all right?" Sam asks. "Will?"

"I'm here."

"Lawrence is gone." Beryll's voice quivers.

"And you should be glad of it." Germaine groans through the dark. "Now why not be useful and turn on the bloody—"

The lights flick on, and I'm squinting and blinking at the faces of Vincent, Germaine, Rubin, Sam, Will, Beryll, Seleni, Lute, and some kid I've never met.

"Nice work," Germaine says, getting to his feet. "You do that, Vince?"

"No. It was automatic." Vincent pushes away from the door and Seleni and me, and gets up to look around the space.

It's a white stone room no bigger than Uncle Nicholae's study, except with no shelves, no windows, and no doors other than the one we just came through. I reach up to ensure my hat's still in place before I sneak a peek at Seleni's grease-and-dirt-creased face. It's still good. She catches my look and mouths, *"You're still a boy."* To which I nod and follow Vincent's cue to move from the door—in case anyone else comes slamming through.

Except the moment my hand releases the handle, the thing dissolves, just like the door in the hedge maze. "What in hulls?" Sam mutters.

"Looks like we're locked in a box, chaps," Will says.

"I believe it's called a sarcophagus," Beryll attempts to joke. No one laughs but Seleni.

Beryll shrugs and strides to the only freestanding item in the room—a narrow table—upon which rest a coin, a book, and an apple. Then he moves on to the far wall where a pad with buttons is attached to the otherwise smooth stone surface. Vincent and Rubin follow, and I'm about to, until the look on Lute's face stalls me.

"Hey, kid."

Lute's staring at Vincent as if he's about to launch across the room and strangle him.

"Kid."

I peer over and—*oh*. Germaine's talking to me. He juts his thick eyebrows at my chest, then Seleni's, then at the new boy. "Names?"

I stiffen. "That's Sedgwick. I'm Renford. Don't know the other."

"Tippin," the new boy pipes in.

"Good. Now you get to come help me, Renford."

I snort, and start to tell him to shove it, but Seleni stops me with a look of warning.

Fine. I stride over to where Germaine is standing along the left wall beneath the only other items in the room—two square clocks hung halfway up, one set right side while the other is upside down, and a giant oil painting mounted evenly between them.

Germaine tips his head at the painting. "The depiction's an exact replica of this room."

"An exact replica, minus us." I scan it for any other anomalies.

"Here, give me a lift. I'm going to inspect it." Germaine puts his foot up and waits for me to link my fingers crisscross under it. When I do, he places his full body weight in my hands and pushes up. I heave forward—toward the wall for countersupport—and try not to imagine how enjoyable it'd be to accidentally slip and drop him on his hindside.

The sound of a scuffle erupts from where Rubin and Beryll are messing with the button box. "Of course it's a code, dimwit," Rubin snaps. "You have to enter the correct combination."

"Hey, boys." Germaine points at the miniature button pad in the painting—the same I've been trying to decipher from my view beneath his bony rear. "It's got a set of numbers," he calls out. "Try 8–8–6–1."

Beryll punches the code in with one finger, and the pad instantly lights up. But that's all it does—until the half-baked voice of Kellen suddenly rattles the air with a chuckle and makes Germaine jerk backward so hard I lose my grip. The two of us tumble together to the floor, and unfortunately my elbow somehow lodges in his rib cage. *Oops.* He gives a satisfying yelp that makes even Lute smile.

"I see you've made it inside." Kellen's voice crackles through the room. *"Well done—although, careful as you go—because upside down and all around your world will slowly turn. Choose wisely, deduce correctly, to open the key to your future. Choose unwisely and you'll fall into the Labyrinth of no return. The question now is simply—how good are you at thinking outside the box?"*

There's a whirring sound, and the button pad lights turn off again.

"Think outside the box," Sam murmurs. "Not funny, gents."

"Actually, it's 'ilarious," his brother says. "Because we're in a room that's like a box, and—"

Sam smacks the back of his messy-hair head.

"Will you two shut it? Here, move over and let me at this thing." Rubin prods Beryll aside with his broad shoulders to try the button pad for himself just as Germaine heads for them, nursing his rib cage, to gape at it too.

I've just turned back to the painting when Lute is beside me. I brace and don't look at him. I don't know how much of my vision he saw. Was it enough to put two and two together? And if he knows it's me, what then?

I squirm and wait for his comments or challenge as to why I'm here, but they don't come. And when I peek up he's not acknowledging me. Instead, he simply indicates the corner of the painting.

I squint and stand on my tiptoes until I can get a good view of what first appears to be the artist's signature but is actually four words swirled together:

Why Are You Here?

"Just like the hedge maze question," I murmur.

Lute reads it aloud before he walks over to the room's corner that matches the one in the painting. I follow. Unlike the portrait, the stone in the real-life recess is blank. I press around for any crevice or levers, then watch as Seleni, Vincent, and Tippin do the same over the rest of the room's corners and floor.

I glance at Lute, then at the painting again.

Why are you here?

"The answer better not be another horror fest," Beryll grumbles. "Because whatever drama that was out in the maze seemed wholly unnecessary."

"Holm probably thinks himself pretty witty giving such deep life questions," Germaine says from the wall pad.

Seleni deepens her tone. "Yes, but what does it mean? The question."

"If the one from the maze outside is any indication," Vincent mutters, "this one's another misdirection, not a clue. He's treating us more like rats than students. And now he's got us caged."

"Okay . . . but what do rats do?" I scan the room looking for anything familiar. "They go back to what they know."

"And what is that exactly?"

But even as he says it, I note he's spent the past two minutes proving my point. He's been staring at the painting's words and retracing them with his slender fingers in dust on the ground. I look closer. He appears to be assigning numbers to them.

I lift a brow. He's seeing if the words are a numerical code.

I peer at Lute again, but he's refocused on Vincent, who a moment later stands, swipes his blond hair back in place, and says, "Germaine, try these." He cites a variety of combinations, which Germaine starts entering in. He inputs one, then another, then another, but there's no reaction other than a one-time replaying of the message from Kellen that we already heard.

I shake my head. The numbers and letters are starting to spin and mix in my head, but there's something wrong with them.

I shut my eyes and try to clear my mind—to concentrate on the question that, just like the one in the maze, Holm must've put here for a reason. *Why are you here?*

Why are any of us here—?

A scream rips through the room and dissipates as fast as it came. It's followed by the sound of metal grinding against stone.

I spin around as the others do the same. "What just bloody happened?" Vincent barks.

Sam points at the floor. "He . . . fell."

"Who?"

"The kid."

I look at who is here. There were ten of us; now there're only nine. I count off—Germaine, Rubin, Vincent, Sam, Will, Lute, Seleni, Beryll, and me. "Tippin?"

"He was standin' right here." Sam is delicately pressing on the stones in the corner where Tippin had apparently been. His face is white as a ghost. "It was lookin' like he'd figured something out and pressed a spot on that wall. Except the bloody floor slid open and swallowed him into a pitch-black shaft."

"Okay, new plan—nobody touch anything without telling the rest of us," Lute says.

"Agreed," Germaine says. "I don't want to die because one of you makes a stupid mistake. Now let's just all walk through this entire room methodically."

We do. And then we do it again. And again. The same walls, same cracks, same levers and corners, minus the one Tippin fell through, and that same painting on the wall that seems to indicate the clue is somehow tied to them all, but we have no idea how.

"Oh you've got to be kidding me." Rubin swears. "If I lose this test because I'm paired with a bunch of idiots . . ." He puffs back his wide shoulders and stares directly at Seleni and Will.

"What about the items on the table?" Will says to the rest of us. He's gone back to them at least five times now, rearranging them to match the picture, stacking them, then pulling them all off before replacing them in their exact spots. "In the painting they're this way. But maybe if we try mirroring them—" He arranges the coin, book, and apple as he talks, but nothing happens other than Beryll hops up to join him, and Rubin scowls before strolling over too.

"Maybe we have to answer the question," Seleni offers.

"Excuse me?" Germaine growls.

"He said maybe we have to answer the question," Lute says in clear warning for Germaine to watch his tone.

Beryll glances up. "What question?"

"The one in the painting." Seleni points. *"Why are you here?* Maybe it's an audible cipher and we have to answer the question in order to release the lock."

"What—like we all take turns answering why we're here? That's ridiculous." Germaine scoffs. "We're here because none of you ninnies can get us out of here, nothing more. Now if you're not going to help, at least let the adults work."

"I'll start."

All eyes turn to Beryll, who shrugs. "There's nothing to lose, right?" He rubs the back of his brown hair and squints down at the dusty floor. "I'm here because my father wants me to be. And to hopefully have the type of future I want."

He's met with nods of agreement from a few of the boys.

In a deep voice Seleni goes next, even as her fingers shake. "I came because I wanted to see what the Labyrinth contest is like."

"Me too." I refuse to look at Lute as I get my turn out of the way. "And I'm here because I want a higher education."

"Well, I think most of you know why I'm here," Germaine exclaims. "To win."

Everyone chuckles, because even if he's an oaf, at least he's honest.

"Obviously we're here for the fame and love connections," Sam says for both him and Will. And everyone laughs again because at least they're honest too.

"I'm here because of the restrictions they're putting on the fishing industry," Lute says quietly. "My brother—he has certain needs. And with my pops gone, it's my responsibility to care for him and our mum." He looks at the skin on his knuckles. "I don't have any imaginings I'll win this thing, but I have to at least find a way to earn a better life for them, you know?"

The room falls quiet. Even Germaine and Rubin have stopped their chortling, and when I glance from Lute to Vincent, the latter is glaring at him with what looks like annoyance. And Beryll . . . Beryll's expression is annoyed too, but in a different way. I swear he looks like he might cry.

Vincent sniffs. "Well I'm here because my parents could use the money. If my way is paid, it'd free up their ability to donate to other things. And I feel strongly about my responsibility to contribute wisdom and talents to better our world."

I study him. That's the shallowest answer I've ever heard from him. Kind of like everything else these days. No heart, just a shell. In the past I would've demanded a real answer from him—a better answer—one that is true of a friend. Except I no longer care.

"Spoken like a politician's kid," Will says beneath his breath, and Seleni nods.

Beryll looks at Rubin. "Your turn, man."

"Well, it's none of your business why I'm here. But just to prove you wrong on this whole confession sesh—I'm here for the fame." He raises his hands and waits. "Annnnd just as I predicted—your sweet assertions didn't do a bleeding thing to get us any freer. In fact, it wasted our time." He goes back to standing at the table near Will.

Germaine and Beryll go back to messing with the number pad, and I take a spot on the floor, from which to study the room and painting. Until, after ten minutes of pressing every combination we all can think of, Germaine throws up his hands and declares the thing broken, and surrenders himself to the floor, too, while Vincent gets up and tries his own attempt at it again. I shut my eyes to tune them all out so I can focus.

Someone bumps my foot and sits down, and even with my eyes closed I know it's Seleni. I can feel her heightened nerves. I open my eyes to smile assurance at her—only it's not her. It's Lute.

He holds my gaze a solid ten seconds—long enough for me to blink—then he looks away.

My stomach hits the floor. Maybe he knows who I am after all.

I sneak him a side glance and am met with my answer clear as day on his somewhat handsome, stony face. Lute waits until Vincent rattles off more number combinations before he bumps his leg against mine and stiffly mutters, "You're wearing pants."

"So are you, thank Caldon."

His lip twitches. "You dress as a boy often?"

"No more than you."

A small smirk appears.

Vincent pivots from the keypad and says to the room, "You know my father would suggest no one rests until we've figured this thing out."

Lute's smile is instantly gone. He drops his tone. "I'm sure his father would also suggest how progressive you are to have followed your beau in here."

Annoyance floods my veins. My mouth goes dry, and I start to whisper that Vincent is certainly not my beau, but Lute's gaze interrupts me. "I saw your fears back in the maze," he says quietly. "Seems like a pleasant future you've chosen, Miss Tellur."

Pleasant?

He tips his head toward Vincent but doesn't move from watching me. Just hardens his jaw beneath a swag of black bangs and says coldly, "He's quite the catch. I'm sure your future will be too."

Is he jesting? What is he talking about? Those were fears, not choices. Before I can reply to his rudeness, he stands and strides off to join Sam, and I am left wondering what in King Francis's name is wrong with him. I glare until a sense of someone else watching me takes over.

I turn to see Vincent staring right at me. Eyes sharp. Blond hair perfectly in place. He furrows his brow, then shifts his interest to Lute.

With a scowl at both of them, I pat my cap to ensure it's still in place, then rest my head on the floor because my brain needs a break from all the talking and Lute's daft assumptions and Vincent being Vincent—whoever that is anymore.

The group of them keep mumbling things, but I tune them out and wander my mind back over the words from Kellen that I've heard three times now thanks to that blasted number pad. *"Up and down and all around . . ."*

"Why are you here?"

My shoulders relax against the cool stone floor.

"Up and down and all around . . ." The words and numbers on the painting are shifting order in my peripheral sight.

I tip my head a little farther upside down from the position I'm already lying in, and for some reason the room looks clearer from that perspective. In fact . . .

I frown and shove my hat tighter on my head—and do a headstand against the wall and take in the view. The room is almost an exact mirror image of itself from the top—with the number pad halfway up the wall, the clocks now flipped around, and, in fact, the painting itself looking more precise.

"Why are we here?" I murmur.

"Hey, kid, what're you doing?" Germaine asks. "This isn't playtime."

"Shh." I lift one finger to measure the distance between the floor and ceiling and that picture hanging much too perfectly to be a coincidence. "Look. Why are we here—instead of . . . there?" I point to the ceiling.

Rubin groans.

"Oh," Seleni says.

It's so simple I almost laugh in embarrassment. How could we have tried every combination but the obvious one? I turn my gaze on the boys. "Gentlemen, I think we're supposed—"

A loud thump shakes the floor, followed by the sound of someone gurgling. I drop and flip back onto my feet to see Will writhing on the floor with foam bubbling from his mouth. The next second Sam's going for Rubin—plowing his head into his chest and knocking him over.

"What the?" Germaine roars and rushes Sam, but Lute and Beryll jump in to stop him.

I scramble to Will. The foam is dripping from his mouth onto his neck and the floor. I tip his head to the side, so he doesn't choke, when I notice the prick of blood on his trembling neck as if he was stung. I frown and peer closer at it. Then at him. His symptoms are very much like . . .

I look up. Rubin and Sam are rolling on the ground, and Rubin's right fist is clenched around something. Lute's already caught sight of it too because he's left Beryll and Germaine's squabble to dart over and set his foot on Rubin's wrist, hard enough to warn him that he'll break it. He leans down as I hurry over and bend Rubin's wrist back enough for me to peel the boy's fingers open and reveal a thorn as thick as my thumb.

"What is it?" Sam demands.

I hold it up. "It's a thorn from the Sleeping Man-Trap hedge," Seleni says.

"That was your blokes' plan?" Beryll bellows at Germaine. "To take us all out with a thorn?"

"Gotta use what the Labyrinth hands you," Germaine says.

Beryll steps back and gapes as if he's forgotten how to breathe. He clenches his hand into a fist and looks about ready to take a swing, even as Germaine's smile says he'll welcome it.

"That's enough." Lute inserts himself between them.

I drop the thorn and Seleni squashes it beneath her boot until the juice runs out and quickly evaporates upon contact with the air, while I return to Will. His body is shaking more violently now, and I press on his pulse to check his blood pressure.

"Hey, Vincent. You want to help here?" Seleni says, and when I glance up she's glaring at him and the fact that he hasn't moved from his spot against the wall where he's watching with a look of passive interest.

I start to agree with her, only to get distracted by Will's weakening breathing and pulse. He's having an allergic reaction—his throat is closing up. I elevate his head and look around for anything to use, but there's nothing here to counteract it with or to open up his windpipe. "We have to get him out of here. He needs help. I think the poison might be cutting off his airway."

I turn to Seleni. "Try the buttons again—punch in 1–9–8–8."

She jumps to press them and, in a sweet mercy of reprieve, rather than a replay of Kellen's voice, there's a *ding* and the entire room starts to shake. "Nobody move, in case he's wrong," Germaine mutters.

Suddenly the floor is rumbling, and a loud metal chain begins clinking, and the entire middle of the far wall slides open.

17

Another loud clink resounds across the room, and just as Beryll gives a soft cheer, the metal wall begins to slide back down. Lute and Sam grab Will's arms and drag him over as we rush to shove everyone through before the panel drops and once again locks us in.

The moment we exit, the whirring quickens and a gear clunks into place and the wall shuts with a heavy thud that vibrates the ground. We tumble to the grass, gasping and coughing and facing up at a night sky filled with stars, on a mountaintop overlooking a part of Caldon I don't recognize.

The sounds of the festival in the distance slowly draw my attention.

I sit up and note the massive stone and hedge wall stretching behind us as far as I can see into the dark. I pause. *It's still dark.*

We've only been gone a few hours.

It's felt like days. My body is already begging to be done—not with the acuity test but with the emotional stress. Because while the first I'd expected, the second—not so much.

I peer around for Seleni and Lute, and instead my gaze falls on Sam. He's looking around with an odd expression, which is quickly turning frantic as he gets up to search the area. "Where's Will? *Will!* Has anyone seen Will?"

Beryll, Lute, Seleni, and I jump up to scan the hill. He was here one moment, then gone the next. Seleni walks over to me to whisper, "We're not going to find him, Rhen. I guarantee Holm pulled him from the test."

"Why wasn't anyone watching?" Sam's voice is rising. "We have to go back and—"

"He's been pulled, mate." Lute's tone soothes as he steps in front of Sam. "Better that than let him stay and maybe die. If the kid here was right about his reaction to the sleeping thorn, your brother needed medical help."

Sam sags back and his breath comes heavy as he glares at Lute's logic. He pinches two fingers over the sides of his temple and holds them there—before he clears his throat and looks up. "All right then. But one of you better keep an eye on *him*—" He points at Rubin. "So I don't kill him."

Rubin's lip curls. "Hey, it's all fair—that's the name of the game. Nothing's personal."

Sam turns to sock him, but Lute grabs his arm. "Let it go, Sam. He just knocked him from the competition—he didn't kill him." He glances my way. "Let's just cool our heads a minute."

Sam acquiesces but keeps his scowl on Rubin, who just shrugs and peers around. "Where to now, geniuses?"

Beryll points to the base of the steep mountain we're on—where the stars are reflecting off a huge lake that surrounds what appears to be an island.

"Now that's more like it," Vincent says, and takes a deep breath. "Give me outdoors any day, mates."

"Well, well, well, what do you know," a voice says. "Seems there are a few players left yet."

I swerve to see a group of boys strolling toward us. They're covered in sweat and look strained, but still more relaxed than we are at the moment.

"Thought we might be the only ones left."

The speaker is a tall boy about Lute's age and build but with an accent and style suggesting he's from one of the far northern lord's houses. He assesses us. "Pity, though. Seeing as the competition is now double from two minutes ago."

Germaine eyes the group behind the kid. "Funny. I don't see any competition."

"Ohhhhh," the boys groan.

"Big words, buddy."

"Maybe you'd like to test that out?"

Beryll puts his hands up. "We're not looking for a fight. We just got here." He addresses the main kid. "Want to tell us what the deal is?"

The guy puckers his lips and continues summing up Beryll. Then Germaine and Vincent and the rest of us. After a second he tips his head toward the area behind him and his group. "We have the tents over there in that divot. You can have the other side of the hill." He indicates one lone tent to the far right of us. "Now if you—"

A buzz reverberates through the air so deafening it stings my eardrums, as if the very atmosphere just came alive. I cringe and cover my ears as Seleni and the others do the same.

"Oh lovely, it appears we're all here then. Even though some of us are not." Kellen's voice ripples through the noise. I frown and twist to find the old man, but the only people I see are the group of boys and my team.

"Where is he?" someone yells.

"Don't know. Shh."

The sound of Kellen clapping his hands ricochets across the landscape. *"Did I mention you've earned a reprieve? A moment to breathe—and I strongly suggest you take it. Only be on guard for what roams these hills, as worse things than my beasts are now seeking to kill."*

"That sounds promising," Vincent says dryly.

"Survive the night and tomorrow your path will be clear. Find your way to that island, beneath which, the key you seek may be near. But fair warning—try it tonight or in dim light, and you'll be risking your life. But for now perhaps you should ponder the thrill—how good are your engineering skills?"

The next moment the buzzing air is gone, and my ears and skin are prickling like sea urchins, and the boys who were facing us moments ago are scrambling back the way they came.

"Did you hear him?" the tall one yells. "He said the island. See if there's a boat!"

"Are they serious? They're going to go for it tonight?" Beryll says. "Holm just said not to."

Vincent shrugs. "Maybe they're just going to confiscate a boat."

"Yeah, but what if there's only one?" Rubin looks at us.

"Did you see the size of most of them?" Germaine says. "We can take them *and* their boat. Besides—" He points down at the water where the glint of metal masts can be seen near a tree line. "I count at least five down there."

"The real question is—by waiting until morning, are we doing what we're supposed to, or is it part of the test?" Vincent glances at Germaine. "Are we supposed to risk it, or is the water actually unsafe?"

"Why don't we ask the fisherman?" Beryll turns to Lute, whose eyes have been scanning the island and water for the past two minutes. Lute tips his head at Sam. "With the wind direction, you'll be facing a pretty strong current. And while I'm not familiar with this lake, the waters around these parts have dangerous whirlpools. I'd be hesitant to test out any water at night that I've not seen during daylight."

Sam is nodding. "Watched a whaling boat get sucked into one last year. Two men died."

"We're not talking about the ocean here; we're talking about a lake."

I ignore Vincent. "So would you two chance it or not?"

Both Lute and Sam shake their heads, and Lute says, "Not if we can wait a few hours for dawn. Might be wise to regain our energy in the meantime." He looks over at Germaine and Rubin and mutters, "I suspect we're going to need it."

Vincent considers this, then nods. "If you boys want to wait, fine by me. You're the water experts, and I'm exhausted." He spins around and, smoothing his hair into place, heads for the tent.

"Plus, I'm sure there's more than one way to get across," Seleni adds. "Right?"

She has a point. Holm said engineering, not just boating.

When no one answers her, I just nod and take off after Vincent. Because the truth is, I'm beat too. And I need water. And I need to pee.

"Is it strange that no one ever sees Holm in normal life?" Sam follows us across the grassy knoll toward the small encampment. "Like Holm is everywhere but nowhere. I wonder how many community events he's been at and no one has any idea."

"I'm sure someone has an idea," Berryl responds. "Otherwise, how would he get invited to them? I mean, there are people who *must know* who he is—at least some of parliament and the university. After all, isn't he on their board?"

"I've seen him," I say quietly. Because I'm now quite sure Kellen and Holm are the same. "At a party once, at a friend's house."

I don't have to look at the group walking behind me to feel their shock and instant questions. Seleni swerves to peer at me and her eyes are enormous. *"You did?"* they seem to say. But all she hisses is, "You never told me that!"

Beryll's tone lifts an octave. "Whose? What was he like? Did he speak to you?"

I shrug as if I don't know, because the truth is, I really don't know much. "He was exactly like he is now. Eccentric. But also kind."

Germaine breaks into a laugh. "Kind? What sort of description is that? You sound like a girl talking about your mum."

Seleni tenses. I don't change my stride, but I flash her a grimace.

"Ah look, you made him blush." Rubin laughs, but the sound dies off the moment we come upon the mountaintop's indent, where a small fire pit and white tent are laid out.

On the side of the tent, four words are written in giant black lettering. Crafted just like the others in the sections we've been through thus far. This time they ask:

What Do You Want?

"A pint of ale and sleep." Rubin groans.

"To relieve my bladder," Seleni says in as male-like a voice as possible, then promptly heads off for one of the numerous rows of low bushes.

Germaine and Rubin aim for a different outcropping of what look like bloodberry bushes entwined with linden vines. I narrow my gaze and consider calling after them not to touch the berries, but they're probably just relieving themselves too.

Vincent's already in the tent moving around. The side rustles and his head pops out the opening long enough for him to toss a clump of bedding rolls at our feet. "Found these, if anyone wants them."

Sam lunges for one and has it spread out before the rest of us have even reached the fire pit. A water bag falls out from the foot of the roll. He picks it up, unscrews the lid, then plops down and glances up to scan the hill again, in the direction of the stone edifice we just came from. His jaw clenches as he moves his gaze toward the bushes that Rubin and Germaine are still behind.

I grab a bed for me and another for Seleni and unroll them so our heads will face each other. Once finished, I nab the water bag that had been tucked in my bedding and wander up in the direction she went. "How are you doing?" I whisper when I get near enough to both relieve myself and not intrude on her privacy.

"Honestly? I think we're insane, Rhen." She gives a shaky laugh, and it suddenly morphs into a sob that suggests she's far more terrified than she's been letting on.

I finish, retie my pants, and scoot over to hand her the water bag. "What's going on? We've been doing so well. Look how far we've made it!"

She shakes her head. "That's not it. Yes, it's been awful, and I couldn't have made it anywhere close to this far without you, but . . ." She tips her frightened face up. "It just occurred to me that no matter what, we're going to get caught. Oh, Rhen—what was I thinking? I was so focused on getting in, I didn't think about getting out! When I lose, I'm going to get exposed, and what will Mum and Father do? *What will Beryll and his family think?*"

Oh.

Well, it's a little late for that now. "Look," I growl to make her snap out of it. "An attack of nerves isn't going to fix anything right now. And you don't even know Mr. Holm *will* expose us. So far he's kicked plenty of people out, but we're still in. For all we know, he's aware of *exactly* who we are and is still allowing it. So he may keep your identity private even when you exit. But either way, the fact we've made it this far when half the contestants haven't? Says something. Which means you need to pull your brain together and act like yourself, for hull's sake."

She gulps. Then takes a deep breath, juts out her chin, and nods. "Okay. Right." She unscrews the water bag and takes a long draught before she passes it back.

"Good." I stand. "Now—you going to be all right?"

"Yes. Other than I hate the way those boys treat Beryll. And that thing they did to *Will*? My parents would be shocked. Those boys' parents should be too." She waves a hand their direction as we start back down to the tent. "And you do realize that if this were a bunch of women competing, they would've set up camp, cooked dinner, and scouted out the boats by now, right?"

I giggle, then tilt my head in second thought. "Depends on what they were competing for."

Her tone falls serious. "I know I'm hardly holding my own in here, Rhen. But I've been watching Germaine and Rubin— and they're not finished. They're planning something more."

"Well then, it's a good thing we're together."

She eyes me with a funny expression. "I've also been watching Vincent. And . . . I think he might be in on it with them."

I pause. *Oh.* I bite my lip and don't reply, mainly because I'm not sure what to think of that. Except that she's rarely wrong. I nod. "Understood." And then we've reached the camp where Lute and Beryll have splayed out their mats beside Sam's and ours around the fire pit, which now holds a roaring flame.

As if in confirmation of Seleni's words, a large handful of bloodberries have been collected and piled next to the tent.

I swerve to the boys. "You guys didn't touch those, did you?"

"No, but Germaine tried to get us to eat them." Sam's brow puckers and his mouth contorts. "Said he and Rubin found food and even pretended to eat some." He shakes his head. "Must think we're bloody fools."

Beryll pulls the water bag from his lips. "Wait, why? What happens if you do?"

"They're used as a quick death for crippled animals." Lute glances at Seleni, studies her a moment, then extends me a questioning gaze while he says, "The three Uppers took off to go look around."

Sam shoves his hands in his pockets and glowers. "After they claimed the tent."

I give Lute a short nod—although I'm not sure whether it's to answer who Seleni is or that, yes, she's okay. Not that it matters because I've just noted that Beryll was not included in the comment about the Uppers. He's out here with the rest of us. More than that, he seems content to be so.

I grab the spot between Beryll and Seleni and try to assess how he's holding up. Is this what he expected? Is it what any of them expected? Beryll's gaze keeps darting around at every single sound. As if he's listening for creatures in the dark. *"The ones seeking to kill,"* according to Holm.

I shiver and reach over to set another log on the fire before I look back up at the words on the side of the tent. *What do you want?*

Lute is sitting beneath them with his eyes half closed but his body tense enough to tell me he's wide awake and taking stock of what's going on. I study him as Seleni burrows into her bedding until only her face is showing. "Wake me when it's time to decipher the next clue," she murmurs.

Voices and laughter chime out loud in the night air from the other camp, and a few minutes later, Vincent, Germaine, and Rubin boisterously stroll up.

"You guys are missing out," Rubin says. "Vincent's got Germaine telling the story of when he got Miss Chamberling to let him kiss her." He chuckles and starts to duck into the tent. Then stops and waves at Beryll. "Come in, mate. Join us."

When Beryll ignores him, he shrugs. "All right. Your loss." And disappears inside.

"What a prig," Sam says. "All of 'em. They win this thing, and they'll end up just like their fathers—arrogant fools. You know Jake's dad told us we should take 'em out while we had the chance?" His caustic laugh sounds like he wishes that were an option.

Beryll's cheeks pale in the firelight, but he remains

uncharacteristically quiet. His brown eyes are focused hard on the coals.

Another bout of laughter from inside the tent makes us jump again. Someone just passed wind. Seleni wrinkles her nose and whispers, "It's a wonder any of them get a woman."

As if on cue, their conversation turns to talk of girls, and Seleni peeks up at me as Vincent says, "It's all right, Germaine. There's always Miss Smith if no one else wants you."

Germaine chuckles. "I think I'd rather go for your mum, and that's saying something."

"What about that sweet fish, Miss Parish?" Rubin adds.

"Now you're talking. Who *wouldn't* love a chance at her? But the only guy she notices is that uni boy from Kingsford."

I freeze. And try not to let on to the fact that my blood just lit fire around my bones. The speaker was Vincent.

"What about you, Beryll?" Germaine calls out from inside the tent. "You into Laura Parish?" They all laugh, and then suddenly they're stumbling out and taking seats beside Sam and Lute and Beryll, clearly unaware that the three boys out here all have their shoulders tensed and expressions narrowed. Even Beryll looks ready for a fight.

"Nah, Beryll's already got his lass," Rubin says. "Seleni'll do anything for him—ain't that right?"

"Don't talk that way about her," Beryll growls.

"Which doesn't make sense because no offense, Beryll, she's way above your league. Even if your parents aren't sweet on her."

"I'd suggest you boys drop the conversation before it goes

any further." Lute's risen from his seat and casually stuck his hands in his pockets even as his eyes darken with anger.

"It's not that they're not sweet on her," Beryll says quietly. "They just don't know her."

"Because they're too highfalutin for their own good. They won't even hang out with Vincent's parents, and his father's the bloody chair of parliament," Germaine crows. "Or maybe it's something about Miss Lake we don't know. You sweet on her because you have to be, Beryll?"

The firelight flickers as Beryll's cheeks redden. "Don't talk about Miss Lake that way."

Vincent chuckles as Seleni stiffens in her blanket beside me. I start to speak up, but her hand lashes out to stop me. *Let it go*, she squeezes.

"Or what? Something we should know, Beryll?"

Beryll rises to stand next to Lute, and his voice is trembling. "I'll ask you once more to mind the way you speak about her."

Vincent lifts a hand to rub his chin and looks straight at Lute. And says slowly, "In that case, how about we talk about Miss Tellur?"

Germaine chuckles and wags an eyebrow. "I hear you're finally proposing to make her legal. And I don't blame you—that girl's a firework. How far have you gotten with her?"

Vincent keeps his eyes on Lute and lets a small smile play on his handsome face. "Not far enough, I can tell you that."

My chest goes still. I can't breathe. I feel my face flood with mortification and I start to stand, but Seleni tightens her grip on my sleeve to pin me to my seat.

"I'd be awfully careful about what you say from here on out," Lute warns. "Rhen Tellur is better than any one of you, and I'd hate for you to leave here in a coffin." The flames illuminate his expression, which is seething.

"I think I can speak of Miss Tellur just fine." Vincent sniffs. "Especially since she's supposedly of no interest to you." He tips his head. "Or . . . is she?"

"Too bad her body's not curvier." Germaine picks up on the challenge. "But man, that mind and sly mouth of hers. She can take your career places."

Vincent never moves his gaze from Lute. Just lifts a brow. "That's what I'm aiming for."

"Plus, if she's half as wild in—"

Lute launches across the fire pit and lands a fist square against Vincent's jaw. Vincent falls back, and Rubin and Germaine lunge for Lute, but Sam is right there with him, swinging at their faces.

"Whoa, whoa, whoa!" Seleni's jumped up, the same as me—face burning with fury. But it's Beryll who's shoved between them and is pushing them apart. I've never seen him look so fierce.

"That's enough," he barks. "Everyone just cool it! There's no need to take this any further."

To my surprise, the boys obey—even Germaine. They sag back, out of breath, and glare at each other. Vincent, Germaine, and Rubin on one side. Beryll and Sam with Lute on the other.

Vincent coughs and stares at them, as if gauging their size.

Then nods, and the next second he's dropped his arm and waved them all off. "Come on, boys. He's right. There's no need to get into it tonight."

He turns and starts to stride off—then quick as lightning stops and leans back toward Lute. "But you and I aren't done with this. Not by a long shot." Then Vincent strolls into the tent with the other two on his heels.

I swallow and don't look at any of them lest my expression give me away. Instead, I stare at the fire and pretend I didn't just hear all that and that my eyes aren't trying hard to blink back tears. I can't afford to give anything away right now. Not here. Not in front of them. Not with the light on my face and too little sleep. At least not yet.

I sit in the silence of the waning night until the fire winds down and even the crickets have stopped their singing. Waiting for the others' breathing to slow and the snores to pick up. When they eventually do, I get up and stride up the small crest behind us and find a spot where I can sit and take a breath.

Except I'm not just taking a breath. I'm taking five in a row, and then I'm trembling, and soon my entire body is shaking. And once it does, it won't stop. Because it occurs to me that while I don't actually care what Vincent and Germaine think about me, I care that Lute and Sam heard it.

That they might think some of those things too.

And that maybe—just maybe . . . some of it is true. That I am good for doing things for boys like them. But not good just for being me.

I scowl down at the tent and Kellen's words written across it. *What do you want?*

What do you want, Rhen? What does the girl without curves want?

I drop my gaze and it lands on Lute—or on where Lute should be. I lean forward. He's not there. The rustle of a breeze and a cracking twig are my only indication that someone else is near. I turn to brace for whatever ghoul it is, in boy or ethereal form, but suddenly Lute's standing in front of me.

His face is as gentle and strong as ever in the moonlight, and it takes all my strength not to tell him not to think less of me. That I'm just hiding up here long enough to find my backbone again.

"Would you mind company, Miss Tellur?"

Heat blossoms in my chest, which only makes my trembling pick up stronger. I eye him and swallow. I don't know. I don't know if it's a good idea right now, especially depending on which mood he's in. "Depends," I say quietly. "Who's asking?"

He lifts a brow. "Pardon?"

"The you who's friendly, or the Lute who gets strange every time Vincent comes 'round? Because I've had enough male shallowness this evening." And maybe that's unfair of me to say because he did just punch Vincent on my behalf, but I'm not in the place for mental games.

He bites his lip, then drops down on the grass two feet away as his bangs slip across one side of his face. "I'm sorry about that. What they said back there—it was inappropriate and it was wrong. And it's untrue." His jaw pops and fury edges his tone. "You are more worthy to win this contest than any of them, Rhen."

His words take a moment to absorb, but when they do they're a light salve on an ache that I hate even exists. My chest relaxes. My heart relaxes. And it doesn't escape my notice that he just addressed me by my first name.

Without looking at me, he quietly adds, "Although, may I point out that I could wonder the same? One version of the Rhen Tellur I know talks about corpses and wipes blood on my coat and enters an all-male contest in disguise. The other one is marrying that arrogant prig down there. For financial reasons I presume, but still . . ."

I swerve to look at him in confusion. I clench my jaw and try to keep my tongue at bay because *what*? "Mr. Wilkes, I can assure you, you are very wrong. And I do not appreciate such assumptions."

"My apologies. The idea of you courting him for romance was so ludicrous I assumed it must be for status. And considering that his father wrote the fishing port restrictions, I'm obviously not as supportive of—"

"Stop." I put a hand up. The trembling in my bones has reached my lungs. "Just . . . stop." I shake my head, and all of a sudden my voice is shaking too. "No man speaks for me, Mr. Wilkes. Not you, and certainly not Mr. King. I never said anything about courting him—you took his word without asking me. And for your information, I've no intention of being tied to Mr. King. I'd rather marry a . . . a goat." I darken my tone. "Now as I said, I've had enough male shallowness for one night, so if you've nothing better to talk about, perhaps you should leave."

His expression has morphed from stiff discomfort to a look of utter relief. His eyes are an ocean of stars as he lifts a brow. And says nothing.

My frown deepens. "Well? *What?*"

He shakes his head and lets out a chuckle that reaches all the way up to the weathered creases around his eyes. "Rhen Tellur, you are the strangest woman I've ever met."

"If this is you apologizing, you're failing."

"I apologize for believing Vincent's word without asking yours. You're right about me doing so, and it was presumptive and wrong."

"You forgot insulting. But thank you."

He rubs his chin. "But you are strange."

I glare at him.

He laughs and leans back on his elbows on the grass. "It's a compliment! I mean, look at you—you even cut your hair. For hull's sakes, what are you doing here?"

"In the Labyrinth? Proving that I can."

"Exactly." He shakes his head at me. "*Untamable.* That's what my mum would call you."

I toss a piece of grass at him. "That makes me sound like the crazy ocean with all its sirens and storms."

A funny look flashes across his face. "Why do you think I love it so much?"

I stall.

And he drops his gaze and looks away to the lake.

After a moment he clears his throat, and the sound is ragged. Dry. "So you won't mind if I accidentally clock Mr. King another solid one, one of these days?"

The warmth in my chest leaps and spreads to my stomach. "Be my guest. I might even help you."

His smile appears momentarily, before his expression turns serious. He tips his head and his gaze finds mine again, and there's something in his demeanor that's a little wild, a little determined, a little *resolute.* "I *am* sorry, Rhen."

I don't know why, but my throat tightens. Like he just offered a sweeter, deeper balm to a bruise I'd already forgotten was there. I bat my lashes and look away. To the lake, the dying bonfire, the tent.

The tent, with those words.

What do you want?

I want my mum to live.

I want the right to earn an education.

I want to be the first female scientist.

I want to create my own happiness.

I want . . .

I peer over at Lute who's lying flat on the grass with his head on his arms, looking up at the stars. The warmth flares and swirls and licks at my blood, sending heat through my veins to my skin. I softly lean over and plant a single kiss on Lute's cheek, and I feel his entire body freeze. I pull back just enough to catch his reaction. His expression glints surprise.

A moment later his gaze falls to my lips and the look turns heavy—like a fog-covered moor when the earth hasn't quite woken yet. I study his mouth—it really is anatomically perfect.

And then he slips his hand to my forehead and brushes aside my bangs, and everything about it feels calm and electric. Like a wildfire racing for a tranquil sea.

His fingers trace my cheek down to my chin, and he holds his hand there. And he is trembling just as much as me. And then I place my lips on his and he is pulling me in, and it is the most delicious sensation I've ever known, as a breeze picks up and my skin is a ripple of goose bumps and heat and home.

I tangle my hands through his hair and down the sides of his face until they have wandered to his neck, beneath which his pulse is crashing like the morning tides. And mine is crashing just as strong. A minute longer, and I pull back. And my heart is racing so hard I swear they can hear it all the way down in the tent.

I blush and it provokes his dimpled smile, and I'm just about to tell him what happens to a person's blood and organs after their body dies, when a low wail picks up in the direction of the island.

Lute sits up and I scoot right beside him so he can slip his arm around me.

As if in answer to the ghoulish moans, a low scream starts out on the lake that prickles the hairs on the back of my head.

He looks at me. "Apparently there are sirens in the water."

I shiver. It sounds like they found whichever boys were attempting to reach the island.

18

The sirens' screams die down eventually, and Lute and I sit like that for the rest of the short night. Me beside him, his hand tucked around mine, listening for other hauntings and keeping watch on the camp below.

I'm not aware I've dozed off against him until I jolt awake in a clammy sweat from a memory playing out like a dream. Vincent had been studying a live virus that'd been causing strange behavior and death in the local cattle population. I'd been focused on the trials Da and I had created for the lung-fluid antibiotic.

"Here, Rhen, check this out." Vincent had lifted a needle

in gloved hands and waved me forward to peer into his scope where he injected some of the live virus into a dish of clean cow blood. Within seconds, the virus began attacking and dissolving the membranes of the healthy cells.

I glanced up and stared at him. It was incredible. Awful, yes, but incredible how such a small organism could act like an army and go to war against a healthy host.

He grinned, and his blond bangs slipped across his cheek. *"We should test it against your antibiotics."*

I laughed and shook my head. *"You know it wouldn't work. And your father is probably wondering where you are by now."*

He leaned in and winked. *"My father is chair of parliament. He couldn't care less where I am right now as long as you and I are increasing my education."*

I blink and feel the memory bring up a small ache that feels unfair after Vincent's behavior last night. I may never have been in love with him, but I did love the camaraderie we had. Or what I'd thought we'd had.

Lute shifts beside me. "You all right?"

"I am." I slip my arms around my chest because I don't want to talk about it, and as if sensing my mood, Lute simply tightens his arm around my back and goes silent. Until the memory ekes away and the sun slides up the eastern horizon, and morning dawns with her brilliant birdsong.

The moment we stand my muscles scream in fifty different places. Lute's, too, by his expression. He grabs my hat and plants it back on my head along with a quick, shy kiss on the side of my forehead before he steps away and we hurriedly return to camp lest they come looking for us. I rouse Seleni, and Lute jabs Beryll and Sam. "Wind's in our favor," he murmurs to Sam. "But there's gonna be a mean riptide."

Sam jumps up, nods, and turns around to relieve himself. "We'll have to work the sails."

I cringe and avert my eyes—tapping the tent before I peek inside. "Mr. King, we're—"

I go still.

Germaine, Rubin, and Vincent are gone.

What the? Their bedrolls weren't even slept in.

"Um . . ." I yank the tent flap wide and scan the hillside. "We have a problem. The Uppers are gone." I look at Lute. *How did they leave without us noticing?*

"Fools," Sam snarls. "How long ago?"

"Long enough apparently." Seleni is pointing halfway down the steep mountainside—where the three Uppers are scrambling for the lake—to a bank just beside a chain of willow trees where a grouping of boats are moored. Four boys are already there struggling to push one into the water. Apparently not everyone from the other camp attempted to cross last night.

"Kids can't even set a proper mast." Sam ties his pants and swings around to look at us. The next second he launches down the hillside after them.

We grab our water bags and scramble to follow him—and it doesn't take long to realize the distance down the mountain is much farther than it looks. We hurtle and slip our way down the steep, grassy incline, and twelve minutes later we are sweating and heaving. By the time we've almost closed in on the Uppers, they've reached the vessels. They climb in and out of one, then another, before Germaine looks up and seems to realize we're just behind them.

"Move!" he yells, and directs the boys to a third boat. Within seconds they've pushed it off the shore and splashed through the water to climb in. Rubin turns around and salutes us with a smirk plastered clear as day on his face.

"You know, I'm really starting to hate them," Beryll says.

We make it ten more paces when a small explosive sound reaches our ears and a puff of smoke goes up from one of the boats they'd climbed in first, then left on the sand. A spark of flames surges up and catches the sails, and thirty seconds later the thing is engulfed. They must've used the coals from last night.

Seleni has just pointed to the remaining two boats when a cry rings out, and we look over to find a group of three boys from the other camp racing down behind us.

Beryll shoves ankle deep in the water and starts pressing his weight against the stern.

"It's no good, mate. Someone got to it." Lute indicates the gush of water pouring into the hull, then joins Sam and me in putting our weight against the other boat.

"Hate to interrupt, but either you hand it over or we'll hurt your friend," a voice calls. An accompanying screech from Seleni cracks the air.

We spin around to see one of the three boys pinning Seleni to his chest from behind, while in his other sleeve-covered hand, he holds bloodberries toward her cheek and mouth.

"Whoa. Come on, guys," Sam says. "Let the kid go. We can all take the boat."

"Says the dead jerk in *our* camp who ate those berries that your friend gave him last night." He yanks Seleni's head backward and waves the berries nearer her closed mouth.

Her eyes go wide as her breathing quickens and her foot stamps around to connect with either his man jewels or his shin. He dodges and moves two of his fingers up, as if to plug her nose. "A life for a life. Or you can give us the boat."

Seleni seeks out my gaze. Her expression is a mix of fear and a confidence that he's bluffing. She drops her eyes to his hands to indicate how bad they're shaking. I frown. She's right. This kid's never killed anything in his life—and from the look of him, he's just as terrified as the rest of us. I bite my lip and calculate the chances if Seleni and I are wrong.

"Fine, take it." Lute lifts his hands in the air and steps away, then looks at Sam and me to do the same. "We'll find another way."

"But—"

"We'll find another way," Lute says to Sam.

"Good choice," the kid holding Seleni says. He tips his head at the two boys with him, who run ahead and promptly push past us to confiscate the boat. When they have it full in the water, the kid drags Seleni backward until he reaches it, then releases her and the berries before he jumps up to hoist himself aboard.

The three loosen the sails, and the wind whips and fills them, and within seconds they are following Vincent and

Germaine and Rubin, whose boat is already bobbing on the waves thirty feet out. And sixty feet beyond them, the first vessel full of the other boys is reaching the quarter point between us and the island.

Sam lets out a low curse and scans the lake's edge. "We could've taken 'em."

Seleni nods even as she rubs her arms to stop from trembling. "He was more scared than me."

"That might have made him more dangerous—simply because it made him incompetent," I say.

From the corner of my eye, I see Beryll. He's been standing in the same place for two minutes, staring at Seleni. He rubs his neck, then looks at me before he turns back to the water and promptly tugs off his shirt. "Guess that means we get to swim."

"There are sirens in the lake," Lute and I say at the same time.

"I suggest we salvage this wood for a raft." Sam indicates the boat taking on water.

"Won't that take too long?" Seleni stares at Beryll's bare chest, which is surprisingly more muscular than one would've thought.

I raise a brow. Then turn back to scanning the bank and then the campsite—with its smoking coals, white tent, and black-painted question that's too tiny to see but keeps asking, *"What do you want?"*

The tent sides ripple in the wind that's picking up. I can almost hear the ropes and white linen snap from all the way down here.

Like a sail from one of the boats we should be on.

I squint. "Lute. What would happen if we attached a sail to a person rather than a boat?"

He follows my gaze and studies the tent with a look of surprise. I can see the wheels turning in his brain. After a moment he nods. "That actually might work. If you three can do some calculations, Sam and I can handle the tents."

Eighteen minutes later, we're standing at the top of the hill. Seleni, Beryll, and I are estimating the size of the sails and how long the rope tethering them needs to be, while Sam and Lute are busy stripping down three tents, two of which they dragged over from the other encampment. Once finished, they rig the ropes and sheets together with nautical knots until they have what appear to be a cross between kites and those festival balloons we saw last night.

"We're doing this by size and weight." Lute holds out a rope to me. "Sam and I will each take one of you smaller kids. Beryll, you'll have to go on your own. Think you can handle that?"

To Beryll's credit, he pushes back any expression of fear, simply tilts his head, and begins tying the rope Sam hands him beneath his arms and around his chest. I watch this braver version of him. What's gotten into him? Apparently Seleni's thinking the same, because when I glance over, her face is alight with admiration. So much so that I nudge her to knock it off and let Sam tie her to himself.

Once Lute has lashed the balloon-sail to his and my rope harness, he fastens me to himself—my back to his chest, my waist to his waist, one of my thighs to his. He tugs and pulls long enough to ensure we're locked in tight, then leans down to my ear. "Ready, Rhen Tellur? Match your steps to mine."

I'm about to ask what he means when we're suddenly running and tripping down the steep hill—testing to see how fast and from what part of the sharp incline we have to launch for the sheets to catch the perfect gust of wind. It's a lot higher and faster than one would guess, which means we end up face-planting into the cliffed slope of grass more times than I care to talk about. As do the others.

But by the time the sun is high enough for its warmth to flood the small valley, we've figured it out enough to believe this might actually work. That or we might die.

"Fingers crossed," Lute mutters. And with that, we take a final run beside Sam and Seleni and Beryll. It's magic the way it happens. How, just before we hit the second ledge of the mountain slope, the air currents catch the sails and yank them up behind us, and then they've lifted us off the ground and we are soaring ten feet off the grass, and then over the mountainside—and then out over the water.

Sam actually hoots, and Lute and I laugh, and even Beryll's high-pitched scream quickly turns to one of thrill and pride. And for a moment—for *this* moment, with Lute's warmth and spirit entwined around mine—I think it's something I could live in forever. It reminds me of watching Mum and Da play at the seaside—the laughter, their salt-swept hair, and long days of Mum's adoring smile. I chuckle and my eyes well with tears from the lashing wind and the painful swell such memories bring.

I refocus on Sam's joyful hollering, which has just turned to deep shouts from Seleni to look out for what's ahead—where the boat confiscated by the three boys appears to be stuck in a whirlpool. We watch them try to adjust the sails, but the water current is too strong, and within minutes they are spinning helplessly and yelling at each other to do something.

We pass by and have just reached what I guess to be the midway point when Lute tips his head to mine and his lips brush my ear. "I have to confess I wasn't actually sure this would work."

I tilt my head to the side and try to look at him. "Then why'd you agree to it?"

His chuckle falls soft in my ear. "Die alone, or die with a risky girl strapped in my arms? Seemed like a good way to go."

I laugh and make a comment about him being the cushion if we go down, so really only one of us will die. Then I'm pointing ahead of us—to the first boat that went out. They're so close to the shore they could walk, but two sirens have caught the boat and are trying to board.

I keep hold of the ropes tied around my chest and lean forward ever so slightly. I've never seen the ocean ghouls this close before, and a chill skitters down my spine. They're a combination of beautiful and terrifying. Half fish, half women, their scales shimmer like blue skies in the light. But their hair and eyes look like sparse, decaying corpses. "Is that how they all are?" I yell.

He nods and sets his lips to my ear. "Legends say they were women sacrificed to the sea, the lord of which saved them by turning them into fish. Their human forms continue to decay while their lower halves are immortal. They've sought revenge on humans ever since."

I nod and watch the boys in the boat tighten their sails and yank free from the fish-women long enough to run the vessel up onto dry land.

"Vincent's boat just made it too!" Beryll's yell is faint, and I scan to the left to see the three Upper boys lunge out of it and promptly disappear into the forest.

"Where to?" Sam calls.

A canopy of thick, low greenery spans in front of us, like a meadow of trees. Lute tugs one of the ropes and the wind yanks us up higher, giving us a better view of the forested island and keeping us from slamming into the branches we're fast approaching.

Sam and Beryll do the same, and a minute later a stone structure comes into view. It looks like a white, spiraled bull's-eye right in the forest's center. "Aim there," Lute calls to the others, to which Seleni nods vigorously, then points at the two groups of boys below who appear to be heading for it too. They're running like wild animals through the foliage, and I can barely make out their shouts to each other to "stick to the path."

"We're coming in too fast," Beryll hollers, and my stomach lurches because he's right. For all the launching we practiced, we didn't prepare to land.

"Aim for the path ahead of where they're running—there's a clearing around it," Lute calls back. "Pull your arms together and start tugging the left side down, like trimming your sails.

Get as close to the ground as you can, and hopefully you'll catch it on a branch! *Or you'll get killed*," he adds, for only me to hear.

Before I have time to holler back that nothing about that sounds like a safe idea, Lute's already showing Beryll how to do it by example. My lungs lodge in my throat as he drops us right above the trees, and a clearing suddenly appears. Lute's muscles are straining against my back as he's leaning forward, his veins rippling along his arms.

He says, "Start running on the count of three." And then I am running, and he is running, and we are no longer running on air but stumbling and hitting the ground in what feels like something between experiencing an earthquake and having a house fall on you.

We skid to a stop and I lose the will to move for the rest of my short life.

Until Lute tugs the knots loose on the ropes and slides them free so he can roll off of me. His face is inches from mine when he grins. "I keep forgetting you cut your hair."

My hand flies up, but my hat is gone. It must've blown off over the water, or more likely during the landing. I try to cover my head with my hands and scramble around to search for the thing, but it's no use. It's gone.

Lute watches me with a glut of amusement. "I would've mentioned it over the water, but I like it. It suits you."

"That's nice." I scoff. "Except now everyone else will know too."

He looks toward where Sam and Seleni are hobbling to

their feet and trying to untangle themselves from the ropes after the death landing. Sam keeps yelping.

"I think they already do." Lute nods to Beryll, who's got one hand on his nose, which appears to be broken, and the other shielding his brow from the sun as he stares at Seleni. Blood is pouring down his chin and onto his bare chest, and he keeps frowning and tilting his head as Seleni attempts to adjust her clothing. Her hat is missing, and her hair's come loose in wild puffs around her face, much like a cat stuck in a windstorm.

Beryll's expression turns to his seventh level of appalled, which I've actually never seen. "Seleni?" he whispers. He blinks, then peers around, and his gaze passes right over me before it swerves back to land square on my face. "Miss Tellur? What are you two *doing*?"

Seleni turns to him and, like lightning, reaches up to grab her hat, only to discover it's gone. She glances at me long enough to take in the fact that my hat is missing too, then straightens, lifts her chin in the air, and walks over to Beryll. She promptly pulls his hand from his nose and says matter-of-factly, "Rhen's here to win obviously, and I'm here to help. Good thing, too, because look at your face, Beryll! Your nose! Here, let me—"

"Sel—Miss Lake! It's fine! Please, I—"

His futile resistance is drowned out by a stomach-curdling yelp emanating from Sam. I clamber over to see what's wrong with him, but I can already tell it's his ankle. I bend down to touch it, noting the skin is turning way too blue too quick. He pulls it away but not before I see the sweat pouring off his face and the swelling setting in around his shoe.

I look up at him and Lute. "It's broken."

"Happened in the landing." Sam groans. "By the way, good to see you, Rhen. You look like a boy."

"Stop talking. We need to stabilize it."

He grits his teeth. "No, we need to get movin' before—"

Shouts erupt from the forest path just behind us as Vincent, Germaine, Rubin, and one of the four boys from the other boat charge out. They hardly give us more than a side eye as they hightail it for the spiral stone building thirty feet in front of us.

"Basilisks!" Rubin yells, and suddenly the ground is shaking and a terrible roar shreds the air.

Lute grabs Sam's arm and swings it over his shoulder to yank him up. Sam screams, but Lute doesn't stop—he just grips Sam tighter and starts to run with him as we head toward the others.

The stone building looks more like a mausoleum than a spiral from eye level—and as we spring for the single visible door, I note the wording etched above it is the same style as on the tent. But I must be tired, because my brain shuffles the letters out of order to read Dining for the Dead, which in the old language would've meant that either only the dead may enter or something is purposefully trapped inside this place.

I don't have time to think more on it because a basilisk the size of a bloody whale bursts through the trees. His thick body snakes across the ground, writhing through the dirt faster than we can run as his beaked face lunges for us.

Lute throws Sam inside and shoves me through just before Rubin slams the door behind us, and the basilisk gives another screaming roar that echoes through the chamber, triggering a string of lanterns to turn on.

The door lock clicks into place from the outside.

"Of all the—"

"That thing came from nowhere!"

"Three of those boys disappeared just before it got them—did you see that?"

Shaking, I ignore Germaine and Rubin and check to ensure Beryll and Seleni made it through. Then peer at Lute, who's eyeing the room we've just locked ourselves in.

Only it's not a room. It's a circular cavern carved into white stone, with crypts lined up along the walls.

Lute lifts his finger to his mouth and turns around slowly until he's facing us. Germaine falls silent. I hear Rubin gulp.

This isn't an underground sanctuary. It's the catacombs of the ancient knights, and the writing above the door outside was a warning.

We have indeed walked into the dining room of the dead.

19

Our every movement echoes too loud. Too intrusive. Sam's groans ricochet off the walls as sweat drenches his shirt. He tries to muffle them in his sleeve, but it only makes the sound of his pain more agonizing.

I turn to shove my shoulder beneath his other arm to help ease the weight on his ankle, and I'm about to help Lute walk him forward when I catch Vincent staring at us.

He takes in my hair, my face, and the dead man's clothes I'm wearing. Any hint of embarrassment and shame on Vincent's face for his behavior last night is quickly replaced by a curled lip and a flicker of suspicion directed at Lute before his eyes reconnect with mine. "Miss Tellur."

I glance at Seleni and Beryll—the latter of whom's chest is now covered in blood from his nose—and Vincent follows my gaze long enough to utter a sharp snort under his breath.

Sam gives another moan and Germaine hisses, "Would someone shut him up, please?"

Lute and I heft Sam higher before Lute points toward the only clear way out of the crypt-lined room. A narrow opening that leads to darkness. I shudder as Seleni whispers, "Beryll, I don't want to do this."

Whatever he says to calm her is between them, but Vincent looks at me again and purses his lips before he nods to Germaine and Rubin. "Let's check the room." Then he murmurs in my direction, "We'll discuss this later."

I raise a brow. *Oh you bet we will.*

The three of them move to inspect the circular space, but they won't find anything. The crypts are old and sealed—as are the walls—and any etchings or grave goods that were here have long since been stolen by weather or ransackers.

We wait until their quick search is done, then follow Germaine, Rubin, and Vincent to the singular opening at the far side of the room. Whatever used to be covering it is now hanging in pieces of thick plaster from metal bars—as if something burst through it at one point and the architecture never recovered.

I shiver again and tighten my hold on Sam as Lute and I duck him through into the next room, which is not a room at all but a passage of steep stairs inside a stone tunnel. Sam's pained breathing bounces off the ceiling and makes the already-stifling air feel thicker. Staler.

It smells of sulfur.

We hobble him step-by-step to the bottom, where we are pushed through another doorway and into another room with a new set of lanterns that flicker on.

Seleni's gasp is as loud as Germaine's curse.

Stone coffins line both sides of the low-ceilinged space. They're pressed into the walls like boxed sentries in perfect measurements of five paces apart, above a floor that slopes sharply downward. And on their front-facing lids is carved the knight's seal of Caldon.

"It's like an army of dead," Vincent mutters.

"At least the coffins are closed," Beryll whispers.

"At least they're actually *dead*," Rubin says.

I keep my mouth shut and don't say anything. Because I'm not so sure they *are* dead.

Lute eyes me as if he knows what I'm thinking, because he's thinking it too—and nods toward the ground that is sloping away from us. I peer down, and after a moment I see what he's indicating.

The passage is taking us farther underground.

I swallow and try to hoist Sam higher to keep his leg from hitting the ground so heavily, even as everything inside me screams that the very atmosphere in here is made of death. And there's no way out but to keep heading down.

"Where's the other kid?" Beryll hisses. "The one who was with you running from the forest?"

Germaine doesn't turn around. Just keeps going as he says, "Oops. Must've locked him outside."

Beryll looks to Seleni, and a flicker of fear crosses his broken, swollen face. Only his expression is not for himself. He's afraid for her.

I don't blame him. I'm scared for all of us.

"You all are talking too loud," Vincent says.

"Hey, we're not the ones carrying a moaning beached siren," Rubin scoffs. "Besides, what's there to fear? Ghouls only come out at night." But he trims his tone and tries to walk softer.

Vincent ignores Rubin to hurry forward toward what appears to be a corner up ahead. "It looks like we follow this path." Except when we reach it, it's nothing more than a deep-set alcove with more coffins. Older coffins. Some of the lids have cracked and crumbled, and scraps of shroud and bones peek out.

He turns and scowls. "Dead end." As if we couldn't tell. Because there's nothing. No other doors. No windows. No way out but to follow the long, sulfur-saturated tunnel in front of us that seems to meld from one passage opening to the next.

The rank scent grows stronger the farther in we go. It pricks my nose and burns my eyes, and even I try not to stare at the endless walls of sarcophagi too long. There's something eerie about them—even for someone who's used to dealing with dead things.

When we reach the tenth opening, leading to the tenth long passageway, the sulfuric smell flares and the atmosphere thickens. The flickering lights are dimmer here, and whether that's from the strange layer of grey haze or simply because there's less air, they sputter slower and cast shadows to reveal older, yellower stone walls marked with a series of carvings missing from the previous passages. I wonder who's buried here and for how long. And how many other contestants have shuffled past them through the years.

A splash of wet hits my nose and splatters on my cheek. I peer up into the shadows as, beside me, Sam shudders too. By my estimation we're under the deepest part of the lake surrounding the island.

Sam suddenly stumbles, and when I glance over, his eyes have glazed and his head has dropped into a faint. I look at Lute. *"He needs to rest,"* I mouth.

Lute firms his chin because we both know that's not going to happen in here. So we keep walking.

Twenty more minutes eke by as we tread more corridors exactly like the ones we've just left, and by the time we hit what is by my count the nineteenth coffin-lined passageway, the moisture is dripping down like misty rain, and the air's so coiled with the smell of rotting eggs that Rubin and Beryll keep gagging. Until Seleni smartly tears two pieces of fabric from her pant legs and has them wrap it around their faces—Beryll's rather delicately.

I push Lute and Sam ahead, then step through the nineteenth doorway, only to freeze in my tracks.

Beryll, Seleni, Vincent, and the others fumble into us, and I move aside enough to let them in, and then they are gasping and motionless too.

The room we've just stepped into is a shorter length than the others, with a doorway at the far end. It's also taller—at least three stories high, with giant, graceful columns spanning floor to ceiling, where stone chandeliers hang from stone chains to suspend lifelessly over long tables that look eerily like cadaver slabs.

Whatever this used to be, it wasn't originally built as a tomb. It was made for a king, and this space is some type of banquet room.

Or maybe it was built as both.

Rubin coughs into his makeshift scarf. "What the?"

Lute leans over to slap a hand over his mouth so fast, Rubin doesn't even have time to react before Vincent also smacks the back of his head. "Shh, you dolt." Vincent lifts a finger to his lips and tips his chin to the walls.

Rubin peers around, and his forehead pales as if it's dawned on him where we are. The same way it's dawning on me too, as my eyes adjust to the shadowed walls.

The crypts lining them are made from the same stone, with the same etchings, same distance apart as the last passage. Except these are open.

And rather than shreds of cloth and crumbling bone, these are filled with ghouls.

Draped in white death robes, their bones and flesh look almost human beneath their closed eyelids. As does their skins' yellow glow, created by the sulfuric air tainting their permanently decaying bodies that never have rest, only slumber.

I look at Lute and point to their arms. The right one of each is thrust out, like an arrow, aimed toward the opening at the far end of the hall. And on the outstretched hand of the ghoul mounted closest to that doorway dangles a thin chain holding a key.

My throat drops into my gut. This isn't just a dead king's dining hall. This is a banqueting lair.

A sudden loud gagging rings out. Rubin is leaning over, losing his face scarf and what little water is left in his stomach. No matter how silent he's trying to keep it, the sound still echoes through the room, and we all jerk toward him as if to mute the trauma. But then he's finished and everyone's slowing mid-movement, trying to let the sound die away as quick as possible without adding anything to it.

We stay paralyzed in place for what seems like an eternity. Standing there. Watching. Waiting.

To see if their eyes will open.

It's an elongated minute before Vincent finally beckons us to move forward.

Lute and I tug Sam up as high as I'm able, to try to keep his feet from scraping the floor. We step slowly through the hall. Eyes wide on the ghoulish faces. Every tread rooted in the fear of their awakening.

Vincent, Germaine, and Rubin move faster than we can and have soon hurried ahead. We've only hit the halfway point by the time they make it to the opening—through which I can see two adjoining rooms. Lute picks up our pace as the three Uppers duck in, except the next instant Vincent reappears and looks our way.

I frown. *What's he?*

He lunges to the side, sets his foot on a coffin ledge, and hefts his body high enough to yank the hanging key off the final ghoul. With a crash he falls backward onto the floor, then is up and racing for the door.

Beryll swears, and Seleni tries to shush him, but it doesn't matter—the ghouls' eyes flash open, one at a time, like a row of lanterns being lit.

Which is when the moans start up.

So deep, so empty, my bones shake from the wretched sounds.

In one swoop Lute grabs Sam and yanks him across his shoulders, then yells at Beryll to get Seleni and me through the doorway. Suddenly it's not just the moans filling the room but the wisps of sulfuric mist. They're coming on so thick, the haze almost obscures the opening.

We rush for the hole in the wall, and the next second we've all five plunged through and are racing into the next room. Only to be stopped by a metal wall Rubin is standing in front of, banging his fist on and yelling. "They went up without us. Hurry, help me! They went without us!"

"Where?" Beryll shouts, but Rubin just points at the metal and keeps yelling.

In unison Lute and I drop Sam, then rush to look—to see which lever makes the wall open and close. My hands search the crevices—every indent and space, but I can't find one. *Oh hulls, I can't find one!*

The room starts shaking from the ghouls' moans.

"They're coming!" Seleni yells.

I turn to glance through the doorway and see them dropping down one by one from their coffins, in some sort of unified reverie. *Of all the—*

I lunge for the side wall—the one that's covered in the same strange, scripted carvings as the tombs—and feel it for any markers. *There's got to be a lever here.*

"I thought Germaine said they only wake at night," Rubin whines.

"Well, apparently they don't," I snarl. "Now move."

The ceiling starts shaking just like the floor, dropping dust and pebbles, and the opening between us and the ghouls' hall is making a grinding sound. I look over to find Lute kicking at a knob in the wall beside it. "I think it's to seal the opening." He groans.

Rubin stares at us. "It's too late. We're all going to die."

"Oh for bloody sake, pull yourself together!" Beryll leaves the metal wall he and Seleni were trying to force up and jumps to help Lute, but the second he does, Rubin lunges for Seleni and pulls her toward the ghouls' hall.

"Rubin!"

Lute and I both leap to grab him, but Beryll is already there landing a solid punch to Rubin's jaw. He stumbles and releases Seleni long enough for Beryll to grab her, and then Sam jumps up and screams just before he throws himself full force into Rubin. He slams Rubin to the ground and they slide to where the ghouls have just converged. And for a second, the screeches of Rubin and the undead combine into one.

And then the lever Lute had been kicking at squeals, and the entire wall and ceiling rumble just as the stone around the opening begins to crumble and fall, and a slab suddenly drops into place.

"Sam! Sam!" I scream for him and scramble for the door. *"Sam!"*

Except it's no good. He and Rubin are stuck outside with the ghouls while we're coughing and choking on a roomful of dust and the horror that is spiraling up my throat.

"Rhen, the door!"

Seleni jumps for the metal door opposite us that just lifted open. Whatever lever Lute hit must've been rigged to raise it while bringing down the other.

I grab Lute and start for it, when Beryll yells, "Wait, I'm stuck!"

I spin around.

Beryll's leg is partially wedged in the crevice between the wall and the now-fallen door.

"Beryll!" Seleni scrambles over to tug him free. When the thing won't move, she starts clawing at it with her nails. I rush to help her, but Beryll holds out a hand to stop us. His bare, bloody chest is turning pale and his face now free of Seleni's scarf is twisted in pain, and when he speaks his tone is more angry than anything. "It's not going to work. I'm not going anywhere until Holm gets me."

I keep digging anyway, as Seleni says, "But you have to move—you have to keep going—we're almost there!"

His cheeks hollow as he sucks in and winces. "It's stuck solid, and—broken I think."

She crouches on her haunches and stares him straight in the eye. "Beryll Jaymes, we are not leaving you down here. Now help us—"

He pulls her face in with both hands and plants a kiss firmly on her lips. "Miss Lake, I'm serious that I'm not going anywhere. So go, and I'll see you soon."

Behind me, the metal door lets out a squeal as if it's going to fall. Lute reaches out to shove his hands up to hold it. "Rhen, this thing is moving."

Seleni turns to glance at him, then looks over at me. She inhales. Then nods. "You two catch up with Vincent and Germaine. I'll stay with Beryll."

I ignore her and keep digging around Beryll's leg, which, judging by the weight of the boulder on it, is most definitely broken. "Not a chance."

The metal door starts shaking, dropping more dust on us. She grabs my hands and yanks them from the rocks. "Rhen, go. I've got this."

I shake my head. "Beryll's actually hurt, Seleni."

"I know. But you can't help us—only Holm can. So go find him." She tugs my hands from the rubble and forces me to stand and look at her as the metal door makes a noise like it's beginning to bow. "I came to support Beryll. And to show what we can do. But I'm not like you, Rhen. I want you to win—I want you to show them you can. But my way of winning is different, and it's my own choice. I've always wanted the life of a wife, and mother, and helpmate to my husband, and I know you may not think much of that, but it's what I want. And I'd be proud of it. Same as I'll be proud of whatever you do."

I look at her and blink. I think I know that. I think I've always known that.

"And I think that desire is just as noble as what you're doing, if that's the life I want and choose. So I'm staying here with what I want. And you are going to go get what you want. Are we clear?"

I bite my cheek and eye her, then Beryll.

Then nod.

Because of course it's clear. Her life may not be for me, but it *is* for her.

The walls shake and dust crumbles into my eyes as the metal door shrieks and strains against its hinges. "Rhen, this thing's coming down," Lute says through gritted teeth.

The expression in Seleni's eyes hardens. "You win this thing, Rhen Tellur. Enough to make Vincent and Germaine regret they weren't born women. And then you burn those horrid dead-boy clothes you're wearing to the ground, because I don't ever want to be seen with you in them again."

With that, she shoves me toward the door Lute's holding up, steps back as a light flickers on, and offers up a wide smile. "See you two on the outside."

The ghouls are still screaming as I step in. The next moment Lute's hands drop and the metal door falls. And suddenly the room Lute and I just locked ourselves in lurches, and the ground beneath me feels like it's plunging away. It takes my stomach with it as the whole thing begins flying upward toward the surface.

20

It's approximately ten point three seconds before the moving room slows and comes to a full stop with a soft thud.

Lute slips his hand into mine and we wait for the door to open.

It doesn't.

He steps over to press against it, while I peer around for another lever, but there is none. The box we're in is made of smooth metal and nothing more.

"Hello?" I yell. "Mr. Holm? Mr. Kellen?"

The overhead light brightens, makes a whirring sound, then it's shining at the wall in front of us, which starts to ripple, and a set of words appears:

I glance at Lute.

He frowns and grips my hand tighter just as the metal wall shudders and squeals, and the door slides open, and we are looking directly into the face of Mr. Kellen. Or rather, Mr. Holm. Whichever is his actual name.

"Welcome, Rhen Tellur from the Port, whose uncle owns a study and who has joined my sport. It's quite nice to see you again." He chuckles and tips his head as if assessing me. "I'm glad you took my advice."

I pause. He knows who I am and that I'm in his contest.

I point to the metal floor and don't ask how long he's known, or what he's going to do about it, or even what advice he's referring to. "Our friends in the catacombs need immediate—"

"Ah yes, your friends. Have no fear, they're already near and soon to be safe. But now . . ." He clicks his teeth. "It appears you are the final two. And yet two others have already come through." As if pleased with this pronouncement, he tugs his pipe from his lavender vest pocket, taps it against his hand, then moves aside to keep from impeding our view any longer. He swags an arm across a stone veranda overlooking a ballroom that's even more magnificent than the ones in Aunt Sara's fairy-tale books.

Lute and I step from the metal lift and onto a marble floor with gold veins running lacy patterns through it. Clusters of dangling chandelier lights catch and illuminate the gold, causing it to glow beneath giant floral arrangements, imposing banquet tables, and frothy fountains. It gives an aura that the whole room's not only alive but the very heartbeat of the house.

Except without people.

I catch Lute's eye. *Where are Vincent and Germaine?*

I turn to Mr. Holm. "Do you know where the two other players went, sir?"

"Two? Two? As I said, they already ran on through." He tips his head and leans in to peer at me, then Lute. Then smiles. "Just as you both will now follow me." He spins on his heel in the direction of an enormous gold door set precisely in the veranda's center. "But best be careful where you step, lest your game become forfeit." With that, he dons an imaginary hat and starts forward with short, clipped steps as he raps that pipe against a coat button.

I glance at Lute long enough for the meaning of Mr. Holm's words to sink in. He's still going to let me compete. Lute flashes me a wink, and then we're hastening to catch up and follow the pattern of Holm's feet. Three steps to the left. Three to the right. Five forward.

It's like a dance, repeated in perfect time, as the sound of his pipe rapping that button is the only thing in my ears, until it becomes like the pendulum of a clock.

Mr. Holm doesn't stop to look back until he's reached the giant ornate door, where he utters an incoherent word and the thing silently swings open in front of him. I whisper to Lute, "Vincent still has the key," but I doubt he hears me because when I turn, we are entering a sitting room the size of a small house and his eyes have gone round as saucers.

The parlor is decorated similar to the ballroom—in white and gold marble, with three lightly draped windows on each side that span floor to ceiling and overlook the hedge maze we came through last night. Instead of floral arrangements and fountains like those out in the hall, a single long wooden table stands in front of us, and set out on it is a selection of laboratory supplies and half-mixed fluids.

I look up to Mr. Holm who's sashaying over to a collection of gilt rugs and blue velvet sofas on the far side of the room where an array of well-dressed attendants lie sprawled out across them.

Lute's breath catches, and then mine does too.

In fact, my whole body goes still.

A person looking years older and far more normal than he does in any painting I've seen sits in one of the formal chairs. And yet—I'd recognize his regal nose, silver ringlets, and emerald-green dress suit anywhere.

We are in the presence of King Francis.

In the wide, jolly-faced flesh.

I hit my knees the same time as Lute, but His Royal Highness is already waving a jeweled hand for us to stand as four guards on our left shift their attentive stance. They wear the same type of chest pieces bearing the knight's crest we saw in the catacombs.

Mr. Holm clicks his heels and the sound echoes through the room. "Now that we're all here, we may begin. Mr. King, Mr. Wells, please join us." He tips his chin at a bench behind me, on which Germaine and Vincent have apparently been waiting. They leave their spot and stride over, and Germaine snickers at something Vincent's just said—until he reaches us and leans in. "Probably shouldn't give up your baking job, girl. We're always in need of women to cook."

Vincent stares straight at me and softly smiles. "Miss Tellur."

"So nice to see we're all here." Mr. Holm raises his voice. "Now allow me to officially introduce your spectator for this final assessment of the test. Our Fair King, Ruler of all Caldon, His Royal Highness King Francis, long may he reign."

I start to bow again, but the king twitches his hand as if it's unnecessary and edges forward in his chair. "I commend you for your efforts." He steeples his fingers beneath his chin with an expression that says this is what he came for. "You have my full attention. Please commence."

With a nod, Mr. Holm comes to stand on the other side of the table in front of us.

"So now we're to be observed while we perform," Germaine says.

"What did I tell you?" Vincent whispers. "Like rats in a maze."

"His Royal Highness is only here to observe, nothing more. However, the task you've been assigned is specifically for him." Mr. Holm doesn't look at Vincent—just turns to the king who tips his head—before he swerves back to indicate a single door directly across the room from us that blends so well into the wall it looks like part of the marble. "You'll note the door behind me requires a key. On the other side of it, you'll find your future with glee. But in order to pass through, you must first accurately complete this final test."

"I've promised His Majesty an extra-special display this evening. Aside from the fireworks, we'll send up kites that will glow like cavern worms into the night sky. It's your job to create the glow compound used to coat those kites. But let me warn you—as with most chemical reactions, time is of the essence."

Holm points to the table holding the laboratory supplies. "In front of you is a bench with four individual stations. Each one has the same equipment, same chemicals, and same compounds. And I'll give you a clue." His voice dips excitedly. "Parts of the process have already been prepared for you. But . . . it's up to you to figure out which solutions have been mixed at what stages, and what assembly steps and chemicals have yet to be finalized."

He steps back, places his hands into his vest pockets, and stares at us.

I frown and look around. Wait—is he serious? Creating a glow compound is tricky, but it's not that tricky. It's more like making a cake—lots of ingredients and detailed timing. But otherwise, it's essentially the same. I peer over at Vincent. He and I used to make these with my da and take them out into the fields to release. They'd last a few hours and look like the stars had come to earth.

Vincent's eyes say he's remembering the same thing. He shakes his head at Germaine. "There's got to be a catch. It's too simple."

Except Germaine says nothing as he stares at his section of supplies. And when I peer over at Lute, his face is a mirror image of Germaine's.

Neither of them knows how to do this.

"Please note, you may speak to one another, trade supplies, and offer small conversation." Mr. Holm's voice trickles around us. "However, you may not share your finished compound. Nor may you share the recipe for how it can be created. Gentle-persons of the Labyrinth exam—the clock starts now."

I turn from Lute to the station in front of me to grab a pair of gloves. Only there are none. I narrow my gaze. Why wouldn't he supply gloves?

Shaking it off, I tug my sleeves to the edge of my fingers and start in.

If I can figure this out fast enough, I can help Lute.

First I analyze the two pitchers of solution that have already been readied. One green, one clear—I just need to figure out which stages. I dip a glass pointer separately into each and dab a bit of their liquid onto a dish to see if I can get a feel for what's already been placed in them. I make a quick list on the available notepaper, then place the dishes under a microscope and begin adding individual chemicals to see if I can narrow down the still-needed components.

Next, I gather the remaining ingredients I think I'll need and begin measuring those, one at a time, beside a third pitcher.

"Seems your boy there is struggling a bit," Vincent whispers. He hovers beside me, peering at my mixture and notes, his gloved fingers resting beside my own bare ones.

I lift a brow. Where'd he get the gloves? "Seems your boy is too."

He grins. "Brings back old times, doesn't it?" He moves on, tracing his gloved hands along the table, then steps around me and does the same to Lute. Then to Germaine.

I shake my head. If he's trying to intimidate us, it's not working. It's just annoying.

Focus, Rhen.

I go back over the ingredients I've measured and begin to combine them in the pitcher. If I've learned anything through the years with Da, it's that sometimes the simplest experiments are the trickiest, simply because I tend to overthink the process or go too fast.

Lute studies the compounds in front of him and writes out their structures on a paper. His bare fingers press against the table and scratch out each chemical as he deciphers it. Smart.

I turn back to my own mixtures and set my hands on the work area to refocus. Then pick up the green to pour into my clear liquid first. I've just added it in when the tips of three of my fingers start tingling. I ignore them and dip in a glass stick to stir the solution.

The tingling picks up. I frown and look down. We should've had gloves.

Except . . .

Except I don't believe any of these chemicals would give such a specific sensation. I rub my fingers on my pants to stop the prickling, but just as I return them to the pitcher, the table jolts and a cry rings out through the room.

21

A second cry rings out, and something hits the floor with a thump. In my peripheral vision I see Germaine slumped over into a fetal position. He's shaking and gasping for air like he's choking.

What the?

The king and his attendants rise just as the knights move to surround His Majesty, even as he's asking what's going on and requesting that something be done for the boy.

I look around for Mr. Holm, but he must be assisting the king too, because I don't see him. My fingers begin to shake. Ignoring His Royal Highness's questions, I drop to where

Germaine is convulsing on the ground and Lute is already kneeling and loosening the boy's collar. He yanks it back so I can check Germaine's pulse. It's racing far too fast for safety.

I scan his body, his chest, his lips, then glance up at the table to Germaine's chemical combinations. This isn't due to the compounds we've been using. Something else is going on. Something is *wrong*.

Vincent.

I veer around to find him still standing at his station, casually pouring the first two of his pitchers together. On his face is a smug look of satisfaction. Not just smug—*chilling*.

I narrow my eyes as he seals the lid on his pitcher, then lifts it up and looks at me. He begins to shake the solution.

My skin ices over. He took out his own friend. In front of the king and Holm, no less.

A hand grabs mine, and Germaine's eyes have grown wide with terror. He's squeezing my fingers as if begging me to help him as his breathing becomes labored. "Vincent . . . ," he chokes out. "What's he done?" Which is when I notice my own breathing feels funny and my throat is tightening. *What did Vincent do?*

Come on, think, Rhen. I lean down to sniff Germaine's breath and catch the slight blue discoloration appearing around his mouth. Except now it's edging the whites of his eyes as well.

Bloodberries?

The tingling in my fingers gets harder. It's spreading up to my elbows.

Lute lets out a cough beside me and then gags, and he's suddenly shaking too.

"Lute!"

I don't know how Vincent did it, but he gave us a dose of bloodberry. I peer up at his passive face again, then at the table where noticeable purple streaks are beginning to appear. Right along the spots where he'd traced his gloved hands.

The gloves. The ones he'd been using have been discarded beside a pile of others—beside *our* gloves. And they have a purple stain on them.

The fact he brought a berry in here, broke it open, and spread it where he knew our hands would touch . . . It's brilliant, and sick, and the thought that he was once my friend makes me want to retch. I turn back to Germaine, whom Lute's still trying to help, and count his pulse again. Considering he's not dead yet means the dose is diluted. Which would make sense if it was absorbed through us touching the wood.

"He used a bloodberry," I say aloud. "The poison's soaking in through our hands."

Lute's hands are trembling as he nods. "How bad?"

"Toxic enough that if we don't counteract it, we'll all be dead shortly."

Lute bends over and pretends he's not trembling, even as the blue stain is starting to edge his lips. "What do you need?"

I spiral back to my studies in the lab with Da. To the natural toxins and their opposites. I rise and look around for a vase of flowers. "I need piphonies."

"Like the arrangements on the veranda?" Without waiting for a reply Lute shoves off the floor and half strides, half stumbles from the room—only to return thirty seconds later with an entire vase of blooms. His legs are shuddering so hard he can barely stand. So are mine. The poison's hitting our lungs and nervous systems.

I help him set it down. *There.* Yellow buds as small as buttons. I ignore the quaking in my arms and torso and begin pulling the blossoms out by the handful. Lute strips the leaves off and drops them to the floor, and then he tips over with his hands clenched at his chest.

I don't stop to help him—just reach up, grab a glass, and use the base of it to grind the petals right there on the marble. As soon as I've finished I grab a damp clump and shove it under Germaine's tongue, then put a wad under Lute's too, then mine, right as my breathing thickens and my vision starts fading.

Through the dimness I see Vincent set down the pitcher of mixture he's just finished with. The liquid inside the glass lights up like a bright blue star.

I want to tell him to go to the underworld, except I don't because my body's suddenly exploding with agony, as parts of me begin quivering and breaking in an internal earthquake. And not just in my nerve endings and fading mind, but in the part of me that knows that Vincent's win means I have failed.

My mum with her illness.

My belief that I could beat this test.

My flimsy hopes for my future.

And as much as I try to block it out, all I can hear in my head is my uncle's suggestion that perhaps I am too much like my parents to become anything different.

The room begins to spin. The king and his friends, the

cold marble floor—it all starts flickering, like a mirage brought on by the poison. I blink and grab Lute's hand as the darkness encroaches and Vincent bolts for the marble-looking door.

The next second, Lute staggers to his feet, pulls me up with him, and pushes us toward where Vincent's fumbling with the key and the lock. Except we only make it two paces when Lute falls. I try to drag him back up as his body starts to convulse like Germaine's.

Lute grits his teeth as if it's taking all his strength to hold on to his clarity and then tips his head toward Vincent. "Go."

"I didn't finish the experiment."

"How do you know this wasn't the experiment? Go."

I yank his arm. "If I go, you go with me."

Lute's hands slide up and cup my face, his skin hot against mine. I can feel his heartpulse in his palms, pressing against my cheeks. "I've already won," he whispers.

He pushes me away. "Now run." And then his hands slip away and my sight is diminishing even as I hear him in my mind, in my ears, in my mouth, and his words are so strong that I shove the fear away and stumble forward.

The room morphs beneath each shaky step. I sprint and fall across space toward the door that Vincent is already tearing open. I lunge for his shirt and scrape my fingers across his back right before a blast of afternoon air throws him against me.

He turns in surprise, then chuckles and grabs my waist to steady me. "This is why I like you, Rhen." He slips his hand to my chin and leans over my face until his lips are an inch away. "You're a fighter. Take me up on my offer, and I'll still give you the world." His hand pinches harder, and with every ounce of rage I have, I jerk back and shove a hand beneath his ribs and into his diaphragm while my shaky knee jerks up to connect with his family jewels.

"Sorry," I gasp. "Your world is too small." I thrust against him, ramming him to the side, and plunge for the doorway where I am suddenly spit out onto the balcony overlooking the Labyrinth entrance and festival grounds in broad daylight as the sea of partiers wavers in and out of my vision.

The light is so bright I shield my eyes. The noise is deafening—but mixed in with it, I can hear the cry of seagulls and smell the port's salty air. Until the rising tide of voices grows clear enough for me to pick out words and phrases.

They're arguing about the fishing regulations.

I squint. Not just arguing—the festival looks half destroyed. The Upper tents have been torn down, and the Lowers have taken over the terraces.

I peer back through the doorway, but Vincent is nowhere to be seen. Only Holm, the king, and his attendees are standing back in the shadows. I want to sink back in there with them. Back to the Labyrinth and Seleni and Beryll and Lute. Especially Lute.

"Gentlepersons and friends," the announcer's voice bellows from somewhere. "Your attention, please."

"Who is that?" one of the spectators yells.

My airway shrinks and I begin heaving. The antidote's not working fast enough.

"What's going on here?" Vincent's father demands. "Where's my son?"

"Friends and community." The announcer's words ricochet off the garden walls and echo out over the lawns with the same intensity that is ringing through my head. "I give you the winner of this year's scholarship contest—Miss Rhen Tellur."

The thunder in the crowd rivals the pounding of my heartbeat in my ears as I stumble forward and drop to my knees. My arms and stomach seize.

Even so, I vaguely note their shock turns to laughter. "Is this a joke? Bring out the real winner!"

"Is that Rhen? What happened to her hair?"

Until they apparently realize he's serious, and their words become:

"What's going on?"

"This is a boys' sport!"

"How was she even allowed in there? *How did this happen?*"

"She's from the Lower Port, that's how!" a voice bursts out.

"One of our own Lowers won!"

"Poor girl's still not even wearing stockings." Mrs. Mench's voice rings louder than the rest. "I knew it."

I look down at the crowds of people and parasol-covered lawns. Then over to see the dean and board members of Stemwick University standing beside the announcer, whom they probably think to be Mr. Holm.

They are not cheering. They're not doing anything at all other than frowning down their long noses.

And everything goes black.

22

At some point my body decides to settle on the fact that I am not dead. It begins to fight against the poison-fueled nightmares and ongoing sensation of falling, despite my mind saying that something's still very wrong. As if my limbs lunged through the winner's exit but my brain knows I haven't really won. That there's something more. That the key to the bigger maze is still missing and I'm walking in circles trying to decipher what that means. *"Like rats in a maze."* Isn't that what Vincent had said back in Holm's parlor?

Except this rat keeps scratching at my skin, trying to get in. With its disease that just keeps morphing, and the vials of blood and tubes filled with live viruses that won't stop floating through my head. Along with memories of Vincent in his better days, running tests beside me.

My blood pounds as the antidote works to clear the poison from my blood and the ghouls from my sleep. But still the rats keep scratching.

Until the day following my exit from the Labyrinth—when I peel my lids up to see the sun and Da's face.

"Ah. Was suspecting you'd wake soon." He smiles.

I offer a weak smile back. "What's the verdict?"

"You'll live."

"I assumed. I meant the other verdict?"

"Your mum and I still love you, and we might even be rather proud of you."

"Funny."

He winks. "There are a few verdicts, if you want to know. The first is that you did indeed win the contest. The official statement is that while there was a final test, Holm never said exactly what it was a testing of—and there's a whole thing about it having to do with character and all that."

"What of the other contestants?" My mind flicks to Lute. Then Sam and Beryll and Will and Seleni.

He fetches me a cup of tea then comes to help me sit up. "Aside from the boy who ate a bloodberry, the rest are alive and have been returned home. Some a bit more beat up than when they entered. Same as every year. And Lute's mum sent word that he woke this morning."

I stop midsip from my cup and breathe out relief. Then

frown. *But how? How are they alive? How did they escape from the sirens and basilisks and ghouls? How did Holm rescue them so fast?*

I don't ask because Da won't have an answer. Nobody ever does but Mr. Holm. What had Da said? *"Same as every year."*

Maybe that's the real magic, or horror, of the strange little man.

I'm sorry for the boy who died, though.

Da clears his throat and taps his own cup. "The second verdict is that the whole Port is waiting to see if the university will agree to let you take their exams—just like we're waiting to hear back on the fishing industry representation. Some of them have"—he sucks his cheek in as if trying to choose the right words—"made no secret of what their reaction will be if either is denied."

I raise a brow. I can imagine some of the names behind such a threat. We both stare at each other. And then he pulls out his notes on a new crippling disease serum he's been developing.

23

It takes another full day for any official news to arrive. According to Mrs. Mench's loud commentary outside to anyone walking by, Stemwick's board has not only been busy arguing policies and a long history of being the highest standard in male-focused education—they've also been weighing the implications of honoring a female as Mr. Holm's scholarship recipient. Particularly when it appears their funding relies far more heavily on Holm's yearly contributions than anyone thought.

And like the Port, the Holm estate has also made its position perfectly clear—either allow me to take the entrance exam or lose the financial support.

Da's agitation grows while he waits. Every five minutes between starting work on a new trial medicine and checking on Mum, he steals a peek out the window when he thinks I'm not looking.

His tension becomes Mum's excuse for why she's begun sleeping so much. "I'm just trying to tune out the stress of his nerves." To which I swallow and pat her hand because I know full well it's not true.

This is the next stage of the disease, and it's not something we can run from.

Although everything in me still wants to—just for a while. To go find Sam and Will as if everything is fine. Or maybe ask Seleni to find Lute and see what's on his mind.

But I don't. Da's set Sam and Will to healing. And Lute has his family to care for, and I have mine. And that is where things lie as I sit with my fading Mum, as the slow fear for what is about to happen creeps upon the horizon. I can feel it twitching and shuddering and . . . waiting.

I don't bake or make deliveries. I don't see Seleni or the sea. I just wait with Da and Mum as I try not to look like I might throw up from the realization that's been sinking in. That even if I did get accepted to the uni, anything I learn won't be soon enough to save Mum. She will die anyway—of that I am sure. Unless Da's new treatment is a miracle.

I wrinkle my nose against the astringent scent of cleaning alcohol and stand in the lab—and stare at the rat cages and experiments and blood samples and try all the harder to unravel what those scratching nudges in my head keep saying. Because

I know I'm missing something. Something right in front of me. I just can't figure out what it is.

And then the letter comes.

I am adjusting Mum's pillows and watching the seagulls through the sunlit pane when Da rushes in with the packet—sealed in a thick, yellow envelope, much like Mum is wrapped up in layers of yellowed blankets.

He holds his breath and watches me weigh it in hand. The thick paper in my fingers is heavier than I'd expect for a simple yes or no answer. I frown. Maybe they've skipped the exams and just sent some sort of disciplinary action. Or maybe it's an application. My chest leaps before logic sets in. I saw their expressions after the contest. To say half of them were furious would be an understatement.

I offer the letter back to Da. "You open it." But he bats it away.

I look at him. Then Mum. Then break the wax seal and lift the contents out, and without peeking at what is written there, I hold the papers six inches in front of Mum's face. "You read it first."

Her eyes turn moist and she nods before she weakly lifts her hand to grab it and scans the first page. We wait. She looks up at me and has me shuffle to the next, then the next, so she can peer over each one. "It's a ten-page packet of qualifiers and caveats," she eventually whispers. "But . . ." She pauses and blinks and directs her gaze back to the first, as if to ensure she won't misspeak.

"Helen, what'd they decide?" Da stands over her with a face so anxious I think he might pass out.

Her lips curve up into a smile, and she starts to cry in thin, barely-there teardrops that drip down her cheeks as she looks up at me. "I'm proud of you." Then she glances at Da.

"The board has agreed to let Rhen take the university entrance examination."

The moment the letter illuminates her face and makes her cry—is the moment the theory hits me. I stand in the sunlight beside the bed in my nightdress, even though it is six o'clock in the evening, and watch Mum's joy spill out in her emaciated voice and smile and loving gaze. I frame that look in my mind, my emotions, because it is exactly who I know my mum to be and also the person she hasn't been for a very long time. And because I don't know how many more times I'll get to see it.

And it occurs to me that no person whose every cell is this full of life could produce such a wretched disease.

What if Da and I were wrong this whole time, and the disease didn't start in humans?

What if it came from a plant or animal? What if it came from . . . ?

The rats.

Da is still focused on the letter and his elation. He drops on the bed and clasps Mum's hands in his as the two of them lock eyes and share parental pride, while the sensation of unease stirs my gut and spreads within me.

I want to tell him. To tell them I have a theory. But to do so would alert Da immediately to what it might mean. That the origination of the rat disease might've been Da and me.

I don't speak. I refuse to ruin this moment for either.

I simply swallow and move the letter so the two of them can be closer. Except Mum grasps my hand and pulls me in. She grips my chin and lifts herself enough to lean forward until our noses are near touching—then whispers, "You take this world and make it what it should be. And don't let the beliefs of a backward system define you. You are the one who has to live with the future, baby girl. So you *live* it. You understand?"

She stares hard in my eyes for a moment longer, until I nod and inhale the feeling of her fingers cupping my skin as firmly as I wish I could hold on to her. I kiss her forehead. "I love you, Mum."

When I get up, Da squeezes my shoulder, and then he's got one hand on Mum's cheek and the other in her hair, and he's smiling down at her. And suddenly he looks frailer than I've ever seen. Sitting there holding her face to his. This woman who isn't just his wife, but also his closest friend.

Whoever said the female is the weaker of a species never tested that theory against the draw of a woman's love.

I give up whatever I was going to say and place a kiss on Mum's arm, then turn to go downstairs to the lab.

As I leave I hear Da singing a soft song just between the two of them.

It's their wedding song.

I head to the shelves in the basement and take down the last sixteen months' worth of blood and disease experiments. And begin to examine them.

24

The celebration party for the Holm scholarship recipient is, traditionally, hosted by the recipient's parents exactly ten days after winning the Labyrinth contest. The entire Port knows it's usually attended by the winner's social circle and is as elaborate as the family can afford. Which means it's normally an extravagant affair bordering on a circus that neither Da nor I is interested in hosting.

In fact, neither one of us brings it up—him, because I doubt he remembered, and me, because my mind is on Da and Mum, and my experiments, and Stemwick's entrance exam that's in four days. Which is what I tell Seleni when she asks.

"That's why Mum and I have decided to do it for you," she chirps.

"Sel, please." I keep my gaze on the test tube I'm working with and shake my head. "This isn't the time."

She tips her head and waits for me to look at her. "You've been down here for days, Rhen. I know you're trying to study for the exam and eager with a new idea for your mum. But you've got to breathe sometime."

I stare at her and don't tell her that I haven't done any studying for the exam. That I've spent every waking minute the last three days re–breaking down the compositions of the lung-fluid illness, the cure I'd come closest to creating for it, and the cow disease Vincent had been studying. And identifying key markers. And starting the beginnings of a new type of cure, just in case I'm right.

I simply say, "Good luck convincing Da."

"Oh, my father will do that. And what of Lute? I assume you'd like me to invite him."

When my only response is to nod and clear my throat, she eyes me with understanding. "Still haven't heard from him, then."

I shake my head and turn back to my petri dish, ignoring the fears that that admission brings.

She disappears up the stairs, and I get back to running my tests.

The next day Aunt Sara appears with a full basket of rich-smelling meats and vegetables—and broaches the celebration suggestion to Mum and Da. When Da politely refuses, Uncle

Nicholae himself strides down to personally insist—and to say that Da is permanently welcome in their home from now on.

"It should've happened a long time ago." Uncle Nicholae sticks out his hand and nods toward Seleni and me. "I hope we can leave the past in the past and move forward as a family."

Da decks Uncle Nicholae a solid punch right in the jaw and sends him backward onto the wood kitchen floor.

I lift a brow and bite back a smile as Seleni gasps. "He deserved that," she murmurs.

"Fair enough." Uncle Nicholae stands and wipes his cheek with the back of his sleeve, then reoffers his hand.

And that is how the party that neither Da nor I really wants to attend—but Mum does—gets planned for the evening of the university's entrance exams.

The exams arrive like sea foam rushing in—too fast—and too soon Da and I find ourselves the morning of sitting over a bazillion notes on the floor of their room with our cups of hot tea, as the sun rises and my leg is jittering something fierce.

"You'll do wonderful," Mum says softly. "Don't forget the smart women stock you come from. Your poor da never could keep up."

Da swerves his gaze to her and laughs, and it takes me a second before the sound sinks in. It's the first honest humor I've heard from him all week, and I swear it's like a ray of light slanted through the window and splayed itself out across his and Mum's bed. I smile and they both grin, and in that moment we are okay. We are *all* okay. Which, I think, is enough of a promise for today.

I get up to pour them more tea as Da gives Mum a second dose of the treatment he's been developing—and I notice Da's still got on the same clothes from two days ago. So has Mum. I wrinkle my brow and study them both. Is that what it will mean if I pass this exam? He'll be here alone to care for Mum—or worse—left without either of us?

The reality of that about drowns me.

I wince and finish pouring their tea just as the clock chimes that it's time. I stoop to collect my scribbled notes that Da is tapping on. "I have to check on something real fast."

I kiss them both before hurrying down to check in on my lab tests again, only to discover that the results of the original crippling disease cells work have revealed what I already had begun to suspect. My stomach turns.

25

The exam takes place in the privacy of a back room at the local constable's home located in the Upper district—while all the boys from the Upper district take it at the university itself.

Seleni has scoffed about it half the walk there. "Let me get this straight. So you can take the university exam. You just can't take it *at* the university like an actual applicant."

"In all likelihood, they're probably just trying to keep the Uppers from filing lawsuits," Da says.

Seleni shakes her head. "Either way it's wrong. Beryll said some of the men requested Rhen be tested separately, out of sensitivity to the boys taking the exam. They feared she'd be a distraction." She snorts. "Apparently your feminine wiles are capable of making them idiots, Rhen."

"They don't need *my* bloody help," I say to keep my nerves from showing. I squeeze both their hands before I take a deep breath, walk onto the porch, and with my head held high stride through the front door.

The constable offers me his arm and wishes me a soft, "Good luck, Miss Tellur," before he ushers me into a room where three university professors and two board members all take their seats at a makeshift setup of a table and seven chairs. The door closes behind me, and without any introduction one of the professors slides over a stack of papers and an ink quill. "Miss Tellur, let's begin."

And so we do.

Only it doesn't feel like a beginning. Rather, it feels like a continuation of something I've been waiting for my whole life and just didn't know it. Like a part of me that's been buried beneath the ground is suddenly peeking its head up to bloom.

Which is exactly what it feels like—*blooming*.

I take a sip of water and answer another question.

Then another. And another—until the combined oral and written exams have gone on for almost six hours, aside from three ten-minute breaks, and a bite of bread and cheese Aunt Sara and Seleni packed. A quarter of the test questions I know without batting a lash, but the rest I struggle through. At one point toward the end of the afternoon, the words and numbers begin shifting order, and my taxed brain breaks into a panic.

Slow down, Rhen. Take a breath.

I shut my eyes and run through the rhythmic species cycles until I can focus again. And then in a matter of minutes we are done, and I'm shaking their hands as a board member informs me, "On behalf of this group that is sanctioned to oversee your testing, we congratulate you on being allowed to do so. You'll know the results along with our decision in a couple of weeks."

The door opens and the constable appears. I follow him out into the parlor, which is wafting with cologne, and when I look up, Vincent and his father are standing there, as is my uncle.

Mr. King is speaking with Uncle Nicholae. "Just came to see how Miss Tellur is doing. Vincent took his exams a few days ago thanks to a private contact, and since he's made a decision to pursue Miss Tellur's hand in courtship, he felt it imperative to lend his support today."

I bite down the bile in my throat.

"Your son tried to kill me and was behind a boy's murder," I want to say aloud. And I would, too, if it'd do a lick of good. Germaine and Rubin already named him as having paid them to help him win, but since nothing could be directly tied to Vincent, they're currently on house arrest while he walks free.

I sniff. He'll make an excellent politician.

And yet . . . even politicians' sins will eventually find them out. Once they realize those sins become a cage.

I stare at him and stroll over. His blond hair's mussed. He looks desperate. Uncomfortable. "What do you really want, Vincent?" I hiss.

His mouth flattens in a tight smile. "To let bygones be bygones."

I raise a brow.

He glances at his father, then lowers his voice. "I'm willing to overlook your little fling with Mr. Wilkes if you're willing to overlook my misdeeds. We can go back to normal and my father won't need to know."

I blink. *Is he jesting?*

"I can appreciate your mind better than most," he continues. "We used to be friends once, Rhen, and I daresay I never once judged you or the risks you took. Even being in the maze. What I'm saying is, you've made your point. You can let it go now. I'll appreciate what your mind can lend me. You'll appreciate my money. Clear as that."

I actually laugh. And it's louder and fuller than I intend, which brings a bright red flush to his handsome face.

How very progressive of him.

"Mr. King, I think I'd prefer to put my mind toward my own future rather than be your—how did you describe us in the Labyrinth—rats in a cage?"

A burst of fear erupts across his perfectly chiseled features. It's pure. Unadulterated. The same fear I saw on him in the hedge maze when facing his visions of the diseased people rising from their graves to come after him.

I slow and tilt my head and study his reaction. Until this moment it hadn't occurred to me how something so ridiculous could be his deepest fear. Or *why*. I feel the scratching in my mind pick up, as if edging me closer to some discovery.

My skin ripples with the memory I'd had in the Labyrinth. Of Vincent suggesting he borrow my lung-fluid vaccine to test on his cow-disease cells.

Of Vincent working beside me the day one of the rats showed the first symptoms of the crippling disease. Of Vincent tipping over a drink he wasn't supposed to have in our lab—and knocking over two of the cages, causing that rat to escape. And of his disappearance the next three days and his change of personality and career choice two months later.

I lift my gaze to him.

And I know.

I know what he's done.

I open my mouth. Shut it. Just as Vincent's father says, "Nicholae, I commend you for encouraging the ideals young minds seem to push for. They rarely come to fruition, but I believe allowing them to realize that on their own is important. Good for you for letting Miss Tellur's passions run their course until she comes 'round."

I bestow Vincent with a smile that quickly twists to outrage. It wasn't Da or me who created the disease accidentally.

It was him.

And if I could, I'd kill him for it.

Instead, I clench my fists and quietly say, "Just like your son's passions ran their course, Mr. King?"

Vincent's eyes flare as his father turns my way. "Pardon, Miss Tellur?"

I lick my lips. "Is that why you suddenly switched career goals, Vince? Because of what you created with your passion in the lab? Being responsible for the crippling disease is quite a feat."

"Miss Tellur, I don't see how my son's—"

As someone who has spent a solid bit of the past few months running, the one thing I never expected to see was Vincent King run. Especially from a girl.

But in the span of the ten-second space between when I finish talking and Uncle Nicholae says, "Is this true, Mr. King?" Vincent has flushed the color of a burnt sunset and launched for the door.

The constable is there to stop him. "Hold on just a minute, friend."

Vincent looks around at us, wild-eyed, like a trapped animal, and I know it shouldn't give me the smallest bit of pleasure, but it does. The disease he accidentally developed is killing my mum, and I can prove it. I'd bet my scholarship on it.

"Miss Tellur . . . Rhen," Vincent says. "You have to understand. I was just messing around with some tests. I thought if we could see what they did on the rats . . . I didn't mean for one to get loose."

"Rhen, go get ready for your and Seleni's celebration party," Uncle Nicholae says. "I think the Kings and I need to have a chat."

I nod. And without giving Vincent another ounce of acknowledgment, I turn my back on him and walk out the door.

26

"To Rhen for winning!" Uncle Nicholae says. "And to Seleni!"

"To Rhen and Seleni!" the guests respond.

Their cheers are accompanied by the clinking of glasses and the trill of a musical serenade, followed by corks popping from a tower of golden bottles as the servers push expensive drinks on every adult in the place.

"To keep everyone docile." Seleni giggles. "At least according to Mum. But I think it's more to keep her and Father calm, because the way they've been acting, you'd think King Francis himself was set to make an appearance." Her voice drops conspiratorially as she plays with the sleeve of her frilly blue dress.

"I even heard her say she might have to dip into Father's snuff later just to survive this—and Father didn't argue. He just looked nervous and put extra hired guards on all the upstairs doors and around the house perimeter in case a 'riot breaks out.'"

I laugh and take in the loud room and outer gardens, all of which are frothing to overflowing with politicians and children and Uppers and Lowers—all of whom seem less interested in rioting than in partying, ever since the Lowers put the Uppers on notice at the equinox festival. The hint at reevaluating the way the fishing restrictions are handled came swiftly after, and since then the interest has mainly been taken up by Seleni and me—the "girls who behaved like boys," an elderly woman says behind us in a whisper.

I glance back at the woman and offer up a wink. "We even kissed boys in the Labyrinth," I say. To which she turns two shades of red and utters something about wondering what young ladies are coming to these days.

Except according to the number of women in the room shyly eyeing Seleni and me, I'm not sure what we're all "coming to" is a bad thing.

"Rhen Tellur, you are terrible." Seleni chuckles, but she dips and plays to the attention all the more. Then emits a sharp gasp. "Beryll's just arrived with his parents. Oh, Rhen." She swerves to me. "How do I look? What do I do? I have to go meet them. Here—wait two minutes, then come over and talk with us. And make me sound good." She plants a quick peck on my cheek, smooths her dress, and trots off to where Beryll is standing in a leg cast and leaning against a cane beside a fashionably dressed couple and an old woman wearing a hat.

I look past them to the open door to see who else came in— and hide my disappointment. It's only them. Da and Mum still haven't arrived. Neither has Lute.

I bite my lip. Perhaps they're having a hard time.

Or perhaps . . .

Perhaps Lute's emotions have calmed and the reality of things has set in.

I lift my chin and turn to go find Sam and Will—only to be met by a woman accompanying two young girls strolling up in ill-fitting, worn cotton dresses and braids tied up above flushed pink faces.

"Excuse me," the older one says. "Will you write something on our kerchiefs?" They both hold out their soiled hand linens and look up with expectant gazes and hands that are shaking a little.

I offer them an embarrassed smile, then take my own kerchief from my sleeve. "Only if you'll sign mine." And then they are grinning as awkwardly as I am, and somehow it doesn't feel so strange.

As soon as I've finished, Seleni is calling my name, and when I turn she's beckoning me. She and Beryll are standing with his parents, looking my way. I put my kerchief away and stride over as someone whispers, "Gordon's son must be getting serious about Miss Lake if both parents are here."

When I reach them, Beryll's parents greet me with muted smiles and reserved nods, and I don't know what I expected, but it's not this. Whereas Beryll is brown haired, his father is a ginger with freckles and a good-humored smile, and his mother is petite. And where I'd believed they'd appear sour in spirit toward Seleni, they both seem to be quite pleasant with her. They smell of cinnamon.

"We were just speaking of Vincent," Seleni says. "Father said he's being held at the constable's until he can be transported to the courts."

"We're sorry to hear about it." Beryll's father looks kindly at me. "What a tragedy for you all."

I nod and reach a hand out to him and his wife. "Thanks. I'm Rhen, by the way. Seleni's cousin."

Beryll blushes. "Pardon. Father and Mum, this is Miss Tellur. Miss Tellur, these are my parents, Mr. and Mrs. Jaymes, and one of their acquaintances—Ms. Danford."

Ms. Danford has turned away to speak with someone, but Beryll's mum smiles at me, then looks around. "Are your parents here, Miss Tellur?"

I return her smile with my own and refuse to let my fears flicker bigger than they already are. "They're hoping to come."

"Oh, they'll be here." Seleni slips her hand into mine and squeezes. "And they'll be glad to know Beryll was just saying he's made a decision." She peers proudly at him. "He's decided to pursue a career in parliament." Beryll's father clears his throat. "My son seems to have taken a concern with social issues as of late."

He eyes Seleni who promptly blushes. "I believe it has something to do with the friends he's made, no?" He sets a hand on his son's shoulder and pats it. "Now, I think my wife and I are due to meet *your* parents, Miss Lake. Miss Tellur. If you'll both excuse us."

I watch them depart when Ms. Danford finishes her conversation and turns our way. She's wearing a bright-green hat over a rather wrinkled face that looks curiously full of mirth. But it's her eyes that catch me. They're lavender.

She lifts her hand to mine. "Miss Tellur, did I hear? How very nice to meet you." Her fingers enfold mine and the oddest sensation nudges me. There's something familiar about her. "I hope you enjoyed your time in the Labyrinth. You certainly proved yourself in there, didn't you?"

I freeze. And blink. Then go to respond, except I'm not sure what to say because all I can think is it couldn't be. I shake my head and move in to peer closer at her, but she abruptly turns and says in a tinkling voice, "Now if you'll pardon me, I believe there's a Labyrinth cake with my name on it somewhere." And she strolls off toward the side hallway.

"There you three are." I jump as Sam's voice rings out. "We've been scouring everywhere for you." He hobbles up to us on crutches with Will by his side—his hair as peacock-ish as ever.

Will grins. "Had to down four desserts on our own since we didn't have anyone to share 'em with. Then we had to start in on this sweet pigeon pie."

"You didn't spike the juice, did you?" I eye them and their full plates, keeping Ms. Danford in my sights as she steps into the hall, which is the exact opposite direction of the food.

"Maybe." Will bows slightly and winks at Seleni. "You're

welcome for any entertainment that ensues. Just don't tell your mum."

Beryll chuckles, before his expression turns serious. "By the way, I approached my father about revisiting the fishing initiative at the House of Lords. He's going to request a fuller impact study be done, to see if anything was overlooked."

"Tell them what else," Seleni quietly squeals and grabs his arm.

She's bouncing on her heels as he blushes. "I have officially informed them I will be courting Miss Lake."

My grin is huge and accompanied by a hug that promises to scream with her later when it won't embarrass Beryll even more. So that's why she's been glowing like a firebug since he walked in.

"Good goin', chap." Will slaps him on the back. Then wrinkles his brow. "So the old man's not against it, eh?"

Seleni slides her arm through Beryll's. "He'd apparently been too shy to stand firm on it."

"Well, in my defense—"

They keep talking but I'm staring at the corner that Ms. Danford disappeared around. I excuse myself and follow her.

She's slipped down the hall toward the partially open parlor door. She stands there a full minute with her back to me as several male voices trickle out from within the room, and I can't tell if she's listening or trying to decide to enter. If Ms. Danford is aware I'm there, she doesn't give any indication.

A second later she stiffens. "Miss Tellur, you're not with the other guests."

I stare.

My mouth goes dry as she turns and peers at me with those lavender eyes above wrinkled cheeks and a pretty blue suit with larger-than-normal buttons. And a voice that sounds very much like the chiming of a clock.

"Did you need something, dear? Or are you just here to *spy*?"

I shake my head. "I don't understand. You're . . ."

Her grin grows wider and she takes a step closer to study me from head to foot before her gaze flashes back to mine. "I'd expect you of all people who've entered my contest to know things aren't always as they appear, Rhen Tellur from the Port." She scrunches her lips and leans back to continue assessing me, then discreetly pulls an empty wooden pipe from her pocket. She lifts it and glances at it, then in one swift movement waves it across the front of herself.

As she does so, her appearance changes into that of the elderly, silver-tuft-haired Mr. Kellen, with a purple waistcoat and an empty wooden pipe.

Before I've had time to blink, she waves the pipe again, like a magician's wand, and shifts back into the female version of whatever she is.

I shut my eyes. Open them. She's still there. I squint. "Who are you?"

She chuckles, and it's the same pleasant sound I heard the other night in the hall outside my uncle's study. "A woman must find her own way, yes? As the only living heir in a long line of Holm men, I couldn't just let the name die with my father. So—" She shrugs. "While I wasn't afforded the education one traditionally needs for running business affairs, he ensured I was trained in . . ." She gives a slight smile and taps her pipe against her hand. "Other things. And now?" Her mouth eases into a sad smile. "If I couldn't attend a school, at least I can influence those who do."

The next moment she gives a delighted clap and bestows me with a smile. "Good evening, Rhen. And congratulations again on your win. I expect you'll do good things for the world of men." She starts back to the parlor.

"But Vincent had the key," I say quickly.

She slows and tilts her head. "He had *a* key, yes, Miss Tellur. I never said whether the actual key was physical or a characteristic. I'd expect someone of your intellectual prowess to have latched onto that by now."

With that, she waves the pipe over herself once more and takes on a completely new appearance—that of a balding middle-aged man in suit and tie—and, giving me a nod, strides through the door to join the men.

And I am left staring at an empty space.

I frown and turn to—to do what? I don't know, but the moment I slip back around the corner toward the party, a voice says, "I hear short hair on females could become all the rage."

Lute.

I don't know whether to melt or laugh or cry. I want to ask where he's been, where we are on things, but his eyes find mine, and those questions are for later as I glance at his clothing and offer a smirk. I don't think I've ever seen him in nonfishing suit pants before. "You look nice."

He swags those dimples at me and sweeps a chunk of black hair from his face. "I was just going to say the same about you." His eyes scan my dress Da bought for me, even though it cost about every penny we've ever saved and I insisted he not. "Good choice." He leans in and lowers his voice as he tips his gaze to encompass the room we've just walked into, even as his tone says he'd rather be anywhere right now than an Upper party. "How you doing with all this?"

I crinkle my face.

He laughs. "Thank Caldon for good food then. And your aunt and uncle seem quite proud." His expression turns serious. "So how do you think the test went?"

"To be honest? I've no idea." I swallow. "But Vincent . . ."

"My mum told me this evening as soon as I got in." Lute's gaze grips mine, and probes deeper—as if trying to read something or maybe tell me something, I'm not sure. Finally, his voice falters, as if laced with exhaustion. "With the weather coming in, my father's men and I had to do a fishing trip. Left straight after I came around from the berry poison, and I only just got in." His hand slips from his hair down to claim my palm, which he squeezes and waits for me to respond.

But I don't because if I do I'll probably curl into him right here. Forget the party, forget the people. This is what I want.

He must read my thoughts because he nods and pulls me into him, and holds me against his chest the same way I've held Mum for the last few months. I tremble and inhale his salty scent, and even with the promise that the new treatment Da's made Mum, or the medicine I've been working on, might be developed in time to save her, I'm surprised by the wave of feelings that comes. I sag against him as the weight of Vincent and the test and Mum about bowl me over. Until at some point I realize he's not just holding up my body—I think maybe he's holding my heart in place as well.

"Can we forget this party and go?" I whisper.

He chuckles, then pulls back enough to peer down at me. "Even I have a healthy fear of your cousin. She'd skin our eyeballs, and Beryll would be appalled." But even as he says it, I sense a change in his demeanor. In his tone. Something tenses. Tightens.

I frown and watch him pull back from me just a bit. With a nod I straighten and glance away, giving him distance. "How's your mum and Ben?"

He shrugs. "Other than scared that I came home on a stretcher, they're good. But the festival was about all the excitement Ben could handle for a few weeks."

"How long are you home for?"

He doesn't look at me. "Not long enough. I have to leave again tomorrow. The men are trying to get in as much fishing as we can in case those regulation negotiations go awry." He starts to say more, but my aunt's voice rings out in an incoherent exclamation, and when I look over, I see my parents. Mum is in a wheeling chair. Da is standing protectively, and uncomfortably, behind her.

Lute nods at them before he ducks to murmur in my ear. "I'd like to speak privately with you later if you have a minute."

He excuses himself before I can respond, to allow them their space with me. And I nod because I've already read in his eyes what is on his mind. It's the same as on mine. The question of whether or not we can make the complexities of our lives collide.

My breathing grows thin. I watch my aunt hug my mum and I choke down a lump of tears, because this is what we all keep coming back to, isn't it? The pursuit of dreams and choices—my mum's and her sister's—their husbands and kids. Lute's and mine. His to stay home and change the world for his mum and brother—mine to pursue university in hopes of changing the world for people like my mum.

I push those thoughts away even as the ache threatens to untether me. My mum and aunt are turning to me with eyes more full of tears than I knew either was capable of. Because Mum is home. In her first home.

I smile at the idea of that.

With a last look at Lute who's gone to find Sam and Will, I stride over to the two women and hug my mum long and hard. Mum's arms feel a bit stronger today. I glance up at Da. His serum seems to be holding off the disease's progression. Maybe mine will be in time after all.

The expression on his face says he'd like to run out of here with all three of us. But he doesn't.

He just stands there looking . . . alone.

Leaving Aunt Sara to show Mum off, I tug Da outside and over to the garden wall, where we can stand in some privacy staring at the sea, next to a newly planted rosebush with a well of dirt still freshly broken and sifted around it. I think it must look a bit like Da's heart these days.

Without a word Da nods, as if he knows what I'm thinking about the fresh dirt and raw heart, then leans his arms on the wall. "I like your friend Lute, by the way."

"So do I."

"You were so busy telling me about Vincent earlier—who, by the way, I will be tearing his bloody limbs off—you forgot to say how the test went."

"I knew maybe a fourth of the material. The rest I had to wrestle with."

He eyes me. "A full quarter, eh? That's my girl."

My girl.

The fear from this morning rears its head. That I am his girl, and soon maybe the only one he's got left. If I go to university, I'm not just losing Mum. I'm losing this life with him too. And Lute. I'm losing everything I've known in my pursuit of something we still don't know if we can have. And if Mum passes . . . I'm causing Da to lose too.

"Da." My voice breaks. "What if I'm wrong? What if it's too late for Mum, and by going to university I'll be leaving you alone?"

He pats my hand. "You follow your dreams, not your guilt, Rhen."

"But what if my dreams aren't that simple?" I almost say. "Maybe that's the problem." What if my dreams aren't just one thing, but instead they are everything? They are education and Mum. They're Da and Lute. They're finding a cure while also holding on to what I have here. Why can't the future, past, and present *all* be my dreams?

I slide my hand into his and face the ocean in all its blue and orange and floating seaweed stretching on to purple sky glory, and I swallow the mouthful of fears.

"I'll miss doing this with you when you're at university, kid."

I grip his hand tighter. And make the hardest and yet easiest decision I've ever made.

"Da. I want to delay going."

"It'll—what? No." He shakes his head. "They're going to accept you—"

"Whether they do or not, I'm going to wait." I squeeze his hand. "Going to university will take time away—and right now you and Mum need me more than ever. We both know the reality is that if my cure doesn't work, I won't learn enough in time to fix Mum." I gulp. "The cure will be either what we're developing now or not at all."

He pulls his hand from mine so he can turn and face me straight on. "You listen here, Rhen. You are going to that university. Of course it takes time. What did you think you were getting into?"

"That's not what I mean." I look past him to the water, then inhale so my voice stays steady. I look back at this man who has been my father and friend my entire life. I'm already possibly losing Mum. I'm not ready to lose him too. Even if it's in a different way. I'm not ready to lose him to his grief.

"I'm going to keep doing research, but we'll do it together. I'm going to stay and care for you both because that's what family does. And when things change, maybe I'll attend university then."

Rarely in my life have I ever seen him angry. Like truly

shaking-in-his-skin angry. But he is now. "Rhen Tellur, you listen and you listen good. Your mum and I did not raise you to abandon family or needs. But we also didn't raise you to sacrifice your dreams to others."

"But what if my dreams are both?" I whisper. "What if I can do both? Just slower?"

He shakes his head as hard as he can, and his breath becomes weary. "What you did—what you've done through that contest—is nothing short of a miracle. And I'm old enough to know that when a miracle comes along, you look it full in the face and accept it as such. So now I'm looking you full in the face and accepting it. Whatever that looks like—whomever that ends up as—you will walk forward with your head held up."

"And you?"

"Rhen, I'm your father, not your child."

"True, but I'm not a child anymore either, Da."

He chuckles and says softly, "Welcome to a part of growing up, kid."

A squeal interrupts him as a mum hurries behind us with her daughter, who's a mess of brown hair and skin and scrawny legs as thin as a chicken's. I watch them shuffle toward the house when the girl glances up and, with a look of surprise then wonder, offers a shy smile.

Da's arm slips around mine and squeezes. "We've gotten a solid seventeen years with you. Maybe some other people need you now. After all, what else is all the research for if not to value the people we do it for? We started our work for your mum. You'll finish it for her and others."

I glance over and blink at him, and ignore whatever else I was going to say. Instead, I lean in to plant a firm kiss on his cheek.

He smiles. "There's my girl." He tips his head toward the door through which I can see Seleni and my friends standing. "Now go finish your fun. I'll go check on your mum. I'll give her ten more minutes, but then I'm taking her back to rest."

I start to argue that I will help, but the look on his face cuts me off. So I just watch him stride away before I follow him back into my aunt and uncle's brilliantly shiny house.

Beryll and Seleni are talking with his parents. Will and Sam are chatting with Moly. And Lute . . .

Lute is quietly speaking with the woman I know as Holm. The two are laughing over something, and it suddenly occurs to me that the crowing rooster was right the day of the Labyrinth. Death was in the air, and it did come. But maybe it was the death of our more fearful selves.

I glance back to Lute and Holm, and she abruptly lifts her gaze to meet mine. Her eyes twinkle with a gentle understanding that says she knows what I'm thinking. That how we use our time is ultimately what matters.

I turn to Lute who must sense it, because he stops in the middle of their conversation and looks straight at me too. And raises a brow in question.

"How about getting out of here?" I mouth.

27

Before we've even reached the main road from Seleni's house, the salt in my blood is tugging, drawing, inviting Lute and me to race for the shore of our small port town. The starlit water glints at us as we run past the fields, over the bridge, and down through the narrow winding streets. I dare Lute to keep up with me in his suit pants that are nicer than anything he's probably ever owned.

"You sure you're not going to rip those things?" I gasp when we reach the road to Sow's pub.

"No promises." He laughs. "But there's some definite chafing."

I launch off a set of cobblestone steps and into another alley, and continue down it until we emerge breathless and laughing onto the long lane in front of the wharf, where Lute's boat is moored amid a long row of others. The silvery water holds the night sky's reflection as the waves rush up in white-foam specks that look like stars.

I slip off the wood-planked ledge as the wind frays my hair out in a hundred short pieces. Our skin catches the rush of the salt spray, splashing wildly against the dock, as Lute hops down to join me on the sand.

My shoes are the first thing to come off.

My dress is the second.

Lute gives a low laugh. "Of course you wore pants under your party dress."

I don't answer—just shrug the skirt up over my head, except I'm tugging and it's not coming off. Something has caught against my neck.

Lute grabs the material and holds it to keep it from ripping. "Stop squirming. You forgot a button." His fingers brush against my back as he untwists the loop.

I wait for him to slip it free—and then the frothy gown is peeling off in his hands and I'm slipping toward the sea in my dead-man pants and blouse from the Labyrinth. I bend down to roll them up, then strip off my stockings while the waves rush up five paces away.

Lute tosses the dress aside and drops down on the sand, then props his arms behind his head as he looks up. The night sky is in full glory tonight—showing off her constellations as if rivaling my gown.

He says nothing.

I say nothing.

We just listen as the waves rush in and the sirens pick up their calls in the distance.

I don't know how long we stay there like that. Him lying flat on his back. Me standing nervous by the water. In the dark, with the sky stretched out like an inky canvas from one side of the world to the other—while the tide rushes in and out, in and out, like a clock or a heartpulse or the steady breathing of Lute's lungs. Neither of us uttering a word.

Until eventually the weight becomes a pendulum swinging between us.

His breathing changes, and he sits up to rest his chin on his knees and looks out at sea.

I watch him. His face. His fingers tracing his knuckles. His eyes that won't look at me. They give nothing away and yet their silence is deafening. He clears his throat and the sound bubbles like the foam now bursting around my toes, so when he finally does speak, his voice is equal parts salt and storm, and I don't know what worries me more—that he still won't look at me or that his face has become set with determination.

"Rhen, I've been thinking—" He rubs a hand through his hair. "I know things are getting ready to change, and . . ."

On second thought, maybe I'm not ready to hear what we're both thinking. I stride the three paces it takes for the ocean to fully wrap around my ankles and the cold to bite at my skin. "Let's not talk about it. Let's just enjoy the moment before we move on."

His eyes cloud over, like the sky just before a rainstorm. Dark. Earthy. Waiting for an explanation. When I don't give one, he nods. "What's going on, Rhen?"

I suddenly can't breathe. Because I . . . I don't know. I just know I want to run.

And I laugh because there's the crux of everything. I constantly want to run away—even from this entire conversation.

But I don't. I stay and redirect my gaze. And allow his question to sink in.

"I think we both understand what's going on," I finally say, and when I turn to look at him again, his face is blank of any readable expression, and he's staring in silence at the water.

My chest clenches. I nod and look down. I pop a tide bubble, then another. "You have your family to take care of, and I have Mum and Da and possibly school. If I get in, I'll be in another town, and—"

"You'll get in."

"You don't know that. But if I do, then—"

"Then I was going to propose an idea—one that wouldn't obligate you but hopefully would support you."

I refuse the emotion to leak out on my face. The hope that maybe he has a plan . . . that while I'm willing to try balancing Mum and Da and uni, maybe he wants to try for this too—whatever this is—just as badly as me.

"I know you're worried about your da and your mum. Worse—your da being alone if you can't help your mum in time. And I know your scholarship will provide them an allowance, but your da also told me they plan to stay living near here.

So I thought . . ." He looks up at me, and his eyes are bright and beautiful and achingly sad. "I want you to know I'll look in on him every day. And when I'm at sea, my mum will."

I blink. Oh.

He pushes a hand through his briny black hair. "There are no strings attached to that—no expectations. Just my offer as a friend."

As a friend.

My heart ripples against my ribs. He's just offered me the world and offered me himself as a friend—and I'm grateful and humbled and sideswiped all at once, and yet I don't know what to do with that. I eye him. "And if I don't get in?"

"You'll get in because we both know this isn't where you belong right now," he says quietly. I stiffen and start to respond—but his expression says those words pained him just as much as me. He shakes his head. "Not until you can take hold of what you want and bring it back to this place."

I choke. Because I know this is how it is. How it has to be. It's how it's always been. I can fit in everywhere but I will never quite belong anywhere. Even to him.

I look away. And say it out loud because I'd rather do it for both of us than hear it from him. "Thank you for the offer. I'm more grateful than you know. If I get in, I'd like to take you up on it. And I agree—I think just staying friends is the best plan. So from—"

"What?" His voice is so quiet it almost drowns in the waves. His eyes flash my way, but I can't tell if it's in challenge or irritation.

"Staying friends is a better plan," I repeat. "Whether I get in or not—"

"That's not what I said," he whispers cautiously.

I freeze.

"Please don't tell me you want just that."

I step from the tide and move nearer to him. To his posture that's leaning toward me, not away.

Those grey eyes are on fire as he sets them on me. "If only friendship is what you want, I'll respect it, but—" He shakes his head.

"You just said I don't belong here right now, Lute. And you . . . you belong out there." I cast a glance at the sea.

In one swift move he rises to his feet, takes my hand, and stares at me for a long minute, his blazing eyes saying a hundred things but I don't know how to decipher any of them as the waves continue to surge and retreat as if, just like me, they don't fully know where they're supposed to be. Belonging everywhere and nowhere all at once in a body that is owned by neither man nor land because the sea is simply her own entity.

The sea is her own entity.

The rhythmic water thrums against my ankles and soon becomes loud in my head. I shut my eyes and let its whispers slip through me, until the next moment it's reaching right into my soul and reshuffling every assumption I've held. The beliefs I've misunderstood.

I frown and look up at Lute. What had he called the sea? *Untameable.*

What if it really is the same with me? What if I don't fully belong anywhere . . . because I belong to myself? Maybe that's the sea's strength, and maybe that's my strength too. It's not that I don't belong. It's that *I belong to me.*

It's why I entered the Labyrinth.

It's how I will survive if I lose my mother.

It's how I'll survive if I end up losing Lute.

I will belong to me.

I let the smile edge my lips and pull Lute's hand flat to my chest where I can feel the *thump thump thump* of my blood pulsing through my heart as I stare at him. This man standing in the middle of the ocean spray, so near, he might as well step into me. The water droplets slide down his hopeful face like fingers across bare skin. They catch on his lashes and lips and chin, and he presses my fingers against my chest before he pulls them away and sets them on his.

To feel his lungs and heartbeat too. Because maybe I also belong *there.*

Finally, he exhales and, leaning in, whispers, "Bloody hulls, please say something. Say you want to conquer the world but that you also might be willing to let me do it with you—even if I'm doing it from here. Because you are the wild sea and unkempt storms and constellations in a world where I am the anchor for everyone I know." He leans forward, as if his heart is stretched as taut as his tone. "And you remind me that I can do impossible things."

He looks at me shyly, as if afraid I'll say no. "I know the university's a day's trek away—but I don't mind the distance if you—"

My fingers on his anatomically perfect lips cut off the rest of his comment. He lifts a brow and waits for my choked-up smile before he slides his hand around the back of my neck and pulls me closer, his thumb tipping my chin up to his. I draw him into me until the atmosphere between us ceases to exist, and it's just us, the sea, and the sky.

He opens his mouth to speak again, but I'm already crashing in at the seams of my being, as the ocean spray around us is swirling and falling into wind and life and magic. And suddenly his hands are in my hair and his lips are on my cheek, brushing down to my chin, then my mouth, and every single inhale I take declares that I am undone.

Hand on hand. Nerve on nerve. Lip on lip. Breath entwined. Burning to the ground. Everything in me belongs to me, but it also belongs to him. To this boy who is willing me to succeed. Who is willing to take on a world with me, and in the process, perhaps we will create a new world of our own.

I pull back and look at him. "I'm sorry you didn't win the contest, Lute."

"It was never mine to win. My Labyrinth was you. Your mind. Your heart. Your trust. In hopes you'd name me your own."

I stand on my tiptoes and cup his face between my hands. "Mr. Wilkes, have I ever explained the decomposition process of an animal corpse to you?"

28

When the letter arrived on the steps of every Pinsbury Port home in the quiet October morning hours, scarcely two weeks following the Autumnal Equinox Scholarship Competition that had thoroughly shocked at least one half of the tiny kingdom of Caldon—Mrs. Mench was understandably appalled. After all, Mr. Holm had sent it without even the slightest consideration to how such things work. Social changes should be given time, as should people, and there had been far too much of the former lately. Propriety must be honored even when some reckless young bucks thought tradition was for toppling.

Mrs. Mench only hoped it wouldn't become a habit. She'd had enough excitement—that hadn't been created by her, at least—for a solid five months. And that was saying something.

Even so, she and everyone else in Pinsbury tore open the sealed parchment the moment the missives hit the cobblestone steps, because for the first time in fifty-five years, no one had any idea what the contents said. Two letters from Mr. Holm within the same year had never been heard of before.

The brief, purple-inked note was hand printed on a parchment made of forty-pound vellum.

All gentlepersons of all ages are cordially invited to attend the celebration of one Miss Rhen Tellur and her full acceptance into Stemwick University for the commencing winter quarter. Festivities will be held exactly one week from today, on 13 October, year of our King Francis (long may he reign), at Holm estate. Guests will appear at six o'clock in the evening in front of Holm Manor's entrance and are welcome to stay until one o'clock the following morning.

For Attendees: Party refreshments will be provided at all times. Sleeping accommodations not provided (hence, please leave by one o'clock). Gratitude and congratulatory excitement toward Miss Tellur are expected. (Those who fail to comply will be tossed out at *our* congratulatory excitement.)

For Dissenters: No one likes a sore pouter—so stay home.

For All: Mr. Holm and Holm Manor bear only slight responsibility, liability, and legal obligation for the future societal changes that may result from your female children believing it is within their power and right to become whomever and whatever they desire—and in doing so, to change the course of history.

Sincerely,

Holm

Dear Reader,

You'll notice a variety of individuals, families, and situations represented in *To Best the Boys*, particularly some reflecting learning struggles and different needs. These are based on specific loved ones within my own family and close friends, and it was their desire and mine to represent them accurately and with honor in this novel. For this reason, they were given absolute control over their word choices, scenarios, and representation within *To Best the Boys* (and in this note). However, we are aware that not everyone agrees on language, word preferences, or portrayal. With that in mind, if anything rings as inaccurate or insensitive to you, please accept our deepest apologies. Rhen is based on my mom (and two brothers) who have dyslexia. Ben is based on my family member who has Down syndrome and autism, as well as a dear friend with Down syndrome. Lute and his mom are based on our families. Our hope is to honor the beautiful people and stories in this world. And in doing so, we hope we've honored you.

Humbly,

~m

DISCUSSION
QUESTIONS

1. Even though the book is a light fantasy, what aspects of *To Best the Boys* mimic our own world today? Specifically consider the political, social, and educational challenges.

2. In *To Best the Boys*, Rhen dreams of being a female scientist in a kingdom that won't allow it. And yet, she believes in herself enough to buck tradition and rewrite society's rules. What dreams do *you* desire to see fulfilled, and what challenges do you face? If you could accomplish anything, what would it be? And what are you waiting for?

3. Vincent and Rhen used to be friends until his choices surrounding a mistake he made changed aspects of his

character. Do you think that happens in real life? Do you think he could've become a better person in spite of the mistake? How?

4. There are multiple men in Rhen's story who are *good* men. They speak, act, and support others in ways that are opposite of Vincent, his friends, and some of the adults. What's the difference between the "good" ones and the others? What specific behaviors made them honorable people? What was the difference between the way Lute and Vincent each treated Rhen?

5. The families in Rhen's story are a reflection of my own community. They all have different needs (some financial, some physical, some logistical)—all of which influence their daily lives and decisions. What needs can you relate to?

6. The politicians in Rhen's world made a decision they believed was good for the environment and the community. Was it a good one? How could they have handled it to make it better?

7. Multiple times throughout Rhen's story, she encounters specific boys talking to her, or about her, in ways that make her uncomfortable. In one instance, Vincent not only defends Germaine and Rubin to Rhen, he gets her to question the legitimacy of her own personal boundaries and beliefs. In another instance, the three boys talk about Rhen, Seleni, and other girls as if all they're good for is to get something from. And in repeated instances, various boys and men (and some women) use words, embarrassment, authority, or condescension to try to

make Rhen submissive to their opinions. How did this make *you* feel? Has this ever happened to you? What was the situation? For some women, such instances haven't been common. For others, those situations occur far too often. And for still others, those types of incidents are just the tip of something far more painful. So allow me to say this: Wherever you are, whatever has been done to you . . . It. Was. Not. Your. Fault. And it was *not okay*. Your opinions and feelings and body and mind are *yours*. They are precious because *you* are precious. And I'm so very sorry. If you have someone safe you can talk to, please do so. And if you need someone, please reach out to the many resources available. A good place to start might be www. womenshealth.gov.

8. At the end of the book, Rhen has a realization that changes the way she views herself and how she fits into the world. She's struggled her whole life with feeling like she doesn't belong fully anywhere, when the truth is—she belongs to herself. What do you think of that concept? How might the way we interact with society and others change if we choose to belong to (love, be true to, own) ourselves first?

ACKNOWLEDGMENTS

I hit a spot in every book I write, always around page 90, when I think, *Well, this is it. I'm officially a fraud at this author thing.* Rudely, without fail, not one person in my life so far has had the gall to believe me. In fact, they tend to go about their business as if I'm legitimately capable of finishing the book. And somehow they've been right six times now. I owe them more than I can say.

These are my page 90 people. I couldn't have written this book without them.

My husband (aka hottest best friend I've ever had). My three muggles, Rilian, Avalon, and Korbin. My biochemist sister, Kati, who brainstormed this story with me and then checked the science of things. Dad, Mom, my siblings, and their families—thanks for all the meals at home and in Croatia.

My sensitivity readers—Susan, Amanda, Mindy, Diane, and others, for guiding this story with your wisdom, words, and heart. And to the Meades and Ulibarris—this story is for you.

Marissa Meyer, C. J. Redwine, Nadine Brandes, Sara Ella, Allen Arnold, Jeanette Morris, and Courtney Stevens.

My #FantasyOnFriday ladies—Jodi Meadows, C. J. Redwine, Beth Revis, Kristen Ciccarelli, Tricia Levenseller, Danielle Paige, Erin Summerill, and Amy Bartol.

Father's House, The Rise, and my lovely Sarah Kathleen Photography.

Lee Hough. Amanda, Bex, Jodi, Paul, Allison, Kristen, Julee, and the rest of the Thomas Nelson team.

My Mad Hatter street team. Let's be wild together. ☺

Every bookstagrammer, blogger, interviewer, reviewer, and book clubber who has read, photographed, or shouted up my books. (Even if you threw them across the room first due to #cliffhangers. Sorry about those. Kind of.)

My readers. You are my people. And you are more than I deserve.

Jesus. Because you are all this heart exists for.

~m

A RECIPE FOR
LABYRINTH CAKES

INGREDIENTS:

Cakes:

1/2 cup butter

4 ounces white baking chocolate

1 cup powdered sugar

2 eggs plus 2 egg yolks

6 tablespoons flour

1 teaspoon grated orange peel

1/2 teaspoon cardamom

1/4 teaspoon cinnamon

Easy caramel sauce:

1 cup brown sugar

$^{1}/_{2}$ cup butter

$^{1}/_{2}$ cup heavy cream

1 teaspoon vanilla

DIRECTIONS:

Preheat oven to 425 degrees. Lightly butter 6 muffin cups and set aside. In a small saucepan (or in the microwave), melt the butter and white chocolate over low heat, stirring regularly until smooth. Remove from heat and stir in the powdered sugar, then add in the eggs and egg yolks and whisk. Blend in the flour, orange peel, cardamom, and cinnamon. Ladle the mixture evenly into the greased cups and bake for 10 to 13 minutes, until puffy and lightly browned.

While the cakes bake, prepare the caramel sauce by combining the sugar, butter, and heavy cream in a small saucepan over medium heat and stirring continuously. Once the sauce is melted and begins to bubble around the edges, stir for 4 minutes more, then remove from the heat and blend in the vanilla. Set aside.

Remove the cakes from the oven and allow to cool 3 minutes before inverting them onto parchment. While still hot, flip the cakes right side up and generously spoon the caramel over them. Sprinkle the tops with orange peel if desired. Allow the cakes to cool, then grab one, your copy of *To Best the Boys*, and a friend to share them with—and enjoy!

The line between virtual & reality is about to EVAPORATE.

What the experts are saying . . .

"A smart, intriguing adventure."
—Wendy Higgins

"A fascinating future with a captivating gaming aspect."
—RT Book Reviews

"Spellbinding conclusion."
—RT Book Reviews

"A well-paced page-turner."
—Kirkus

Available in print, e-book, and audio!

CONNECT WITH ME

Mary loves to connect with readers! Here's where you can find her online:

maryweber.com

Instagram:
MaryWeberAuthor

Facebook:
Mary Weber, Author

Twitter:
@MChristineWeber

School, Skype, or
conference visits:
mary@mchristineweber.com

ABOUT THE AUTHOR

Photo by Sarah Kathleen Photography

Mary Weber is the award-winning HarperCollins author of the bestselling young adult Storm Siren Trilogy and The Sofi Snow duology. An avid school and conference speaker, Mary's passion is helping others find their voice amid a world that often feels too loud. When she's not plotting adventures involving tough girls who frequently take over the world, Mary sings '80s hairband songs to her three muggle children and ogles her husband, who looks strikingly like Wolverine. They live in California, which is perfect for stalking LA bands and the ocean.